URSUN'S TEETH

KASPAR WAS SUDDENLY aware of the silence of the guns and his worst fears were confirmed when he saw his runner's horse galloping back through the smoke, its rider's headless body still clutching the reins. He saw howling beasts rampaging across the artillery ridge, smashing aside wicker gabions and hurling severed body parts before them.

The monstrous creatures were drunk on blood, frenzied to the point of intoxication by the slaughter. The beasts smashed through the gun emplacements and ran downhill towards the Ice Queen, bellowing in ferocious hunger.

Kaspar dragged on the reins of his horse and shouted, 'Kurt!'

Kurt Bremen had already wheeled his mount and yelled, 'Knights Panther, with me!'

More Graham McNeill from The Black Library

· WARHAMMER NOVELS ·
THE AMBASSADOR

· WARHAMMER 40,000 NOVELS ·
NIGHTBRINGER – A Uriel Ventris novel
WARRIORS OF ULTRAMAR – A Uriel Ventris novel
STORM OF IRON

A WARHAMMER NOVEL

URSUN'S TEETH

GRAHAM McNEILL

*...and this one's for Michele.
You gave me this ending.*

A BLACK LIBRARY PUBLICATION

First published in Great Britain in 2004 by
BL Publishing,
Games Workshop Ltd.,
Willow Road, Nottingham,
NG7 2WS, UK.

10 9 8 7 6 5 4 3 2 1

Cover illustration by Paul Dainton.
Map by Nuala Kennedy.

A CIP record for this book is available from the British Library.

ISBN 1 84416 076 9

Distributed in the US by Simon & Schuster
1230 Avenue of the Americas, New York, NY 10020.

Printed and bound in Great Britain by
Cox & Wyman Ltd, Reading, Berkshire, UK.

See the Black Library on the Internet at
www.blacklibrary.com

Find out more about Games Workshop
and the world of Warhammer at
www.games-workshop.com

THIS IS A DARK age, a bloody age, an age of daemons and of sorcery. It is an age of battle and death, and of the world's ending. Amidst all of the fire, flame and fury it is a time, too, of mighty heroes, of bold deeds and great courage.

AT THE HEART of the Old World sprawls the Empire, the largest and most powerful of the human realms. Known for its engineers, sorcerers, traders and soldiers, it is a land of great mountains, mighty rivers, dark forests and vast cities. And from his throne in Altdorf reigns the Emperor Karl-Franz, sacred descendent of the founder of these lands, Sigmar, and wielder of his magical warhammer.

BUT THESE ARE far from civilised times. Across the length and breadth of the Old World, from the knightly palaces of Bretonnia to ice-bound Kislev in the far north, come rumblings of war. In the towering World's Edge Mountains, the orc tribes are gathering for another assault. Bandits and renegades harry the wild southern lands of the Border Princes. There are rumours of rat-things, the skaven, emerging from the sewers and swamps across the land. And from the northern wildernesses there is the ever-present threat of Chaos, of daemons and beastmen corrupted by the foul powers of the Dark Gods. As the time of battle draws ever near, the Empire needs heroes like never before.

URSUN'S TEETH

Prologue

KAR ODACEN KNEW that the lightning bolt he had waited his entire life for would strike the mountain long before it split the sky. A mighty peal of thunder rolled across the heavens, the rain falling in an unending torrent, as though the seas of the world had been carried into the sky by the gods and now flooded forth in an attempt to drown all the lands of men.

He could feel the power of the lightning seething above him, summoned to the land below by the magicks he and every shaman of the Iron Wolves before him had drawn to these mountains since time before memory.

The jagged peak above him was a dark spike against the flickering sky, the gods battling in the clouds casting their ghostly lights across the highlands of the World's Edge Mountains. He felt the hairs on his scarred and becharmed arms stand erect as he passed a column of bleached skulls, fully as tall as the greatest warrior of the Wolves, the tip of the copper pole they were impaled upon protruding a span above the topmost skull. Ripples of blue fire danced along the length of the column of bone, flickering within the empty eye sockets of the grinning skulls, imparting them with a malicious anime. Hundreds of such tribute poles ringed the peak of the mountain, a sign to the Old One who slept beneath the world that he was remembered; that the warriors and shamans of the Iron Wolves had not forgotten him. These mountains were old when the world was young and the Iron Wolves had never dared forget their duty to them.

The high zars of the Iron Wolves had laid a thousand times a thousand skulls from a hundred lifetimes of war at their shamans' feet and, as the centuries passed, each generation would add more skulls on their copper poles to the mountain. In preparation for his attack into Kislev, the High Zar of the Iron Wolves, Aelfric Cyenwulf himself, had bade his shaman raise countless skulls in honour of the Dark Gods.

Kar Odacen passed one such tribute pole, a sense of fearful anticipation growing within his breast. He had awoken from a dream in which packs of the ravenous, black-furred wolves of the north chased a solitary white wolf across the heavens. Upon the shimmering white wolf's back was a mighty-thewed warrior clad in furs who wielded a great warhammer, and though this wolf was powerful, it could not outpace its hunters. The white wolf turned at bay atop a tall peak of ice-slick rock and together it and the rider fought the snapping packs of northern wolves. Man and wolf fought hard and well, spilling the blood of hundreds of their foes, but even as they took heart in their slaughter, the dark wolves changed to become a roiling storm cloud of impenetrable darkness, pierced only by lava-hot spears of lightning that opened great gashes in the flesh of both man and wolf.

Though he could not see within the cloud, Kar Odacen's dream-self knew that something unimaginably ancient and monstrously evil lay at its heart. And even he, who had sent his spirit into the realm of the dae-monkin, knew to dread its power.

Without warning the dark storm suddenly swelled to swallow the man and his wolf whole and Kar Odacen had woken knowing that the night his distant predecessors had prophesied had finally come. He had set off into the darkness, climbing breathlessly for hours as the rain pounded like hammer blows on his shaven, tattooed head and his feet were torn bloody by razor sharp rocks.

Another boom of thunder, like the gods' footsteps on the world, rolled across the sky, but Kar Odacen did not bother to look up, knowing in his bones that it was not yet time.

He reached a plateau of sheared rock, two hundred yards or more below the peak, his breath like hot smoke in his lungs, and dropped to his knees with arms raised above him in praise of this most holy night. Even over the unceasing roar of the rain he could hear the crackling from the skull columns below him grow louder, feeling the heat of the fire that danced between them as it reached deep into the heart of the mountain.

The skies rumbled and the mountain shook, as though bracing itself for what must happen next and Kar Odacen felt a swelling of dark and terrible power. He looked up as the heavens split apart with a vast, incandescent sheet of lightning that struck the highest peak of the mountain, its brightness searing the sight from his eyes.

The mountaintop exploded, disappearing in a gigantic cloud of rubble and smoke. Rocks were hurled hundreds of yards into the air, tumbling down in an avalanche of blasted shale. Kar Odacen screamed the name of his Dark Gods as the rubble smashed down all around him, pulverising the slopes of the mountain, but, impossibly, leaving him unscathed. Blood dripped from his ears and he blinked the searing after-image of the lightning from his eyes as he felt the hard rain cease and the deafening echoes of the thunder and explosion fade to nothing, leaving him swaying and alone on the smashed mountaintop.

Kar Odacen lowered his arms, feeling a tremor of dread run through the rock of the mountain. A similar feeling of fear and awe took him in its grip. The sudden silence of the mountains after the violence of the storm was more terrifying than anything he had known before.

A creeping horror slowly overtook him, rising languidly through his bones as the throat of something that had seen the birth of the world took its first breath in uncounted ages. Blinking away tears of rapture and terror, Kar Odacen saw a writhing column of impossibly black, lightning-hearted smoke rise from the smashed caldera of the mountaintop, its sapphire innards crackling with a horrifying, fiery urgency. Though no breath of wind disturbed the night, the smoke gathered itself together, and slid down the mountainside like a dark slick upon the air.

The mountain shuddered with the tread of something magnificent and terrible, rocks crushed to powder beneath its weight and power. The baleful glow from the smoke's innards grew fiercer as it approached the paralysed shaman, the horror concealed there pausing to regard him with as much interest as a man might pay an ant before continuing on its thunderous journey towards the new world below.

Kar Odacen shivered and let out a juddering breath, shaking like a newborn foal.

'The End Times are upon this world...' he whispered through trembling lips.

CHAPTER ONE

I

BUILT ATOP THE *Gora Geroyev*, the city of Kislev was an impressive sight. High walls of smooth black stone were topped with saw-toothed ramparts and constructed with the practicality common to its northern inhabitants. Tall towers jutted from either side of the thick timber gate and enfilading cannon positions covered the road leading towards the city with their bronze muzzles.

The tops of tall buildings reared above the walls, as if daring an attacker to try and sack them, and the tips of the spears carried by the fur-clad soldiers who walked the ramparts glittered in the low, evening sun. Surrounding the base of the walls were thousands of refugees, people driven from their homes in the north of the country by the warriors of High Zar Aelfric Cyenwulf, a bloodthirsty war leader of the Kurgan tribes.

A sprawling canvas city housing thousands – tens of thousands – gathered around the city, clinging to the walls as though seeking safety by virtue of their proximity.

'Precious little protection to be had here,' whispered Kaspar von Velten, ambassador of the Emperor Karl-Franz, pulling his cloak tighter about himself as a blast of freezing air whipped across the packed hillside. The Tza-rina had been forced to bar the gates to prevent further refugees from entering the already overcrowded city. When the High Zar's army came south, as soon it must, the city would quickly starve should the entirety of the fleeing populace be given sanctuary within its walls.

'No,' agreed Kurt Bremen, leader of the group of Knights Panther who rode with Kaspar. 'It will be a slaughter.'

'Perhaps,' said Kaspar. 'Unless Boyarin Kurkosk can stop the Kurgans north of here.'

'Do you think he can?'

'It's possible,' allowed Kaspar. 'I'm told the boyarin is a great warrior and he gathers nearly fifty thousand men to his banner.'

'For these people's sake, let us hope he is a great leader of men as well as a great warrior. The two are not always the same thing.'

Kaspar nodded, guiding his horse along the frozen, rutted roadway between twin rows of makeshift camp-sites and riding towards the gates of the city. Cold, frightened people glanced up as he and his knights passed, but their misery was too complete for them to pay much attention to them. He felt his heart go out to them, brutalised as they were by months of war and hardship, and wished he could do more to help them.

The gates of the city groaned open as his weary group approached, crowds of desperate people gathering what meagre belongings they had managed to carry from their stanistas and hurrying towards the gates, pleas for entry pouring from every mouth.

Kossars in long, padded coats and green tabards emerged from within and blocked the gateway with long-hafted axes and shouted oaths. Fierce-looking men with helms of bronze and long, drooping moustaches, they pushed the wailing refugees back without mercy and Kaspar had to fight the urge to shout at them. These were their own people they were condemning to the freezing temperatures, but the part of Kaspar that had once been a general in the Emperor's armies knew that they were only obeying orders that he himself would have given were he in charge of the city's defences.

He eased his silver-maned steed, Magnus, through the yelling crowds, turning as a weeping woman pulled at his snow-limned cloak. She wore a threadbare pashmina over a coarse black dress and thrust a swaddled babe towards him, pleading with him in snatches of rapid Kislevite.

Kaspar shook his head, 'Nya Kislevarin, Nya.'

The woman fought off the kossars' attempts to pull her away from Kaspar, screaming and fighting to place the baby in his arms. Even as she was finally dragged away, Kaspar could see that her efforts had been in vain: the child was long-dead, blue and frozen.

Fighting back his sadness, he rode through the cold darkness of the gateway, pathetically grateful to emerge into the cold, miserable confines of the winter-gripped city. The scene inside the walls was little better, the streets lined with gaunt, fur-wrapped people, huddled together and shuffling aimlessly and fearfully along the city streets.

Though he knew his actions in Kislev over the last few months had already saved many lives, having stopped a corrupt Empire merchant from profiteering from stolen supplies destined for the people of Kislev, Kaspar felt fresh resolve to do more.

His personal guard of Knights Panther; mighty armoured knights atop enormous Averland destriers were weary after nearly two weeks spent out in the frozen wilderness of Kislev. They followed him inside, all visibly struggling with the idea of leaving these people outside the walls.

In the centre of the Knights Panther rode Sasha Kajetan, once the most beloved and heroic figure in Kislev, a swordsman beyond compare and leader of one of the Tzarina's most glorious cavalry regiments. Kajetan was now a broken man, virtually catatonic and skeletally thin after his flight into the oblast.

Kajetan's hands were bound before him, his true nature as a brutal murderer having only recently come to light when he had killed Kaspar's oldest friend, before abducting and torturing his physician.

But Kajetan was now captured and though the feared *Chekist* would surely want him hung, Kaspar was determined to delay the swordsman's fate for as long as possible to try and fathom what had driven the man to such murderous extremes.

Kajetan caught Kaspar's look and nodded weakly in acknowledgement. Kaspar was surprised; it was the first human gesture the swordsman had made since they had fought their way through the Kurgan scouting party in the oblast nearly a week ago.

Kaspar watched as the gates closed, pushed shut by nearly a score of kossars and barred with thick spars of hardened timber.

'Sigmar forgive us…' he whispered, turning his horse and riding along the Goromadny Prospekt towards Geroyev Square in the centre of the city.

During the summer and spring months, the square was traditionally the site of a thriving market, thronged with trappers selling their wares, horse traders and all manner of merchants. When Kaspar had first come to Kislev, enthusiastic crowds had gathered, yelling and cursing around a corral of plains ponies, the bidding spirited and lively, but now the square was packed to capacity with innumerable campsites, clusters of tents and sputtering cookfires covering every inch of ground.

It was a sight typical around Kislev, a city in which there were many wide boulevards lined with hardy evergreens – most of which had long since been cut down for firewood. The hulking iron statues of long-dead tzars watched over their people's misery impassively, powerless to aid them in their time of need.

The Winter Palace of the Ice Queen dominated the far side of the square, its white towers and gleaming marble walls of ice glittering like glass in the low evening sunlight.

'The Ice Queen left the gates open too long,' observed Kurt Bremen. 'There are too many people within the walls. Many of them will starve to death when Kislev comes under siege.'

'I know, Kurt, but these are her people, she could not leave them all to die. She would save her city, but lose her people,' replied Kaspar, riding along the edge of the square towards the Temple of Ulric and the Empire embassy that lay behind it.

'Unless there is some better news from the Empire, she may lose it anyway. With Wolfenburg gone, it is doubtful the Emperor will send his armies north when there are enemies within our own lands.'

'They will come, Kurt,' promised Kaspar.

'I hope you are right, Ambassador.'

'Have you ever met the Emperor?' asked Kaspar, turning in the saddle to face the knight.

'No, I have not had that honour.'

'I have, and Karl-Franz is a man of courage and honour,' said Kaspar. 'He is a warrior king and I have fought alongside him on more than one occasion. Against orcs, Norse raiders and the beasts of the forests. He has sworn to aid Kislev and I do not believe he will forsake that oath.'

Kurt Bremen smiled. 'Then I too will believe it.'

II

BOTH RATCATCHERS WERE so inured to the reek of shit that neither now paid it any mind. Hundreds of tonnes of human and animal waste flowed through the sewers below the streets of Kislev, carried through the oval tunnels dug through the rock and earth of the *Gora Geroyev* to empty far downriver into the Urskoy.

Commissioned by Tzar Alexis and designed by the ingenious Empire engineer, Josef Bazalgette, the tunnels below Kislev were amongst the greatest engineering marvels of the north, effectively eliminating the scourge of cholera from the Kislevite capital. Mile upon mile of twisting tunnels extended in a labyrinthine maze beneath the streets like the tunnels beneath the Fauschlag of Middenheim; though these tunnels were formed of bricks and mortar rather than from the natural rock.

A pair of small dogs padded before the two ratcatchers along the ledge that ran alongside the foaming river of effluent, their tails erect and ears pressed flat against their skulls. The rushing of the sewage echoed from the glistening brick walls, keeping conversation to a minimum.

Both men were clad in stiffened leathers, crusted with age and filth, and high, hobnailed boots. They wore thin metal helmets, padded with matted fur and scarves around their mouths and noses. Though they barely noticed the smell any more, they wore the protective scarves through force of habit. Each man carried a long pole over one shoulder, a single rat dangling by its tail from each of them.

'A poor day, Nikolai, a poor day,' said the shorter of the two ratcatchers with a weary shrug that made the rat on his pole dance in an imitation of life.

'Aye, Marska, few vermin to catch today,' agreed his apprentice, Nikolai, casting an irritated glance at the two dogs. 'What shall we eat tonight?'

'I think we shan't be presenting these sorry specimens to the city authorities for a copper kopek,' sighed Marska. 'I fear we may be dining on rat again, my friend.'

'Perhaps tomorrow will be better. We could sell some to the refugees?'

'Aye, maybe we can,' said Nikolai doubtfully.

Winter's icy grip and the bloodthirsty ravages of a Kurgan barbarian war leader, whose armies were even now closing on the city, had displaced thousands of people from their homes on the steppe and many now huddled, cold and frightened, around the walls of the northern capital. It was true that the refugees who flocked to the camps outside the city walls were willing to eat pretty much anything and there had been some nice money in selling rat meat to them. But that had been before the cold had killed most of the rats and the few emaciated creatures they had managed to trap were the only food that they themselves could expect to see for some time.

The two men trudged on in silence for some time until Nikolai nudged Marska as he saw the two dogs suddenly stiffen and draw their jowls back over sharp teeth. Neither dog made a sound, their vocal chords having long since been cut, but their bowstring-taut posture told both ratcatchers that they had sensed something they didn't like. Ahead, Marska knew the passage widened into a high-domed chamber where a number of divergent effluent tunnels converged before heading out to the Urskoy.

Marska unhooked a small hand crossbow from his belt and eased back the string, wincing when the mechanism clicked as it caught. But to keep the weapon cocked would lose the tension in the string and reduce the power in the bolt. The weapon was an indulgence; most ratcatchers could only ever afford a sling and pebbles for shot, but one glorious summer, Marska had discovered a body floating in the sewers with a purse bulging with gold coins. He had hidden the coins about his person for many months before daring to spend them. Nikolai slipped a rounded pebble into his sling and eased himself past the two dogs, his footsteps silent for such a big man.

Ahead, Marska could hear voices, muffled and obscured, but years of working below the streets of Kislev had given him a good ear for picking out sounds that wouldn't normally be expected here.

Nikolai turned and gestured quizzically along the length of the tunnel to a sprawling pile of debris, bricks and mud that lay on the ledge that ran alongside the effluent. The rubble looked for all the world as though it had been pushed from the wall and Marska wondered who in their right mind would want to tunnel *into* a sewer. The dogs padded along silently, stopping as they reached the tumble of debris, dipping their heads to sniff at something on the ledge.

Marska ghosted forwards and crouched beside the mud that had spilled from the hole in the wall. Tracks, but tracks that didn't make any sense. They were smudged and deep, as though whoever or whatever had made them had been carrying something heavy, but that wasn't the first thing Marska noticed that was odd. It was hard to be sure, but the prints looked as though they only had four toes on each foot, and from the conical depression a little beyond each toe, it appeared as though they were clawed…

It was obvious that whatever had made the tracks walked on two legs, but what manner of man had only four toes and claws? An altered perhaps, or one of the beasts of the dark forests come down from the north? Marska felt a flutter of fear race up his spine at the thought of one of these hideous creatures loose down in his sewers. As a child, he had seen such a beast when a band of Ungol horsemen had ridden through his stanista with the corpse of one of these monstrous, horned creatures and Marska remembered the terror he had felt at the size of the beast.

The voices came again, thrown from far away by the curve of the tunnel. Only fragments of conversation echoed back towards the ratcatchers, but Marska knew that they must be talking about something important. After all, people did not meet in the sewers to discuss the latest harvest or the weather.

As a member of the Guild of Ratcatchers, Marska was also part of the network of informers who worked for Vassily Chekatilo, the ruthless killer who controlled everything illegal in Kislev, a dangerous man who traded in stolen goods, narcotics and flesh. Part of his power came from knowing things that he should not know and the ratcatchers were an important part of that, for who paid any attention to the filthy peasant covered in shit who cleared your house of vermin?

Taking great care to tread silently, the two ratcatchers crept forward, at last reaching the edge of the fallen pile of brickwork. Now that they were closer, Marska could see that the hole in the wall disappeared into the darkness for some way.

Moving slowly so as not to draw the eye of any observers, Marska and Nikolai eased their heads above the level of the rubble.

The domed chamber echoed with the lapping sewage, ripples of reflected light dancing on the vaulted ceiling. A circular ledge, some six feet wide, ran around the circumference of the chamber and eight, half submerged, pipes disgorged their filthy cargo into the central reservoir that drained downriver. On the far side of the chamber stood four figures beside a ramshackle cart, like that used by the collectors of the dead. An apt choice of conveyance, thought Marska, seeing a bronze coffin sealed with a number of rusted padlocks atop the cart. Two figures dressed in rippling robes that appeared to change colour stood closer to the wall of the chamber, while another pair stood beside the cart.

These last two figures were smaller than the others, hunched over, and even over the reek of the sewers the stench emanating from the nearest was overpowering. Dressed in excrement-smeared rags and bound around the arms and chest with weeping bandages, it was bent almost double by a collection of thick, brass edged books tied to its back. A cracked bell hung from a rope belt around its waist and its face was, thankfully, obscured by its patchwork hood. Its companion was hidden in the shadow; so well that Marska had very nearly missed him. Swathed from head to foot in black robes the figure clutched what appeared to be a long-barrelled musket of some kind, though it was festooned with brass fittings, coils and pipes whose purpose escaped Marska.

The tallest of the figures in the multi-coloured robes took a hesitant step forward, holding a metal box, some six inches square. The filth-smeared figure beside the bronze coffin raised its head, as though scenting the air, its head darting quickly from side to side. Marska watched as the lid of the box was opened and a soft, pulsating emerald green light radiated from inside it, bathing the chamber in a fearful, sickly glow.

'Your payment,' said the figure holding the box, its voice smoky and seductive.

The filthy hunchback snatched the box with a squeal of pleasure, almost quicker than the eye could follow, and stared deep into the glowing depths, as though inhaling the scent of whatever lay within.

'And this is what you bring me?' asked the former owner of the box, reaching out a delicate hand to touch the coffin.

A blur of motion, black on black, and a clawed hand snatched out and grabbed the hand reaching for the coffin. Marska was amazed; without seeming to move, the black robed figure with the musket had darted from the shadows to intercept the hand reaching for the coffin. No man could move that fast; it was inhuman.

The filthy book-carrier shook its head slowly and the hand was withdrawn.

Marska turned and cupped his hands around Nikolai's ear, whispering, 'Nikolai, get back to the surface. Chekatilo will want to hear of what's happening down here.'

'What about you?' hissed Nikolai.

'I want to see if I can hear anything else, now go!'

Nikolai nodded, and Marska could see that his young apprentice was glad to be leaving. He didn't blame him, but he had to stay; if Chekatilo found out – and he would – that he had seen these events and not learned all he could, he might as well slit his throat now.

As Nikolai slipped away, Marska turned his attention back to the drama unfolding before him in time to hear the rotten, bandaged figure reply to an unheard question, hissing a single word that sounded as though it came from a mouth never meant to speak the tongues of men.

'Eshhhiiiiin…' it said, bobbing its head, pointing to the figure dressed in black. As it did so, Marska saw what looked like a long, fat worm waving in the air behind it. His lip curled in distaste before he realised that he was not looking at some serpent as people were often wont to claim dwelled in the sewers, but a tail. A pink tail, hairless save for a few mange-ridden patches of coarse, wiry fur.

Revolted, he drew in a sharp breath, and in that moment knew he had doomed himself as the figure in black's head snapped in his direction.

'No…' he hissed, pushing himself to his feet to sprint away.

He had barely risen when a flurry of silver flashed through the air and struck him in his chest. He grunted in pain, turning to run, but his legs wouldn't obey him, and the ground rushed up to slam into his face as his limbs spasmed violently. Marska rolled onto his back, seeing a trio of jagged discs of metal with dripping blades protruding from his chest. Where had they come from, he wondered, as he felt his muscles jerk and his lungs fill with froth?

He tried to move, but was helpless, dying.

With the last ounce of his strength he yelled, 'Run, Nikolai, run! They're coming!' as a dark shadow enveloped him, darker even than that pressing in on his eyes.

Marska looked into the face of his killer and realised that Death had a sense of irony after all.

III

THE GOROMADNY PROSPEKT was busy despite the late hour. People with no homes to call their own wandered the streets, rightly fearing that to lie down in the cold snow would be to die. Snow drifted up the sides of buildings, the central thoroughfare of the city trodden to brown slush. Those few taverns with any wares left to sell burned what fuel they had to keep the worst of the cold at bay, but it was a futile gesture against the aching, marrow-deep cold of Kislev.

Families huddled together for shared warmth in doorways, fur blankets pulled tight around them, yet still shivering in cold and fear.

Harsh times had come to Kislev, but worse was yet to come.

The scrape of metal on stone was the first hint that something out of the ordinary was happening, but most folk ignored it, too cold and hungry to pay any mind to matters beyond their concern.

A rusted iron manhole slid through the snow, grating on the cobbles, bloodied hands reaching up from below the street. A man, covered in muck and screaming in terror hauled himself from the sewers, jerking like a marionette as he rolled in the slush.

Something fell from his dirty clothing, a short-bladed dagger with a curved blade; a blade that had caught in the folds of his leather tabard and nicked the surface of his skin.

The man thrashed the ground, desperately trying to put as much distance between himself and the entrance to the sewers. His back arched as he convulsed and his screams of agony moved even the hardest hearts to pity.

As curious onlookers cautiously approached, the man screamed, 'The rats! The rats! They're here, they've come to kill us all!'

People shook their heads in weary understanding, now seeing the man's ratcatching apparel, guessing that he had simply spent too long below ground and thus fallen prey to lunacy. It was sad, but it happened, and there was nothing they could do. They had troubles of their own.

As the onlookers dispersed, no one noticed the venomous yellow eyes that stared out from the blackness below, or the clawed hand that reached up to slide the manhole back in place.

IV

IF KASPAR HAD been grateful to see the spires of Kislev as they rode from the oblast, it was nothing compared to his relief at returning to the Imperial embassy. Snow clung to its walls and long daggers of ice drooped from the high eaves, but a warm homely glow spilled into the night from the shuttered windows and smoke spiralled lazily from the chimneys. He and his knights rode up to the iron, spike-topped gates, blue and red liveried guards eagerly opening them and welcoming their fellow countrymen back.

A tutting farrier took the bridle of Kaspar's horse and he dismounted, wincing as the stiffness of two weeks in the saddle pulled at his aged muscles. The wound he had received from the leader of a Kurgan scouting party pulled tight, the stitches Valdhaas had pierced his flesh with still raw beneath a fresh bandage.

The door to the embassy opened and Kaspar smiled as Sofia Valencik strode along the path towards him, a heartfelt smile of relief creasing her handsome features. His physician's long, auburn hair was pulled in a tight ponytail and she wore a green dress with a red, woollen pashmina wrapped around her shoulders.

'Kaspar,' she said, throwing her arms around him, 'it's so good to see you.'

'And you, Sofia,' replied Kaspar, returning the embrace and holding her tight. He was pleased Sofia was on her feet again; the last time he had seen her, she had been confined to bed, recovering from her brutal kidnapping by Sasha Kajetan. Her left hand was still bound with bandages where he had severed her thumb.

Thinking of the captured swordsman, Kaspar opened his mouth to speak.

'Sofia–' he began, but she had already seen her former captor being pulled from the saddle by one of the Knights Panther. He felt her go rigid in his arms.

'We were able to capture him, Sofia, as you wanted,' said Kaspar softly. 'I've sent word to Pashenko that we'll bring him to the *Chekist* building tomorrow and–'

But Sofia appeared not to be listening, pulling free of Kaspar's arms and marching stiffly towards Sasha. Kaspar made to follow her, but Kurt Bremen gripped his arm and shook his head slowly.

Sofia hugged her arms tightly about herself as she neared Kajetan, the swordsman's emaciated frame held aloft by two knights. Kaspar could see how much courage it took her to face her abuser and felt his admiration for Sofia soar once more. Hearing her steps, Kajetan turned and Kaspar saw the swordsman shudder in… what? Fear, guilt, pity?

Kajetan met the woman's eyes for as long as he could before dropping his head, unable to endure the cold heat of her accusing gaze any longer.

'Sasha,' she said softly, 'look at me.'

'I can't…' whispered Kajetan. 'Not after what I did to you.'

'Look at me,' said Sofia again, this time with steel in her voice.

Slowly Sasha's head rose until once again their eyes met. Tears streamed down Kajetan's cheeks and his eyes were violet pools of sorrow.

'I'm sorry,' he choked.

'I know you are,' nodded Sofia. And slapped him hard across the face.

Kajetan didn't flinch, the red imprint of her hand bright and vivid against the ashen pallor of his face. He nodded and said, 'Thank you.'

Sofia said nothing, wrapping her arms around herself once more as the knights led Kajetan to the cell beneath the embassy. Kaspar moved to stand behind Sofia as the Knights Panther attended to their mounts and the embassy guards closed the gates once more.

'Why did you bring him here?' asked Sofia without turning.

'I wasn't about to hand Sasha over to Pashenko before getting some assurances that he wouldn't hang him the minute my back was turned,' explained Kaspar.

Sofia nodded and turned to face him once more. 'I am glad you are home safely, Kaspar, I really am, and I'm happy that you managed to bring Sasha back alive. It was just a shock to see him there like that.'

'I understand, and I'm sorry; I should have sent word ahead.'

'It brought it all back, the terrible things he did to me. I almost couldn't move, but...'

'But?' asked Kasper when Sofia's words trailed off.

'But when I saw what had become of him, I knew that I wasn't about to let what he'd done beat me. I'm stronger than that and I had to show him that, even if it was just for my own sake.'

'You are stronger than you know, Sofia,' said Kaspar.

Sofia smiled at the compliment and linked her arm with Kaspar's, turning him around and walking back to the embassy with him.

'Come on, let's get you into a hot bath, you must be frozen to the marrow,' said Sofia playfully, 'I don't know, a man of your age gallivanting outside in the middle of winter like you're some kind of young buck.'

'You're starting to sound like Pavel,' chuckled Kaspar, his grin fading as he saw Sofia's face darken at the mention of his old comrade in arms.

'What's the matter?'

Sofia shook her head as they entered the embassy and shut the door behind them. Kaspar immediately felt the warmth of the building envelop him as one of the embassy guards helped him off with his frosted cloak and muddy boots.

'It is not my place to say,' said Sofia archly.

'But I can see you're going to anyway.'

'Your friend is *nekulturny*,' she said. 'He spends all his time drinking cheap *kvas*, and falling into the blackest of moods. He hasn't been sober since you left to go after Sasha.'

'He's that bad?'

'I don't know what he was like before, but he seems intent on drinking himself into the Temple of Morr as soon as he can.'

'Damn it,' swore Kaspar, 'I knew something was wrong before I left.'

'I don't know what it is,' confessed Sofia, 'but whatever it is, he needs to sort it out soon. I don't want to have to stitch a shroud for him.'

'Don't worry,' growled Kaspar. 'I'll get to the bottom of it, that's for damn sure.'

V

VASSILY CHEKATILO THREW a handful of thin branches onto the crackling fireplace and took a drink of *kvas* from a half-drained bottle, enjoying the comfortable warmth filling his chambers at the rear of the brothel. His establishment was busy tonight – as it had been for the last few months since the refugees had begun streaming south – and several whores sprawled on chaise-longues in various states of undress and narcotic oblivion, waiting to be called back to the main chambers.

Most of them had once been pretty. Chekatilo only employed pretty ones, but they were now shadows of their former selves, the rigours of their profession and the escape of weirdroot soon robbing them of whatever beauty they might have possessed. Once, he had thought that having such nubile creatures around his chamber gave it an air of exotica, but now they merely depressed him.

Though sumptuously furnished with many fittings and furniture he had extorted from the previous ambassador from the Empire, Andreas Teugenheim, his chambers were nevertheless assembled with the taste of a peasant. His criminal enterprises had garnered him great wealth and many fine things, but there was no escaping his humble origins.

'A piece of shit in a palace is still a piece of shit,' he said with a smile, watching a pair of black-furred rats gnaw on something unidentifiable in the corner of the room.

'Something funny?' asked Rejak, his flint-eyed assassin and bodyguard, who had entered the room without knocking.

'No,' said Chekatilo, masking his annoyance by turning and drinking some more *kvas*. He offered the bottle to Rejak, but the assassin shook his head, circling the room and unashamedly ogling the naked women sprawled around the room. As he reached the chamber's corner, his sword flashed from its scabbard and stabbed downwards. A pair of squeals told Chekatilo that the two feasting rats were dead. Trust Rejak to find something to kill.

'Did you see the size of those creatures?' asked Rejak. 'I swear the damn things are getting bigger every day.'

'Wars are always good for vermin,' said Chekatilo.

'Aye,' agreed Rejak. 'And ratcatchers, well, except for the poor bastard they pulled from below the Goromadny Prospekt today.'

'What are you talking about?'

'Oh, just something that happened earlier tonight. One of the guild ratcatchers who sometimes feeds me information was hauled off to the Lubjanko screaming that the rats were coming to kill us all. They say he climbed from the sewers like all the daemons of Chaos were after him and started acting like a lunatic. I think he hit some people before the watch came and dragged him away.'

Chekatilo nodded, filing the information away as Rejak wiped his sword on a dark rag before sheathing it and slumping into a chair before the fire. Chekatilo sat opposite his assassin and stared into the fireplace, enjoying the simple act of watching the flames dance and listening to them devour the new wood in the grate. He sipped the *kvas*, waiting for Rejak to speak.

'Damn, but it's cold out there,' said Rejak, shifting his sword belt and holding his hands out to the fire.

Chekatilo bit back a retort and said, 'What news from the north? What are people saying?'

Rejak shrugged. 'The same as they've been saying for weeks now.'

'Which is?' said Chekatilo darkly.

Finally catching his master's mood, Rejak said, 'More people are coming south every day. They say that the armies of the High Zar are getting bigger with every passing week, that each of the northern tribes he defeats he swears to his banner. And that his warriors leave nothing alive behind them.'

Chekatilo nodded. 'I feared as much.'

'What?' said Rejak. 'That the Kurgans are coming south? They've done that before and they'll do it again. Some peasants will get killed and once the fighting season is done, the tribes will return to the north with fat bellies, slaves and some plunder.'

'Not this time, Rejak,' said Chekatilo. 'I can feel it in my bones, and I've not lived this long without trusting them. This time it will be different.'

'What makes you say that?'

'Can't you feel it?' asked Chekatilo. 'I can see it in every desperate face that comes here. They know it too. No, Rejak, the High Zar and his warriors do not come for the plunder or rape, they come for destruction. They mean to wipe us from the face of the world.'

'Sounds like the kind of talk I hear in the gutter grog shops,' said Rejak: 'Old men telling anyone who'll listen that these are the End Times, that the world is a more wicked place than when they were younglings and that there is no strength here any more.'

'Perhaps they are right, Rejak, did you ever think of that?'

'No,' confessed Rejak, placing his hand over his sword's pommel. 'There is still strength in me and no bastard is going to kill me without a fight.'

Chekatilo laughed. 'Ah, the arrogance of youth. Well, perhaps you are right and I am wrong. It is a moot point now anyway.'

'You are still set upon leaving Kislev then?'

'Aye,' nodded Chekatilo, looking around his drab chamber, his eyes fastening upon another mangy rodent feasting upon the bodies of the dead rats in the corner. Rejak was right; these damned rodents *were* getting bigger.

He put the rats from his mind and said, 'This place will be no more soon, of that I am sure, and I have no desire to end my days spitted on a Kurgan blade. Besides, Kislev bores me now and I feel the need for a change of scenery.'

'Did you have anywhere in particular in mind?'

'I thought Marienburg would be an ideal destination for a man of my talents.'

'A long journey,' pointed out Rejak. 'Dangerous too. A man travelling with wealth would find it hard to reach his destination intact without protection.'

'Yes,' agreed Chekatilo, 'a hundred soldiers or more.'

'So where are you going to get a hundred soldiers? It's not as though the Tzarina is going to let you have a regiment of kossars or her precious Gryphon Legion.'

'I thought I might ask Ambassador von Velten.'

Rejak laughed. 'And you think he'll help you? He hates you.'

Chekatilo smiled, but there was no warmth to it. 'If he knows what's good for him, he will. Thanks to Pavel Korovic, the ambassador owes me a favour, and I am not a man to allow a debt like that to go unanswered.'

CHAPTER TWO

I

DESPITE THE BITING chill of the morning and the stiffness in his muscles from two weeks in the saddle and sleeping on the cold ground, Kaspar's spirits were high as he rode through the busy streets of the city. Last night he had enjoyed a long, hot bath to wash off the grime of his adventures in the desolate wilderness of the Kislev oblast, before retiring to bed and falling asleep almost before his head hit the pillow.

Awaking much refreshed, he had dressed and sent word to Anastasia that he would call upon her for an early breakfast. He looked forward to seeing her again, not least because it had been many years since he had been sharing his bed with an attractive woman, but also because she was a tonic for his soul. He found her playfulness and unpredictability fascinating; keeping him forever guessing as to her true thoughts. She was at once familiar and a mystery to him.

He wore his freshly cleaned and dried fur cloak over a long black frock coat with silver thread woven into the wide lapels, and a plain cotton undershirt. A tricorned hat with a silver eagle pinned to it sat atop his head, its design old fashioned, but pleasing to him. Four Knights Panther rode alongside him, clearing a path for the ambassador with their wide-chested steeds.

Word had spread to the people of the city that Kaspar had been instrumental in the apprehension of the Butcherman, and there was much doffing of hats and tugging of forelocks as he passed.

The streets widened as his journey took him into the wealthier parts of the city in the north-eastern quarter, though even here, there was no escaping the depredations of war. Families and scattered groups of Kislevite peasants huddled close to the walls, utilising their meagre possessions to fashion rough lean-tos and shelters from the worst of the cold winds that whistled through the city. He rode past cold and hungry groups of refugees towards the Magnustrasse and Anastasia's house, turning into the wide, cobbled boulevard to find it similarly inhabited.

The stand of poplars opposite Anastasia's house was gone, hacked stumps all that remained of them, and as Kaspar rode through the open gateway in the dressed ashlar walls of her home, he saw several hundred people camped within. Anastasia's home was tastefully constructed of a deep red stone, situated at the end of a long paved avenue that was lined with evergreen bushes – though Kaspar noticed that many of these were afflicted with a sickly discolouration of their greenery. Perhaps the cold was too severe even for these normally hardy plants, though the low temperatures did not seem to bother the darting rats that scurried through the undergrowth.

Dressed in a white cloak edged with snow leopard fur and with her long, jet-black hair spilling around her shoulders, Anastasia Vilkova was an unmistakable sight. Kaspar watched as she distributed blankets to those most in need.

She looked up at the sound of horses' hooves and as he drew nearer, Kaspar saw her face flicker before breaking into a smile of welcome.

'Kaspar, you're back,' she said.

'Aye,' nodded Kaspar, 'I promised you I'd come back safely, didn't I?'

'That you did,' agreed Anastasia.

He swung his leg over the saddle and dismounted, saying, 'Though two weeks in the oblast is more than enough for any man.'

Anastasia, still carrying an armful of blankets leaned up to kiss him as he handed Magnus's reins to a green-liveried stable boy.

He returned her kiss fiercely, revelling in the softness of her lips against his own until she pulled back with a wicked sparkle in her eyes.

'You *have* missed me, haven't you?' she laughed, turning away and handing out the last of the blankets to the people camped within her walls.

'You wouldn't believe how much,' nodded Kaspar, walking alongside Anastasia as they made their way towards her home. 'You seem to have a great many guests just now.'

'Yes, I have space within the grounds here, and it seemed to make sense to allow these poor people to make use of it.'

'Always trying to help others,' said Kaspar, impressed.

'Where I can.'

'Regrettably, people like you are rare.'

'I remember saying something similar to you once.'

Kaspar laughed, 'Yes, I remember, the first time I called upon you. Perhaps we are two of a kind then?'

Anastasia nodded, her jade eyes flashing with secret mirth, and said. 'I think you might be more right than you know, Kaspar.'

They reached the black, lacquered door to Anastasia's home and she pushed it open, saying, 'Come inside, it's cold out here, and I want to hear all about your adventures in the north. Was it hard? How silly of me, I suppose it must have been. To catch and kill a monster like Kajetan can't have been easy.'

Kaspar shook his head. 'It was hard, yes, but I didn't kill him.'

'Of course not, I suppose it was one of those brave knights who killed him.'

'No, I mean Sasha is not dead, we were able to take him alive.'

'What?' said Anastasia, her jaw dropping open and her skin turning the colour of a winter sky. 'Sasha Kajetan is still alive?'

'Yes,' said Kaspar, surprised at the sudden chill in Anastasia's tone. 'He's in a cell below the embassy and once our meal is over I shall be taking him to Vladimir Pashenko of the *Chekist*.'

'You didn't kill him? Kaspar, you promised! You promised you'd keep me safe!'

'I know, and I will,' said Kaspar, confused at the passion of her reaction. 'Sasha Kajetan is a shell of the man he once was, Ana, he won't be hurting anyone. I promised you I wouldn't let anyone hurt you again and I meant that.'

'Kaspar, you promised,' snapped Anastasia, her eyes filling with tears. 'You said you would kill him.'

'No,' said Kaspar firmly. 'I did not. I never said I would kill him. I wouldn't say such a thing.'

'You did, I swear you did,' cried Anastasia. 'I know you did. Oh, Kaspar, how could you fail me?'

'I don't understand,' said Kaspar reaching out to put his arms around her.

Anastasia took a step backwards, folding her arms and said, 'Kaspar, I think you should go, I don't think I can talk to you just now.'

Kaspar started to say that he would still keep her safe, but his words trailed off when he saw the frosty hostility in Anastasia's eyes and felt a flash of anger. What did she want of him? Had he not ridden into the depths of the harshest country imaginable for this woman?

'Very well,' he said, rather more sharply than he had intended. 'I will bid you good day then. Should you wish to see me, you know where to find me.'

Anastasia nodded and Kaspar turned on his heel, snapping his fingers at the stable boy to bring his horse. He would hand Kajetan over to the *Chekist* and that would be the end of the matter.

II

HIS BREATH MISTED before him, the thin blanket his gaolers had given him doing little to prevent the cold of the cell penetrating him to the marrow. Sasha Kajetan sat on the thin mattress that, save for the night-soil bucket, was the only furnishing within the small cell beneath the embassy. He shivered, the pain of his many wounds dulled by the numbing cold.

His upper body was crisscrossed by freshly stitched scars – wounds taken in battle with Kurgan tribesmen – though his greatest wound was to his thigh, where the ambassador had driven his sword after denying him the death he knew he deserved.

Sasha wished that Ambassador von Velten *had* killed him. The woman who had slapped him – the woman he had once believed was his beloved matka – had promised him that the ambassador would help him, but she had lied. The ambassador had not helped him to die, but had spared him, prolonging the agony of his existence and he wept bitter tears of frustration, knowing that he was too weak to end his life himself and hearing the mocking laughter of the trueself as a hollow echo in the depths of his mind.

The trueself was still there, lurking like a sickness, though instead of swallowing him whole as it had done for so long, it gnawed and worried at the frayed ends of his sanity. He held his shaking hands out before him, the blackened tips of his fingers raw where exhuming his mother's corpse from the frozen ground and frostbite had claimed them.

There was nothing he could do to atone for what he had done, though he had hoped that the ambassador's blade would grant him the absolution he craved. He knew that the *Chekist* would hang him for his crimes and, while he welcomed the oblivion the hangman's rope promised, he was tormented by the suspicion that death would not be enough of a punishment. Why the ambassador had not killed him, he did not know. Surely someone he had wronged so terribly should have cut him down like the animal he was?

But he had not and Sasha was consumed with the need to know why.

With a clarity borne of the acceptance of death, Sasha understood that his and the ambassador's fates were still intertwined, that there were dramas yet to unfold between them.

Von Velten had not killed him and as he felt the true-self continue to erode his reason, Sasha Kajetan just hoped that the ambassador did not live to regret that clemency.

III

PAVEL KOROVIC OPENED his eyes and let out a huge belch, his mouth gummed with dried saliva. Bright spears of light streamed through the high window, stabbing through his eyes, and he groaned as the hammer blows of a crushing headache began to build.

'By Tor, my head…' he mumbled, rubbing the heel of his hand against his forehead. Gingerly, he rose from his bed, grimacing as the headache worsened and he felt his stomach lurch in sympathy.

Pavel smelled the stench of himself, stale sweat and cheap *kvas*, and saw that he had fallen asleep in his clothes again. He didn't know when he had last bathed and felt the familiar sense of shame and self-loathing wash over him as his memories swam to the surface of his mind through the haze of alcoholic fog. He needed to eat something, though he doubted if he could keep anything down.

He swung his legs from the bed, knocking over a trio of empty bottles of *kvas*, which shattered on the stone floor. The fire in the grate had long since burned to ash and the cold knifed through his clothing as he pushed himself upright, careful to avoid the pile of broken glass.

Where had he gone last night? He couldn't remember. Some darkened, backstreet drinking den no doubt, where he could lose himself once more in the oblivion of *kvas*.

The guilt was easier to deal with that way; the guilt of what Vassily Chekatilo had forced him to do – many years ago and recently – did not eat away at him when he could barely remember his own name.

Though it had been six years ago, Pavel could still remember the murder he had committed for Chekatilo. He could still hear the sickening crack as he had brought the iron bar down on Anastasia Vilkova's husband's skull; see the brains that had spilled onto the cobbles and smell the blood that gathered like a red lake around his head.

The killing had shamed him then, and it shamed him still.

But to Pavel, the worst betrayal had been at his own accord when he had knowingly placed Kaspar, his oldest and truest friend, in debt to Chekatilo. He told himself it was to help the ambassador find Sasha Kajetan, but that was only partly true…

By trying to erase one mistake, he had made a greater one and now it wasn't just him who would pay for it.

How could he have let himself sink so low?

The answer came easily enough. He was weak; he lacked the moral fibre that made men such as Kaspar and Bremen such honourable figures. Pavel put his head in his hands, wishing he could undo the pathetic waste of his life.

Despite the vile taste in his mouth, the headache and the roiling sensation in his belly, he wanted a drink more than anything. It was a familiar sensation, one that had seized him every day since he had gone to Chekatilo's brothel and sold what shreds of his dignity and self-respect remained to a man he hated.

He pushed his giant frame from the bed, swaying unsteadily and feeling his legs wobble under him. His grey beard was matted with crumbs and he brushed it clear of the detritus of long ago meals, stumbling over to a polished wooden chest sitting in the corner of the room.

Pavel dropped to his knees before the chest and lifted the lid, hunting through his possessions for the bottle of *kvas* he knew lay within.

'Looking for this?' said a voice behind him.

Pavel groaned, recognising the icy tones of Sofia Valencik. He turned his head to see her standing beside his open door, an upturned and very empty bottle of *kvas* held in her hands.

'Damn you, woman, that was my last bottle.'

'No it wasn't, but don't bother looking for the others, I emptied them too.'

Pavel's shoulders slumped and he slammed the lid of the chest down before standing and turning to face the ambassador's physician.

'Now why would you go and do that, you damned harpy?' snapped Pavel.

'Because you are too stupid to see what it is doing to you, Pavel Korovic,' retorted Sofia. 'Have you seen yourself recently? You look worse than the beggars on the Urskoy Prospekt and smell worse than a ratcatcher who's fallen in the sewer.'

Pavel angrily waved her words away and returned to his bed, reaching down to lift his boots from the floor. He sat on the edge of the bed, dragging them on and fighting down the urge to vomit.

'Where are you going now?' asked Sofia.

'What business is it of yours?'

'It is my business because I am a physician, Pavel, and it is not in my nature to stand by while another human being attempts to destroy himself with alcohol, no matter how stubborn and pig-headed he may be.'

'I am not trying to destroy myself,' said Pavel, though he could see that Sofia didn't believe him.

'No? Then go back to bed and let me get you something to eat. You need sleep, some food and a wash.'

Pavel shook his head. 'I can't sleep and I don't think I could eat anything anyway.'

'You have to, Pavel,' said Sofia. 'Let me help you, because you'll die if you carry on like this. Is that what you want?'

'Pah! You are exaggerating. I am a son of Kislev, I live for *kvas*.'

'No,' said Sofia, sadly, 'you will die for *kvas*. Trust me, I know what I'm talking about.'

'I don't doubt it,' said Pavel, rising from the bed and pushing past Sofia, 'but before you try and save someone, make sure that they want to be saved.'

IV

A FOG HAD descended upon Kislev by the time Kaspar returned to the embassy, wrapping the city in a muffling blanket of icy mist. The cold was worse than Kaspar could ever remember, even in the far north when they had pursued Kajetan into the wilderness.

The Knights Panther had prepared Kajetan for his journey to the *Chekist* gaol, wrapping him in furs and a hooded cloak to obscure his features. It had now become common knowledge around the city that the Butcherman murders had been committed by Sasha Kajetan, and Kaspar was taking no chances that a lynch mob would take the law into their own hands to administer vigilante justice on the swordsman.

The fog would help also, and as he tightened the saddle on Magnus, he watched Valdhaas help Kajetan onto the back of a horse, since, with his wrists and ankles bound, the swordsman was forced to ride sidesaddle.

Kajetan looked up, as though sensing Kaspar's gaze and gave him a vacant look, utterly devoid of human emotion that chilled Kaspar worse than the cloying scraps of fog.

Kaspar shuddered, sensing the hollow emptiness of Kajetan's soul. The man was a void now, drained of emotion and humanity. The swordsman had been unresponsive and lethargic when they had taken him from his cell, and Kaspar feared that he would learn little of whatever twisted fantasies had driven him to murder so many people.

'We're ready to go, ambassador,' said Kurt Bremen, startling Kaspar from his reverie.

'Good,' nodded Kaspar. 'The sooner he's gone from here the happier I'll be.'

'Aye,' agreed Bremen. 'I have lost good men thanks to him.'

'Very well then, let's get this over with, I'm sure Vladimir Pashenko is eager to get his hands on the Butcherman.'

'Do you think he will keep his word and not hang Kajetan the first chance he gets?'

'I don't know,' admitted Kaspar. 'I do not like Pashenko, but I believe he is a man of his word.'

Bremen gave him a sceptical look, but nodded and turned to accept the reins of his horse from his squire. 'What is it you hope to gain by keeping Kajetan alive anyway?'

Kaspar planted a foot in his stirrup cup and hauled himself onto the back of his horse, adjusting his cloak over the animal's rump and tightening his pistol belt.

'I want to know why he killed all those people, and what could make a man do such vile, unthinkable things. Something made him the way he is and I want to know what.'

'I remember asking you on the oblast if you were sure you really wanted to know the answer to that. The question still stands.'

Kaspar nodded, guiding his horse to the embassy gates.

'More than ever, Kurt. I don't know why, but I feel that much depends on knowing those answers.'

Bremen raised his mailed fist and the knights set off, with Kajetan riding in their midst, a ring of steel preventing the swordsman's escape or his murder by a vengeful mob.

Kaspar and Bremen led the way, walking their horses along the street that led to Geroyev Square, the fog so thick that they could barely see the walls to either side of them.

The solemn procession emerged into the square, the fog deadening sounds and forcing them to keep to the edges of the square for fear of losing their bearings. The jingle of the horses' harnesses and their muffled steps through the snow the only sounds that disturbed the eerie silence that had descended upon the city.

They passed shadowy outlines of small encampments of refugees and saw the occasional glow of cooking fires, but even with these touchstones, the silence and sense of isolation were unnerving, especially in a city so thronged with people. People moved like ghosts in the fog, drifting in and out of sight as they moved from the horsemen's path

Eventually Kaspar and Bremen reached the Urskoy Prospekt, the great triumphal road that led to the Tzarina's Winter Palace and housed the *Chekist* building. Named for the great reliquary at its end that housed the remains of Kislev's greatest heroes, the wide boulevard was also strangely quiet as they rode along its length, though, looking up, Kaspar could see the weak rays of the sun finally beginning to penetrate the fog.

Ahead, Kaspar could see the grim outer walls of the *Chekist* building emerge from the mist, a pair of armed men in black armour standing before the imposing black gates. He twisted in the saddle, pulling on the reins and drawing level with Sasha Kajetan. The swordsman glanced up as Kaspar rode alongside him, but said nothing, returning his gaze to the snow.

'Sasha?' said Kaspar.

The swordsman did not reply, lost in whatever thoughts were echoing within his tormented soul.

'Sasha,' repeated Kaspar. 'Do you know where we're going? I am taking you to Vladimir Pashenko of the *Chekist*. Do you understand?'

Kaspar thought he was going to have to repeat himself again, but almost imperceptibly, Kajetan nodded.

'They will hang me...' whispered the swordsman.

'Eventually, yes, they will,' said Kaspar.

'I am not ready to die. Not yet.'

'It is too late for that, Sasha. You killed a great many people and justice must be done.'

'No,' said Kajetan, 'that's not what I mean. I know I deserve to die for things I have done. I meant that there are things I have yet to do.'

'What do you mean? What kind of things?'

'I know not yet,' admitted Kajetan, raising his head and fixing Kaspar with his dead-eyed stare. 'But know that it involves you.'

Kaspar felt a thrill of fear slick across his skin. Was the swordsman threatening him with violence? Unconsciously, his hand slipped towards his pistol, his thumb hovering over the flint, as he realised just how far away the Knights Panther were from him. It was a few feet at best, but it might as well have been a mile, for Kaspar knew how quick and deadly Kajetan could be. Had Kajetan simply feigned docility so that he might now escape and continue his grisly work?

But it seemed that Kajetan did not have violence in mind, his head drooped again and Kaspar let out a long breath, his eyes narrowing and his brow knitting in puzzlement as he saw something peculiar.

A flickering glow of green light wavered on Kajetan's stomach. Kaspar watched as it slowly eased up his body until it settled in the centre of his chest.

Mystified, Kaspar could see a pencil-thin line of green light, a light that would surely have been invisible but for the fog, tracing an arrow-straight course from Kajetan's chest upwards into the mist.

He waved his hand through the light, feeling a tingling warmth through his thick gloves as he broke its beam. He tried to follow the line of the green light. He soon lost it in the fog. As a breath of wind parted the murk for an instant, he saw a dark, hooded shape atop one of the red-brick buildings of the prospekt silhouetted against the low sun, holding what looked like one of the long rifles made famous by the sharpshooters of Hochland.

Kaspar's heart raced and he reached for one of his flint-locks as he realised what he was seeing.

'Knights Panther!' he yelled, reaching out and dragging Kajetan from his saddle as he heard a sharp crack from above. Instinctively, Kajetan twisted free of Kaspar's grip and the two men tumbled to the snow as something slashed past Kaspar's head and exploded against the wall behind them, blasting bricks and mortar to powder.

Kaspar rolled, the wound in his shoulder flaring as the stitches tore open. He flailed against Kajetan as the swordsman sprang to his feet.

'Kurt! On the roof! Across the street!' shouted Kaspar as the Knights Panther hurriedly wheeled their horses and closed on the struggling pair. Another bang echoed along the prospekt and Kaspar watched horrified as the closest knight was spun from his feet, his shoulder blown out in a shower of red. The knight fell screaming and, behind him, Kaspar could see a smudge of greenish smoke from where the shots had been fired.

He clambered to his feet and took hold of Kajetan as the knights formed a protective cordon of armoured war-riors around them. Valdhaas lifted the downed knight to his feet as Kaspar drew his pistol and hurriedly aimed at the rooftop across the prospekt. The chances of hitting anything were negligible, but he fired anyway, the pistol bucking in his hand and further obscuring his view.

'Ambassador!' shouted Kurt Bremen. 'Are you hurt?'

'No, I'm fine, but we need to get off the street! Now!'

Bremen nodded, shouting orders to his knights and the group made its halting, stumbling way towards the *Chekist* building. Kaspar half carried, half dragged Kajetan onwards, the bindings on his ankles limiting the speed at which he could move considerably.

'Pashenko! Vladimir Pashenko!' bellowed Kaspar. 'Open the gates! This is Ambassador von Velten! For the love of Sigmar, open the gates!'

The black armoured soldiers Kaspar had seen standing before the gates emerged from the mist, cudgels at the ready, and, as they saw the desperate group of Imperial knights hurrying towards them, turned to open the gates behind them.

Kaspar knew a disciplined handgunner could load and fire between three and four aimed shots a minute, but a long rifle took somewhat longer, with its finer powder and more exacting preparations. Exactly how much longer, he didn't know and as each second passed, he kept waiting for another shot to pitch one of their number to the snow.

But no shots came and they gratefully hurried through the thick gates of the *Chekist* building, emerging into a wide, cobbled courtyard before the fortress-like headquarters of Kislev's feared enforcers. Two *Chekist* hurriedly shut the heavy gate behind them as Kaspar pushed Kajetan to the ground. He took out his other pistol and pointed it at the swordsman, lest he use the confusion of the attack to make his escape. But the prisoner merely knelt in the snow with his head bowed.

Valdhaas lowered the screaming knight to the ground, hurriedly unbuckling his breastplate and shoulder guards to get to the wound. Blood steamed in the cold air as it sheeted down the man's armour. *Chekist* were running from the building's main door and Kaspar could see Vladimir Pashenko amongst them.

'Is anyone else hurt?' shouted Bremen.

No one else was, and Kaspar felt himself relax a fraction when another crack echoed and a portion of the gateway was blown to splinters as something smashed through. A man screamed and Kaspar saw a *Chekist* in front of him drop, a bloody hole blasted through his chest. Knights and *Chekist* alike threw themselves to the ground, horrified that anything could have penetrated the thick timbers of the gateway.

'Everyone inside!' yelled Kaspar, rolling aside and finding himself face to face with Pashenko.

The head of the *Chekist* nodded and helped Kaspar drag Kajetan towards the doors of the building. The knights and *Chekist* soldiers backed towards the entrance, anxiously scanning the tallest rooflines for the would-be assassin.

Pashenko kicked open the door and Kaspar fell through it, collapsing in a heap with his back to a corridor wall. Kajetan rolled onto his back, moving out of the way of the open door.

Kaspar did likewise as the last of the knights entered the safety of the building and Pashenko slammed the door shut. He threw heavy iron bolts across before sliding down the wall to rest on his haunches.

'Ursun's blood, what just happened here?' said Pashenko, his face a mask of fury.

'I don't know exactly,' said Kaspar. 'We were riding along the Urskoy Prospekt when someone started shooting at us.'

'Who?' asked Pashenko.

'I didn't see him clearly, just a dark shape, maybe with a hood, on the rooftop.'

'What in Ursun's name was he firing? It penetrated nearly a span of seasoned timber with enough power left to kill one of my men. Save a cannon, what manner of weapon could do such a thing?'

'No blackpowder weapon capable of being carried by a man, that's for sure,' said Kaspar. 'Even the contraptions designed by the College of Engineers in Altdorf are not that powerful.'

'Trouble has a habit of following you,' observed Pashenko.

'Aye, don't I know it,' agreed Kaspar, as two *Chekist* soldiers lifted Kajetan and led him towards the cells below.

'I would suggest you remain here for a while, ambassador,' said Pashenko, picking himself up and straightening his uniform. 'At least until my men ensure that whoever attacked you is not still lurking and waiting for you to emerge.'

Kaspar rose to his feet and nodded, though as he watched Kajetan's disappearing back, he had the strong impression that whatever the purpose of this attack had been, he had not been the intended target.

V

NIGHTS IN THE brothel were always busy, filled with men afraid to die affirming that they were alive in the most primal way possible. Chekatilo did not usually trouble himself to visit the main floor, but for reasons he could not fathom, he had decided to drink and smoke amongst the common herd tonight. Most people here had come from the north and would not even know his name, let alone be fearful of him, though the imposing figure of Rejak, standing behind his chair, left no one in any doubt that he was a man not to trifle with.

Chekatilo watched the crowd, seeing the same sick desperation in every face. He saw a young boy, probably barely old enough to need a razor, enthusiastically coupling with a woman draped in red silks and furs. He was watched by a similarly-featured man, old enough to be his father. Chekatilo guessed that this was a father's last gift to his son: that if he were to die, it would be as a man and not a boy.

Such pathetic scenes were played out throughout the brothel: old men, perhaps desiring one last memory to take to the next life, young men for whom their existence was one long indulgence and those who had already resigned themselves to the fact that life had nothing more to offer them.

'This places reeks of defeat,' muttered Chekatilo to himself. 'The sooner the Kurgan burn it to the ground the better.'

Watching the parade of human misery before him made him all the more sure that he was making the right decision to leave Kislev. He had no great love for his country, and its dour, provincial nature was suffocating for a man of his ambition. Marienburg, with its bustling docks and cosmopolitan nature, was the place for him. He had made a great deal of money in Kislev, but no matter how much he possessed, he would never escape his birth. Respect and esteem were for those of high birth, not for a filthy peasant who had managed to haul himself out of the gutters and fields.

In Marienburg, he would never have to worry about freezing winters and raiding northmen. In Marienburg, he could live like a king, respected and feared.

The thought made him smile, though as Rejak had pointed out, it was a long way to Marienburg – through Talabheim, on to Altdorf and finally westwards to the coast. He would need help to get there safely, but knew exactly how to get it.

The door to the brothel opened and Rejak said, 'Well, well, look who's back again.'

Chekatilo looked up and smiled as he saw Pavel Korovic enter, shivering and stamping his heavy boots free of snow.

'Pavel Korovic, as I live and breathe,' laughed Chekatilo. 'I would have thought he'd had enough of this place to last a lifetime.'

'Korovic?' said Rejak. 'No, ever since he came begging for you to help the ambassador, he's been coming here, swilling bottle after bottle of *kvas* till dawn before somehow managing to stumble out the door.'

Chekatilo saw Korovic notice him, and blew a smoke ring as the big man nodded curtly before making his way to the bar and tossing a handful of coins to its surface. Korovic snatched the bottle of *kvas* the barman brought and retreated to an unoccupied table to drown his sorrows. Chekatilo toyed with the idea of going over and speaking to him, but dismissed the thought. What did he have to say to him? Korovic knew his place and Chekatilo had no wish to bandy words with a drunkard.

He caught a flash of swift movement in the corner of the hall and jumped as something bristly rubbed against his leg. Startled, he looked down and saw a sleek, black-furred shape dart beneath his chair.

'Dazh's oath!' he swore disgustedly as another rat, this one the size of a small dog, joined the first. 'Rejak!'

Even as he shouted the name he saw more rats, dozens, scores, hundreds of them, boiling out from unseen lairs to invade his brothel. The screams started seconds later as the tide of vermin attacked, a swarming, squealing mass of furry bodies, pointed snouts and razor-sharp incisors that bit and clawed at exposed flesh.

Chekatilo surged from his chair, toppling it as Rejak stamped down on a rat and broke its spine. He stumbled backwards, horrified as he saw the young boy dragged down by the sheer weight of rats, his face a mask of blood as they ripped off long strips of his flesh. Men and women crawled across the blood-slick floor, unable to believe that this was happening to them as frenziedly biting rats clung to their bodies.

A naked man struggled with a pair of rats while yet more bit and clawed his lower body to the bone. He smashed one rat's skull to splinters against the wall, but another leaped from the stairs and fastened its teeth around his neck, biting out his throat with its powerful jaws. Bright arterial spray spattered the walls as the man collapsed and the scent of so much blood drove the swarming rats into an even greater frenzy.

'Come on!' yelled Rejak, pushing Chekatilo towards the door that led to the chambers at the back of the brothel. Screams and sobs of pain filled the air, mixed with the sounds of breaking glass, smashing furniture and squealing rats. Hundreds of darting black shapes sped through the rooms and corridors of the brothel, as if directed by a malign intelligence, snapping and squealing in a frenzied mass as they attacked with teeth that cut like knives.

A frantic woman, flailing at a rat caught in her hair and biting her neck and shoulders, knocked a lamp from its mounting on the wall. It fell and smashed on her head, spraying blazing oil across her and the floor. She screamed as the flames hungrily seized her clothing, blundering blindly through the brothel and igniting furnishings, spilled alcohol and other patrons as she went. Fire roared through the place with horrifying speed in her wake.

As Rejak pushed him towards safety, Chekatilo saw Pavel Korovic under attack from a dozen or more rats that were biting his legs and arms and raking his chest with their sharp claws. He slashed at them with a broken bottle and stamped on others as he backed towards a shuttered window. A pair of rats leapt towards the giant Kislevite, but he dropped the bottle and caught them in mid-air, slamming them together and dropping the limp corpses as he tore the window shutters from their hinges and leapt through the glass to the street.

Chekatilo yelled as he felt a sharp pain and forgot Pavel Korovic as a rat took a bite from his ankle. He reached down, grabbing the rat by its neck and tearing it from his flesh, ignoring the pain as blood poured from the wound.

The rat twisted and bit his hands, claws like razors drawing blood with every slash. Chekatilo wrung its neck as he saw Rejak sheath his sword and draw a short-bladed dagger, the longer weapon too large to wield effectively against such small, nimble opponents. He stabbed and slashed at any rats that approached, stamping and kicking at those he couldn't kill with his blade.

Rats were closing in around them and Chekatilo barged open the door to the back as another huge rat launched itself at him. He ducked and the rat slammed into the wall behind him. Before it could recover, he turned and hammered his boot down on its chest, hearing a satisfying crack as its ribs shattered.

Smoke, heat and flames filled the brothel as Rejak pushed him through the door, hauling it shut behind him as several heavy thumps slammed into it from the other side. The door shuddered in its frame as the rats hurled themselves at it. Chekatilo could hear splintering, scratching noises as they began gnawing their way through.

'Come on!' shouted Rejak, setting off up the corridor. 'The door won't hold them for long!'

Rejak ushered him into his chambers as he heard wood splinter and saw a pointed snout, wet with blood, push its way through the closed door. Giant teeth ripped the hole wider and Chekatilo watched in disbelief as an enormous rat pushed its wriggling body through. The creature landed on the floor and fixed him with its beady black eyes. It squealed in a high, child-like manner, spraying pink-flecked saliva, and the pounding and scratching noises from the other side of the door doubled in their intensity.

Chekatilo followed Rejak numbly, unable to believe the single-minded intelligence of the rats, and shut the door behind him. Who could believe that vermin would attack in such numbers and with such ferocity? He had never heard the like and could only shake his head at such madness.

He could hear the roaring flames crackling through the door, over the diminishing screams from the main hall, and knew that this place was finished. It was of no matter, he had other places and its loss would barely affect him.

But as he and Rejak made their escape from the burning brothel, he felt a chill in his blood over and above the horrors he had just witnessed. He thought back to the rat that had gnawed its way through the door and locked eyes with him. He had seen its feral intelligence and had been seized by a sudden unshakeable intuition.

He was sure the rat had looked at him with something other than hunger in its eyes.

It had been seeking him.

CHAPTER THREE

I

IN THE CLOSING days of Uriczeit, word reached Kislev that Norscan raiders had sacked Erengrad. Hundreds of longships with sails bearing the marks of the old, northern gods had sailed into the port and disgorged thousands of berserk warriors who had swept through the city and killed thousands in their bloody rampage.

The Kislevite priesthood, never the most optimistic fraternity, took to the streets of Kislev and proclaimed that the doom of a wicked mankind was at hand, that these were the End Times as prophesied in the Saga of Ursun the Bear and that everyone should prepare their souls for death. Some of the more eloquent fanatics attracted quite a following and on some days the wide boulevards of Kislev were filled with marching columns of flagellating priests and crowds of zealots who mortified their flesh with scarifying belts, hooks and whips.

Such displays of fanatical piety inevitably led to the zealots taking it upon themselves to root out those they perceived as the cause of the city's woes. Lynchings and beatings became a daily occurrence and over two-dozen people were killed – for no more a crime than hailing from the blighted city of Praag – until Vladimir Pashenko rounded up the most vocal of these doomsayers and locked them away. But the sense of fear they had fostered within the city was harder to dispel. Stories of battles fought between armies in the west and north were told around every campfire and in every tavern.

Sorting fact from fiction proved more difficult than anyone could have guessed. Riders from various parts of the country provided many contradictory tales which were often embellished beyond recognition by the time they reached those who desperately needed accurate information.

To add to Kislev's woes, it soon became apparent that a pestilence had taken hold in the poorest quarters of the city. At first, the outbreak was not recognised for what it truly was, as physicians denied that plague could take hold in such cold conditions and many of the initial deaths were thought to have been caused by the freezing temperatures. But as Uriczeit turned to Vorhexen, it could no longer be ignored and soldiers with scarves soaked in camphorated vinegar wrapped around their mouths and noses were drafted in to quarantine several districts.

Riverboats from the Empire continued to arrive, carrying much needed supplies, but none lingered longer than they had to and their frequency was growing less and less as famine began to take hold in the land of Karl-Franz and the Emperor was forced to husband his resources for his own people. Anastasia Vilkova continued to lead caravans of wagons into the refugee camps as well as those of the Kislevite and Empire regiments to distribute food and water to the soldiers there. With her distinctive, snow-leopard cloak, she soon became known to the soldiers as the White Lady of Kislev.

But such symbols of hope were rare and the coming days would require them like never before.

II

KASPAR SAT ATOP his horse at the base of the *Gora Geroyev*, watching as his embassy guards sparred with the Knights Panther, enjoying the simple spectacle of good soldiers learning quickly. Kurt Bremen's punishing training regime had worked wonders with the embassy guards, transforming them from the slovenly layabouts he had inherited from Andreas Teugenheim into soldiers he could be proud of. Leopold Dietz, a young soldier from Talabecland, had assumed the leadership of the guards – a role Kaspar was happy for him to have. The lad was confident, skilled and understood how to motivate his men; qualities Kaspar knew were essential in a leader of warriors.

The cold was still numbing, but Kaspar could tell that the worst of the winter was over and that these warriors would be called upon to fight when the snows broke. The fighting season was a month away at most and soon an army that had driven thousands of people from their homes would be coming this way. It was now not a matter of if, but when.

Kaspar was pleased to see that the officers of the Kislevite and Empire regiments realised this also and had begun a program of marching and drilling to prepare their men for the coming conflict.

He returned his attention to his own soldiers, walking his horse forward as he saw that Kurt Bremen had called a halt to their training for today. The knights' squires and lance carriers distributed fresh water and food to the soldiers while the knights gathered in a circle for prayer.

Kaspar rode up to Leopold Dietz, who sat on a bare rock and chewed his meal of bread and cheese with gusto.

'My compliments, Herr Dietz. Your men are looking good.'

Dietz looked up, shielding his eyes from the low sun and stood, straightening his uniform and running a hand through his unruly dark hair.

'Thank you, sir. I told you they was good lads, didn't I?'

'Yes, you did,' agreed Kaspar. 'It does the heart proud to see.'

Dietz beamed at the compliment and Kaspar rode on, allowing the men to eat their food. He did not interrupt the knights at their prayer and wheeled his horse as he heard the sound of iron-rimmed wagon wheels clattering along the roadway.

Anastasia sat on the buckboard of an empty wagon, expertly guiding it towards him with a shy smile. He had not seen her since they had argued at her house. A wilfully stubborn streak had prevented him from visiting her, and, despite wishing to appear calm, he couldn't help but smile as she drew nearer.

'Hello, Kaspar,' she said as she drew level with him.

'Hello. It's good to see you, Ana,' he said, dismounting from his horse as she climbed down from the padded seat of the wagon.

They faced each other in awkward silence, neither quite knowing what to say, until Anastasia finally said, 'Kaspar, I am sorry, I shouldn't have been so hard on you. I just–'

'No,' interrupted Kaspar, 'It's alright, you don't need to apologise.'

'How I've missed you, Kaspar,' said Anastasia, opening her arms and hugging him tightly. He was surprised, but held her close, smelling the perfume of her black hair and the scent of her skin. He wanted to say that he too had missed her, but settled for simply holding her and enjoying her nearness.

He stroked her hair and she lifted her head, allowing him to lean down and kiss her on the mouth. The taste of her full lips and tongue was like the forgotten taste of a fine wine suddenly and forcefully recalled. He felt a thrill of arousal and broke the kiss, taken aback by the force of the sensation. A man of passion, but outward reserve, Kaspar was not normally given to such public displays of affection and as he heard the good-humoured wolf-whistles drift from his guards, he felt his skin redden.

Anastasia laughed. 'You are blushing, Ambassador von Velten.'

Kaspar smiled, and it felt good. After the violence of taking Kajetan to the *Chekist* and the recent turmoil in the city streets it felt good to smile again.

'Come on,' he said, 'let's go back to the embassy.'

III

KASPAR AWOKE HEARING people moving downstairs and yawned, shifting his position in the bed to slip his arm from around Anastasia's shoulders. She gave a little moan, but did not wake and Kaspar watched her sleep for a few moments, enjoying the softness of her features and the heat of her pale skin.

They had returned to the embassy the previous evening and made a pretence of having a light supper, but there was little doubt in either Kaspar or Anastasia's mind that they had an urgent physical need to be with one another.

Unlike their previous lovemaking, which had been gentle and tentative, this was fierce and passionate, surprising them both with its intensity. They had tired one another out, satisfying their pent up needs before falling into a contented and dreamless sleep.

Kaspar leaned down and kissed Anastasia's cheek before sliding towards his side of the bed. As he moved, she turned onto her side and said, 'Kaspar?'

'I'm here, Ana, it's morning.'

'Are you getting out of bed?' she said sleepily, sliding towards him and draping her arm across his chest.

'I should, I arranged to speak with Sofia, she has been working with the apothecaries and city officials to try and halt the spread of the plague. I think she wants to make sure I'm not coming down with anything.'

'No…' whispered Anastasia, 'stay here with me. Given your performance last night, I think I can safely say that you are in rude health.'

Kaspar laughed. 'Thank you, but I do need to get up. There are ambassadorial duties I have to attend to as well.'

'More important duties than staying in bed with me for the day?' grinned Anastasia, playfully reaching below the bedclothes.

'Well, if you put it like that,' said Kaspar rolling towards her.

SEVERAL HOURS LATER they lay back, pleasantly exhausted and covered in a light sheen of perspiration. Kaspar propped up his pillows in order to sit upright and allow Anastasia to lie with her head on his stomach. He reached over and poured himself a glass of water from a pewter jug. It was a day old, but refreshing nonetheless.

He offered the cup to Anastasia, but she shook her head.

'So what ambassadorial duties *did* you plan to do today?' she asked sleepily.

Kaspar stroked her sculpted shoulder and said, 'I had planned to visit the officers commanding the Empire forces outside the walls and keep them informed of what news there is from the field.'

'From what I hear, there's not much to tell. No one seems to know for sure exactly what's happening. There are all kinds of wild stories going around.'

'Aye, there are, but I have it on good authority that Boyarin Kurkosk has inflicted considerable damage on a large army of Kurgans massing in the north-west.'

'Really? That's wonderful news. Where is Kurkosk now? Does he march to Kislev?'

'No, his army divided for the winter, ready to gather when the fighting season begins again.'

'Oh, so he's not coming here?'

'I don't think so. Kurkosk gathered the pulk at a place called Zoishenk, so I think he will muster his warriors there in the spring when the Imperial armies march out.'

'Your Emperor is sending his armies north, how wonderful.'

'Yes, I received word that the counts of Stirland and Talabecland muster their men in readiness to march north. An army of the Empire is a fine thing to see, Ana, rank after rank of disciplined regiments, trains of cannon and hundreds of armoured horsemen, their banners and guidons like a rainbow of colour across the landscape. If any army can defeat the Kurgans it will be an Imperial one.'

Kaspar spoke with the fierce pride of a man who had led such fine soldiers in battle and the regret that came of knowing he had passed on the responsibility and honour of such duties to other, younger men.

They lay in silence for a little longer before Kaspar finally extricated himself from the bedclothes and dressed in a simple doublet and riding britches. As he picked up his boots, Anastasia propped herself up on her elbow and hesitantly said, 'Kaspar?'

He turned, hearing the tremor in her voice, and said, 'Yes?'

She asked, 'Kaspar… have… have you seen Sasha since you handed him over to the *Chekist*?'

'Sasha?' he said warily, remembering her reaction the last time they had spoken of the murderous swordsman, but unwilling to make himself a liar. 'Yes, I have. I saw him the previous week.'

'And what was he like?'

Kaspar considered the question for a moment. 'He's not the man he once was, Ana, and he won't be hurting anyone ever again. He's gone; there's nothing left of Sasha Kajetan as far as I can see. I think whatever made him human died out in the wilderness.'

'Were you able to learn why he did all those terrible things?'

'Not really,' said Kaspar, pulling on his boots. 'I could barely get him to speak at all, in fact.'

'That doesn't surprise me, Kaspar. It's plain now that Sasha was evil, simply evil, so you shouldn't waste any more time with him. Are they not planning to hang him soon anyway?'

'Eventually they will, but I've persuaded Pashenko to give me some more time to try and get through to the man before they send him to the gallows.'

'I think you're wasting your time, Kaspar.'

'Perhaps, but I have to try.'

Anastasia did not reply, drawing the sheets up to her neck and rolling over so that she had her back to him.

Kaspar knew when not to push a point and opened the door to his study, leaving Anastasia in bed. He strolled over to his desk to see if any correspondence had been delivered while he had tarried in bed, but there was nothing that demanded his immediate attention and he walked over to the frosted window that looked out over the snow-capped roofs of Kislev.

If not for the fact that he knew the city was full of desperate, cold and hungry people and that soon there would be an army coming to destroy it, the serene view would have calmed him. He cast a glance over his shoulder at the door to his bedroom, seeing a sliver of pale flesh as Anastasia shifted in the bed.

Her dismissal of his attempts to understand Kajetan disturbed him, but he had no real reason he could put his finger on to feel that way. After all, he was not the one who had been close to Sasha Kajetan before it came to light that he was a killer. Indeed, Anastasia had been the object of Kajetan's obsessive infatuation for some time and perhaps she felt that that was a convenient enough explanation for his crimes. But Kaspar could not so easily believe this, and Anastasia's refusal to countenance any other motive sat ill with him.

He scratched his chin, unsure as to what to think, when there came an urgent knocking at his door.

'Come in,' he said, turning from the window as Sofia Valencik entered, not bothering to close the door behind her. He could see from her face that something terrible had happened.

'Sofia, what is it?'

'You need to come downstairs now,' she said.

'Why, what's the matter?'

'It's Pavel.'

IV

AT FIRST KASPAR did not recognise his old friend, so bloody and covered in filth was he. The sleeves and trouser legs of his long coat were shredded and bloody, stinking of the filth of the street and his normally robust frame was a shadow of its normal size. His skin was the pallor of a corpse and his forearms and face were lined with deep cuts that had healed badly and, in some cases, were clearly infected. Kaspar could see thin splinters of glass still embedded in his face.

The giant Kislevite lay unconscious on the floor of the embassy vestibule, his breathing ragged and his eyes glazed. Two guards stood beside the open door, and Kaspar saw that both of them had angry bruises flowering on the sides of their faces. Kaspar knelt beside his comrade in arms and clenched his fist as he felt his anger build towards whatever brute had done this.

'What happened?' he demanded. 'And close that bloody door. Do you want him to freeze to death?'

The shorter of the two guards answered, his words coming out in a rush as the other closed the embassy door. 'We was on gate duty as normal and we saw Herr Korovic staggering towards us, except we didn't know it was him at first. He tried to get in the gate, but we weren't having any of that. We thought he was some mad beggar or something.'

The other guard picked up the tale as Sofia bent to examine Pavel's wounds.

'Aye, then he comes up and tries to barge through the gate. Course, we weren't having none of that and showed him the business end of a halberd, but he weren't taking no for an answer.'

'Then what?' snapped Kaspar as the guards shuffled embarrassed from foot to foot.

Sofia waved over a group of Knights Panther, who had emerged from their quarters at the rear of the building upon hearing the commotion, and ordered them to carry Pavel to his room.

Kaspar straightened as the knights struggled to lift Pavel's weighty body upstairs, following close behind and indicating that the guards should follow him.

'Well, sir...' said the first guard, hurrying to keep up. 'We tries to stop him, but he just shouts something in Kislevite and starts laying about with his fists. He knocked Markus flat on his arse, then put me down next to him sharpish. Then he pushes open the gate and marches right through to the door, raving something about rats before collapsing in a heap. That's when we recognised who he was and called for Madame Valencik.'

Kaspar turned to face the guards as the knights carried Pavel into his room. 'You did the right thing. Now get someone else to man the gate and have someone take a look at your faces. Dismissed.'

The guards saluted and returned to the vestibule. Kaspar strode along the corridor to Pavel's room to find Sofia barking quick-fire orders at the knights.

'Prepare a warm bath as fast as you can! A warm bath, mind, not hot, you understand? And get me some clean, warm water in a basin and some cloths to wash these cuts with. Heat as many blankets as you can find as well, we need to get him warmed up quickly. Someone get my satchel as well, the one with my needles and poultices. And prepare some sweet tisane, it'll help his body fight off the cold from within.'

As the knights hurried to obey her commands, Kaspar said, 'What can I do?'

'Help me get his clothes off. It looks and smells like he's been outside on the streets for a week or more. These cuts have festered with dirt and it looks like some of them have gone septic.'

'Sigmar's blood, how could this have happened?'

'Knowing Pavel, anything's possible,' said Sofia, cutting away Pavel's trousers using a long, thin bladed knife with a serrated edge and Kaspar winced as he saw the hurt done to his friend's body.

Kaspar began pulling off Pavel's shirt, tearing it where necessary and tossing the bloody scraps of linen to one side. The ashen skin of his friend's shoulders, face and upper body were scored with deep gashes, many of which still glittered with glass fragments and were crusted over with dried blood. He saw that his fingers and arms were similarly crusted with blood, though the wounds there were much smaller.

As Sofia finally cut away Pavel's trousers and undergarments, Kaspar saw that his ankles and lower legs were covered with similar wounds to those on his arms and wondered again what had happened. These smaller wounds looked like bites, but what could have caused them?

'Holy Sigmar,' whispered Kaspar when he saw the full extent of the damage done to Pavel. 'What the hell trouble has he gotten himself into now?'

'We can worry about that later, Kaspar,' snapped Sofia. 'We need to get him cleaned up and warmed up. He's almost frozen to death and if we don't raise his body temperature he may die anyway.'

News of Pavel's condition spread quickly throughout the building and the embassy staff hurried to procure everything Sofia had asked for. Anastasia had joined the effort to help Pavel also, cutting linen bedsheets into swathes of bandages and helping to warm water for a bath. The fire in the grate was lit and warmed blankets were wrapped around Pavel's shivering body while Sofia used thin forceps to remove the jagged splinters of glass from his cuts.

As each wound was cleaned, Kaspar gently doused a cloth in warm water and washed it as gently as he could. Pavel moaned, but did not regain consciousness as they carefully cleansed him of dried blood.

Kaspar heard the door open behind him and a group of knights, Kurt Bremen among them, dragged a heavy iron bath into the room. Water splashed over the side and Sofia said, 'Put it in front of the fire and lift him in. Carefully now.'

The knights lifted the naked form of Pavel and gently lowered him into the warm bath. More water splashed onto the floor, as the bath was too small for someone of Pavel's size, and under any other circumstances, the sight of such a big man in the bath would have been comical.

'Is there anything else we can do?' said Kaspar, suddenly very afraid for his friend.

Sofia shook her head and put her hand on Kaspar's arm. 'No, all we can do now is hope that his body temperature has not dropped too far. We'll need to leave him in the warm water for a while then get him dried off and just keep him warm. Then we need to worry about those bites. I'm pretty sure they are rat bites.'

'Rat bites? Is that what they are?'

'Yes, and I am worried that they might be infected. It's possible Pavel's been wandering the streets delirious and in a fever for days. It's a wonder he found his way back here at all.'

'But so many bites? I've never heard of so many rats attacking a grown man.'

'And there is something else,' said Sofia.

'What?'

'Some of the city doctors think the contagion that's broken out in the city is spread by rats, so we're going to have to keep everyone out of here from now on in case Pavel is infected.'

'Oh no, Pavel…' whispered Kaspar as a wave of sadness threatened to engulf him. He had lost one great friend in

Kislev already and fervently hoped he would not lose another.

'I'm sorry, Kaspar,' said Sofia as Pavel stirred, muttering something under his breath.

Kaspar knelt beside the bath and said, 'I'm here, old friend.'

Pavel's eyes flickered open, though Kaspar saw no recognition there, and he tried to speak, but only succeeded in making a series of barely audible groans.

'What is it Pavel?' said Kaspar, though he was unsure if Pavel could even understand him. 'Who did this to you?'

He placed his head next to Pavel's as his deathly ill friend tried to speak once more, uttering a string of slurred Kislevite. Kaspar listened intently, his expression hardening into one of cold, lethal anger as he made out a single word amongst Pavel's delirium.

He stood and marched swiftly to the door, saying, 'Look after him, Sofia.'

'Wait, what is it, Kaspar? What did he say? Did he say who did this to him?' asked Sofia, hearing the murderous edge to Kaspar's voice.

Kaspar gripped the door, his knuckles white and face flushed.

'He said "Chekatilo".'

V

'AMBASSADOR, THINK OF what you're doing,' said Kurt Bremen.

'I don't want to hear it, Kurt,' snapped Kaspar, buckling on his pistols and looping his sword belt around his waist. 'You saw what he did to Pavel.'

'We don't know that for sure,' pointed out the knight. 'This is Pavel we're talking about, anything could have happened to him.'

'He said Chekatilo's name, damn it, what am I supposed to think?'

'That's just it, ambassador, you are not thinking. You are allowing your hatred of Chekatilo to blind you to reason.'

Kaspar pulled on his long cloak and turned to face the leader of the Knights Panther, who stood between him and the door.

'This is something I need to do, Kurt.'

Bremen folded his arms and said, 'I told you once before that we could not perform our duties to you if you behaved in a manner that forced us to violate our order's code of honour. I am telling you that again.'

'So be it,' snarled Kaspar, moving towards the door.

Kurt Bremen's hand shot out and gripped the ambassador's shoulder, holding him fast. Kaspar's eyes flashed with sudden anger and his fists bunched.

As clearly and evenly as he could, Bremen said, 'If you murder Chekatilo then neither my knights or I will remain oath-bound to you.'

Kaspar locked eyes with the knight, knowing that he was right, but too consumed with anger to countenance any other course of action. He reached up and slowly lifted Bremen's hand from his shoulder.

He looked straight at the grim-faced knight and said, 'Either come with me or get out of my way. Because one way or another, I am going through that door.'

'Don't do this, Kaspar. Think about what you are about to do.'

'It's too late for that, Kurt. Much too late.'

Kaspar pushed past the knight and hurriedly descended the stairs to the vestibule. He paused at the bottom as he heard Kurt Bremen coming down after him, and looked up to see him buckling on his own sword belt.

'What are you doing, Kurt?'

'Sigmar save me, but I'm coming with you.'

'Why?'

'I told you, I won't help you murder Chekatilo, but someone has to try and keep you from getting yourself killed, you damn fool.'

Kaspar smiled grimly. 'Thank you.'

'Don't thank me too soon,' snapped Bremen, 'I may have to put you on your arse to do it.'

THE COLD OF the early evening could not cool the heat of Kaspar's rage, but he was wholly unprepared for the sight that greeted him when he and Kurt Bremen rode up to the brothel where they had last met with Chekatilo.

Instead of the nondescript building of sagging black timbers and random blocks of rough-hewn stone, there was only a swathe of fire-blackened timbers and rubble. Soot-coated fragments of coloured glass and the burned remains of a crimson sash flapping from the melted finial protruding limply from the ruins were all that remained of Chekatilo's brothel. The buildings to either side of the brothel had escaped the fire's worst attentions, saved from destruction by the snows that had doused the blaze and allowed the fire watch to extinguish the conflagration before the entire quarter went up in flames.

Not that Kaspar imagined there would have been much of a public-spirited attempt to save Chekatilo's establishment. The people huddled in the lee of the buildings were a pathetic sight, wrapped in furs and covered with a fresh dusting of snow, and Kaspar could not picture them helping Chekatilo. If anything, he imagined they had simply gathered to enjoy the fleeting warmth offered by the burning structure.

'What the hell happened here?' wondered Kaspar as he dismounted. He kicked a scorched piece of timber in frustration.

'Perhaps someone with a grudge against Chekatilo?' suggested Bremen.

'Well that only leaves an entire city full of suspects,' replied Kaspar, crunching through the snow towards the remains of the brothel. Even in the chill air he could smell a sickeningly cloying aroma he knew to be burnt human flesh. He had lit enough funeral pyres in his time to recognise the familiar smell.

Kaspar pointed to the people gathered in their shelters against nearby buildings and said, 'Kurt, you speak more Kislevite than I, ask these people if they know what happened here.'

Bremen nodded as Kaspar hitched Magnus to a protruding spar of timber and clambered over the rubble of the destroyed building to begin sifting through what little wreckage remained of the brothel. It had been thoroughly scavenged by the people of Kislev, those timbers not completely burned to ash taken for firewood and any trinkets that had survived stolen that they might be traded for a little food. As he was about to give up, Kaspar noticed the corpses of several rats, their bodies burned and twisted into unnatural angles by the heat of the flames. As he studied them, he was amazed at their size – fully eighteen inches or more from tip to rump.

He knelt beside the charred corpse of a rat and used a broken piece of furniture to turn its stiff body over. Its black fur had been crisped from its body, but the flesh of its back still remained and Kaspar could see three crossed red welts on its skin that formed an uneven triangle.

'What is it? Have you found something?' called Bremen from the edge of the ruins.

'A rat, and a big one at that,' said Kaspar, 'but it looks for all the world like it's been branded with a mark.'

'Branded? Who in their right mind would bother to brand a rat?'

'I have no idea,' said Kaspar, 'but…'

'But what?'

'I was just thinking of something Sofia said about the plague. She said that the city's doctors feared that it was being spread by rats. I'm seeing this brand and wondering if it is possible that such a thing could be somehow directed by someone?'

'You're saying that the plague is deliberate?'

'I don't know, maybe,' said Kaspar, standing and brushing ash from his britches. 'Did you find anything out from these people?'

'Not much,' admitted Bremen. 'Their Reikspiel is as almost as bad as my Kislevite. The few that were here when it happened say they heard screaming from inside just before it went up in flames.'

'That's it?'

'That's it,' nodded Bremen with a shrug. 'I couldn't understand much more than that.'

'Damn, there's something important here, I can feel it, but can't see it.'

'Maybe the *Chekist* or the city watch know something. They are bound to have been here already.'

Kaspar nodded. 'True, I can't imagine Pashenko won't have taken an interest in one of Vassily Chekatilo's haunts being burned to the ground.'

'Even if he does, do you think he will tell you anything?'

'It has to be worth a try,' said Kaspar, emerging from the brothel and climbing back onto his horse. 'The worst he can do is say no.'

Bremen took a last look into the ruined brothel and said, 'I wonder if Chekatilo was inside when it burned down?'

Kaspar shook his head. 'No, I don't think we could be that lucky. I'll wager that bastard is too slippery to be killed that easily.'

KASPAR FELT A flutter of nervousness as he and Bremen turned their horses into the Urskoy Prospekt, remembering the last time they had come this way and the carnage that had followed. The Knight Panther who had been shot had lost his arm and shortly after succumbed to a malignant sickness that Sofia could do nothing to halt.

They kept to one side of the thronged prospekt, Kaspar noticing that Bremen too was scanning the rooflines and dark windows that overlooked the street and taking comfort in the fact that he was not alone in his caution.

A group of armoured kossars marched down the centre of the street, resplendent in scarlet and green and armoured in a mix of iron and bronze breastplates. They carried wide-bladed axes and had short, recurved bows slung at their sides. All wore furred colbacks and had thick scarves tied around the lower portion of their faces. The black armbands they wore told Kaspar that they had been detailed to those areas of the city closed off because of the plague and he saw that the people camped in the prospekt shrank back in fear from the soldiers.

Kaspar nodded to the leader of the kossars, but the man ignored him and he and his men passed, barely registering their presence.

Eventually they reached the *Chekist* compound and announced themselves to the two guards at the gate. Both men seemed taken aback by Kaspar's request for entry, more used to people begging *not* to be taken within. But, recognising the Empire ambassador, they opened the gate with some difficulty and allowed Kaspar and Bremen to ride through into the cobbled courtyard beyond.

As the gate closed behind them, Kaspar saw it had been heavily reinforced with thick spars of timber, the hole blasted by the marksman's weapon patched with a sheet of iron. Pashenko was obviously taking no chances that a skilled marksman might use the same hole to put another bullet through.

The black door in the grim façade of the *Chekist* building opened and the leader of the *Chekist* emerged into the evening's twilight, his dark armour reflecting the light from the torches either side of the entrance.

'Ambassador von Velten,' said Pashenko in his clipped tones. 'This is a coincidence. I do hope you are not bringing trouble to my door once more.'

'No, not this time,' said Kaspar. 'And why is it a coincidence?'

'Never mind, why are you here?'

'I have just come from where a brothel belonging to Vassily Chekatilo once stood. Do you know anything about what happened?'

'It burned down.'

Kaspar bit back an angry retort and said, 'I wondered if you might have had any idea who might have done it.'

'I might, but it would take from now until this time next year to arrest all the possible suspects. Chekatilo was not a well-liked man, ambassador.'

'A friend of mine is badly hurt and may die. I think he might have been there the night the brothel burned down. I just want to find out what happened.'

Pashenko waved a pair of stable boys forward to take Kaspar and Bremen's horses and said, 'Come inside, there is little I can tell you about the fire you probably do not already know, but as I said, it is a coincidence that you have come here tonight.'

Kaspar and Bremen handed their reins to the stable boys and followed Pashenko into the *Chekist* building, removing their heavy winter cloaks as they entered.

'So you have said, Pashenko. Why?' said Kaspar, his patience wearing thin.

'Because less than an hour ago, Sasha Kajetan began begging to be allowed to see you.'

VI

FLICKERING LAMPLIGHT ILLUMINATED the brickwork passageway that led to the cells beneath the *Chekist* building and Kaspar felt his skin crawl as a low moaning drifted from below. The echoes of their footsteps on the stone steps rang from the walls and, though he had never been particularly susceptible to claustrophobia, Kaspar had an instinctive dread of this place, as though the walls themselves had seen too many miseries and could contain them no longer, bleeding its horror into the air like a curse.

Flaking paint coated the walls and old stains the colour of rust were splashed across the brickwork. Pashenko led the way, carrying a hooded lantern that swayed with his every step and cast monstrous shadows around them.

How many men had been dragged screaming down these steps, never to return to the world above, wondered Kaspar? What was the word Pavel had used? Disappeared. How many people had been disappeared in the cold darkness below this feared place? Probably more than he dared think about and he felt his loathing for Vladimir Pashenko grow stronger.

He saw the leader of the *Chekist* reach a solid iron door with a mesh grille set at eye level and bang his fist against it, the sound booming and somehow dreadful. A light grew behind the grille and Kaspar heard the rattle of keys and the sound of several iron bolts being pulled back. The door squealed open and Pashenko led them through into the cells.

They descended into a wide, straw covered gallery that stretched off into darkness, the brick walls pierced at regular intervals with narrow doors of rusted iron. The stench of stale sweat, human waste and fear made Kaspar and Bremen gag, but Pashenko appeared not to notice it.

'Welcome to our gaol,' smiled Pashenko, his underlit face looking daemonic in the lamplight. 'This is where we keep the enemies of Kislev, and this is our gaoler.'

The gaoler was a heavyset man with thickly muscled arms who carried a hooded lantern and a spike-tipped cudgel. His face was obscured by a black hood with brass-rimmed eyepieces fitted with clear glass and a thick canvas mouth filter. He wore an iron breastplate, leather gauntlets studded with bronze spikes and heavy, hobnail boots, putting Kaspar in mind of the handlers of the lethally exotic beasts kept by the Emperor in his menagerie at Altdorf. Were the captives kept here as dangerous? The thought gave him pause and Kaspar shared an uneasy glance with Kurt Bremen.

'Where is Kajetan?' asked Kaspar, wanting to leave this cursed hellhole as quickly as he could. Pashenko chuckled and pointed along the ink-black corridor.

'On the left, the cell at the end,' he replied, leading the way. 'He is securely chained to the wall, but I would not recommend approaching him too closely.'

'Has he become violent again?' asked Bremen.

'No, he is just covered in his own filth.'

Kaspar and Bremen followed the *Chekist* along the corridor, the gaoler bringing up the rear. Kaspar could hear desperate shuffling and muffled pleas for help or mercy from behind each cell door as they passed.

'Truly, this place is hell,' whispered Kaspar, unconscionably grateful when they reached the end of the bleak, soulless passage.

'If it is hell,' said Pashenko, 'then everyone here is a devil.'

The gaoler stepped up to the cell door, searching on his belt for the correct key; his actions slowed by the thick gauntlets and cumbersome hood he wore. At last he found the correct key and spun the tumblers of the lock, opening the door for them.

Pashenko stepped inside the cell and Kaspar followed, the stench of human excrement almost overpowering him. The lamplight threw its flickering illumination around a square cell of crumbling brickwork, the floor dank and glistening with patches of moisture. Kaspar covered his mouth with his hand to ward off the stench and felt his skin crawl as he saw the naked form of Sasha Kajetan curled in a foetal ball in the corner.

The swordsman had been a shell of his former self when Kaspar had last seen him, but he was now little more than a beaten wretch, his body covered in a patchwork of bruises and cuts. The lamplight threw the shadows where his ribs poked from his emaciated frame into stark relief and his cheeks had the sunken hollowness of a famine victim.

He whimpered as they entered, covering his eyes against the light, the thick chains securing him to the wall rattling as he moved. Despite the horror of his crimes, Kaspar could not help but feel pity for any man subjected to such brutal conditions.

'Kajetan,' said Pashenko. 'Ambassador von Velten is here.'

The swordsman's head snapped up and he tried to stand, but the gaoler stepped forward and slammed his cudgel into the side of his thigh. Kajetan grunted in pain and collapsed into a groaning heap, streamers of blood running down his leg.

'Ambassador...' he hissed, his voice hoarse and cracked. 'It was all for her...'

'I'm here, Sasha,' said Kaspar. 'What did you want to tell me?'

Kajetan's chest heaved, as though every breath was an effort, and said, 'The rats. They everywhere here. Just when you think you all alone, I see them. They keep watch on me for her. Tried to kill me once already, but happy now just to watch me suffer.'

'Rats, Sasha? I don't understand.'

'Filthy rats! I see them, I feel them!' wailed Kajetan and Kaspar feared the swordsman's mind had finally snapped in this intolerable place. 'Above in the city, I hear their little feet as they plot and plan with her.'

'With who, Sasha? I don't understand,' said Kaspar approaching Kajetan.

'Ambassador,' warned Bremen, 'be careful.'

Kaspar nodded as he listened to more of Kajetan's ramblings. 'The pestilent clans of the Lords of Vermin are here. Evil in me can feel them, brothers of corruption we are. Told you once I was tainted with Chaos and so are they, but they glad of it. I feel them in my blood, hear their chittering voices in my head. They bring their best sickness and death here for her, but it won't take me. It won't take me!'

'Sasha, slow down, you are not making any sense,' said Kaspar, reaching out to touch Kajetan's shoulder.

With a speed that belied his pitiful form, the swordsman's hand snapped forward and seized Kaspar's wrist.

'Their sickness won't take me because I am like them, creature of Chaos! You not understand?'

Kaspar pulled away as Kajetan released him and he tumbled onto his backside as the gaoler leaned in and hammered his gauntleted fist into Kajetan's face. Blood exploded from the swordsman's nose and he gave a wild, animalistic howl, but rolled with the punch, lunging forward to wrap his hands around the gaoler's neck.

But Kajetan's strength was not what it once was and the gaoler was no apprentice when it came to dealing with violent prisoners. He slammed his spiked gauntlet hard into Kajetan's solar plexus, driving him to his knees, but the swordsman refused to let go, his chest heaving with violent spasms.

The gaoler raised his spiked cudgel, but before he could land a blow, Kajetan vomited a froth of gristly black blood over the man's breastplate. Kaspar watched horrified as the viscous liquid spilled down the armour, melting it with a noise like fat on a skillet. Stinking smoke hissed from the dissolving metal and the gaoler howled in pain as his armour was eaten away. He dropped his weapon and struggled to undo the straps that held the liquefying breastplate to his body.

Bremen rushed to help him and, between them, they were able to strip the armour off and hurl it to the ground where it crackled and hissed as Kajetan's tainted vomit completed its destruction.

Kajetan slid down the wall of his cell, weeping and rubbing the heels of his palms against his forehead. Bloody vomit dripped from his chin, displaying none of the corrosive properties towards him as it had to the armour.

'Sigmar save us!' cried Bremen, dragging Kaspar to his feet and hauling him from the acrid reek of the cell. 'He is an altered!'

The gaoler stumbled from the cell, his padded undershirt burned away and his chest raw and bleeding. Pashenko, who looked more terrified than Kaspar could ever remember seeing a man, closely followed him. The head of the *Chekist* shouted at the stumbling figure of the gaoler. 'Lock the door! Shut that monster in now!'

Kurt Bremen kicked the cell door shut and the gaoler eventually managed to find the key to lock Kajetan away once more.

'Ursun's blood,' breathed Pashenko, coughing at the foul stink still emanating from Kajetan's cell. 'I have never seen the like.'

Kaspar's senses still reeled from the horror of what he had just seen, his skin crawling at his proximity to a creature surely touched by the power of the Dark Gods. He had thought that Kajetan's claim to be a creature of Chaos on that lonely hilltop in the oblast was the delusion of a madman.

Now he knew better.

Without another word, he and Bremen fled the cells of the *Chekist*.

VII

KASPAR AND BREMEN returned to the embassy in silence and darkness, still in shock at what they had witnessed. The moon was high by the time they reached it and upon entering the warmth of the building, one of the embassy guards gestured towards the receiving room where guests would await the ambassador's pleasure.

'Someone to see you, Ambassador von Velten,' said the man.

Kaspar was in no mood for visitors at this hour and said, 'Tell them I am–'

But the words died in his throat and his pulse raced as he saw the three men within the receiving room.

The first was a man he knew to be a cold-eyed killer; the second a dishevelled man he did not recognise, but the third...

'Good evening, ambassador,' said Vassily Chekatilo.

CHAPTER FOUR

I

KASPAR COULD NOT believe that Chekatilo dared set foot in his embassy and for a moment he was stunned rigid, shocked that this piece of filth had actually sought *him* out after the events of the past few days. Chekatilo's killer, Rejak, stood beside him, taut like a stretched wire, with one hand resting on the pommel of his sword, the other gripping the filthy collar of a man smeared with dirt and of wild, unkempt appearance.

Before another word could be said, Kaspar whipped his pistol from his belt, pulling back the flintlock with his thumb and raising it to aim at Chekatilo's head.

'Kaspar, no!' shouted Bremen as Rejak released the man he held and moved with blinding speed, his sword slashing from its scabbard like a striking snake.

Bremen drew his own sword, but Rejak's blade was at the ambassador's neck before the weapon had cleared its scabbard.

'I'd lower that pistol if I were you,' said the assassin.

Bremen raised his sword, ready to strike at Rejak's heart. 'If you so much as draw a single drop of the ambassador's blood, I will kill you where you stand.'

Rejak smiled, predatory, like a viper. 'Better men than you have tried, knight.'

Kaspar felt the steel point press into his flesh and calculated his chances of pulling the trigger and evading a killing stroke of the blade at his neck. He felt Rejak's icy resolve and knew he wouldn't even manage to fire the pistol before the assassin opened his throat.

He saw Chekatilo disdainfully turn away from the unfolding drama and Kaspar felt his finger tighten on the trigger. How easy it would be to shoot this bastard, who had caused so much misery to the city of Kislev. He pictured the path the bullet would take, the terrible, lethal damage it would do to Chekatilo's head and was shocked to find that he *wanted* to pull the trigger. When commanding men in battle he had killed his foes because he had been ordered to, because that was what his Emperor had commanded. And when he had fought the kurgan horsemen in the snowbound landscape around the Kajetan family estates, he killed those men because they were trying to kill him.

But now he wanted to shoot someone who was not actively trying to kill him and whom he had not been ordered to put to death.

'You cannot do it, can you?' said Chekatilo without turning. 'You are not able to murder me in cold blood. It is not in your nature.'

'No,' said, Kaspar releasing a shuddering breath and lowering his arm. 'Because I am better than you, Chekatilo. I despise you and I will not become like you.'

'Sensible,' said Rejak.

'Take your sword away from his neck, you bastard,' hissed Bremen.

Rejak smiled and put up his sword, sheathing it with a flourish and stepping away from the ambassador. Kurt

Bremen quickly stepped forward and, keeping his sword drawn, put himself between Kaspar and Rejak. He reached for Kaspar's pistol and carefully eased the flint down.

Hearing the click, Chekatilo turned and smiled at Kaspar. 'Now we have necessary show of bravado out of way, maybe we can get to talking, yha?'

Kaspar walked over to a long sideboard and carefully put his pistol down, gently – as though it were a piece of delicate crockery – feeling the tension slowly drain from his body. His heart was pounding fit to crack his chest and he gave thanks to Sigmar that he had not become the very thing he hated: a cold-blooded murderer.

'Why are you here, Chekatilo?' asked Kaspar.

'Same reason you wanted to kill me tonight,' said Chekatilo, sitting in one of the receiving room's large, leather chairs. The filthy man he and Rejak had brought whimpered as the giant Kislevite passed him, and curled into a foetal ball.

Chekatilo tugged at the drooping ends of his moustache as he continued, 'Someone has attacked me and now I want to hurt them back.'

'And what has that to do with me?' asked Kaspar.

'Because I think ones who tried to kill me are same as attacked you in Urskoy Prospekt and hurt your friend. More happening in Kislev than you or I know. Perhaps we can help each other, you and I?'

'What makes you think I would help you with anything?' laughed Kaspar. 'I loathe you and your kind.'

'That not important, Empire man,' said Chekatilo, with a dismissive wave of his hand.

'It's not?'

'No, what important is that we have common enemy. Like I said, those who try and kill you try to kill me too. There is old Kislev saying, "Enemy of my enemy is friend".'

'I will never be your friend, Chekatilo.'

'I know this, but we can at least not be enemies for now, yha?'

Kaspar considered Chekatilo's words, fighting not to let his loathing for the fat crook cloud his judgement. If what Chekatilo was saying was true, then he would only be putting himself and others in harm's way by ignoring this offer of co-operation. And after the terror of what had happened to Sofia and now Pavel, he was unwilling to run that risk again. He nodded warily and said, 'So what would this help cost me?' asked Kaspar.

'Nothing,' said Chekatilo. 'You help me, I help you.'

'Kaspar, no, you cannot trust this man,' protested Kurt Bremen.

'Your knight speaks true, you should not trust me, but I not lie.'

'Very well, suppose I believe that you are sincere,' said Kaspar, ignoring Bremen for the moment, 'who do you think orchestrated these attacks?'

'I not know, but think on this: on same day my brothel overrun by every rat in Kislev, you shot at by killer with gun that can see through walls and kill a man through thick timber. Same day. I not believe in coincidences, Empire man,' said Chekatilo, reaching down to haul the dishevelled man that Rejak had been holding to his knees. He stood and pulled the whimpering man to his feet. In all the excitement, Kaspar had quite forgotten that this sorry specimen of humanity was still in the room.

The man was tall, but Kaspar could see his spine was hunched, as though he had spent long years stooped over. He wore little more than a filthy smock of stiffened linen, and Kaspar could see he was absolutely terrified, his face alive with tics and twitches. His hair and beard were long and unkempt, his eyes darting to the skirting and corners of the room as though afraid of something that might be lurking there.

'Who is this?' asked Kaspar.

'This sorry specimen is Nikolai Pysanka,' said Chekatilo, 'and I just fished him from the Lubjanko.'

Kaspar knew of the feared Lubjanko, the dark-stoned building on the eastern wall of Kislev that had once been a hospital, but was now a dumping ground for the dying, the crippled, the sick and the insane. Its dark, windowless walls carried a terrible weight of horror and Kaspar had felt a nameless dread of the place when he had seen it.

'Nikolai was once a ratcatcher who worked in sewers and homes of rich and powerful people. I pay ratcatchers for the nuggets of information they bring me. It is great profit to know the thing they tell me.'

The wretched man flinched at the sound of his name, his eyes filling with tears. He squirmed in Chekatilo's grip, but had no strength left and eventually ceased his struggles.

'What happened to him?' asked Bremen.

'That I not so sure of,' admitted Chekatilo, 'he raves much of time, screams about rats coming to kill everyone. Now, I see many ratcatchers go mad from time in sewers and most hate rats, but Nikolai screams fit to burst lungs if he see one now.'

Kaspar felt a shiver up his spine, remembering similar thoughts spoken by another madman that very night. Kajetan had spoken of rats too and the similarity in these lunatics' words was chilling.

'I pay no mind to this at first, but then my brothel is attacked by rats so large I think they are dogs. Giants they were, with fangs to bite a man's hands off.'

Chekatilo lifted his arm, exposing several deep cuts and bites, and Kaspar recognised them as identical to the bite marks on Pavel's body.

'The rats kill everyone in brothel – ate them up, snap-snap!'

'I saw them, their bodies I mean,' said Kaspar, 'when I went there tonight.'

'Rats that big not natural, eh?'

'No,' agreed Kaspar.

'So, Rejak here has told me of Nikolai earlier and now I think maybe he not as mad as people think, so we go and speak to him. He not do so good now, no one does in Lubjanko, and he even madder than when they put him in. People they put in there not good people, do terrible things to each other, but who cares, eh? I speak to Nikolai and not get much sense out of him, but he says some things that make me interested.'

'Like what?' said Kaspar, thinking of the triangular brand on the burnt rat's corpse.

'He say he saw things in sewer,' whispered Chekatilo. 'A box that glow with green light. A coffin. And rats that walk like men.'

Kaspar laughed, feeling the tension in his limbs evaporate. He had heard the tales of the ratmen who supposedly lurked beneath the cities of the Old World and plotted the destruction of man, but did not believe them – what civilised man would?

'I too have heard of the ratmen,' scoffed Kaspar, 'but they are nothing more than stories to frighten children. You are a fool if you believe that, Chekatilo.'

Chekatilo pushed the ratcatcher to the ground and snarled, 'You are the fool, Empire man. You think you cleverer than Vassily? You know nothing.'

He knelt beside the quivering ratcatcher and pulled up his smock, exposing his scrawny naked flesh. Chekatilo held the struggling man down and said, 'Look at this and tell me I am fool!'

Kaspar sighed and knelt beside the convulsing Nikolai, his eyes widening as he saw what Chekatilo was pointing at. On the ratcatcher's side there was a small wound, little more than a scratch.

But the wound suppurated, weeping a thin gruel of pus, and the flesh around the wound was a peculiar shade of green, a spiderweb of necrotic jade veins radiating outwards from the cut. Kaspar had seen many wounds that had become infected, but had only ever seen something like this once before…

In the shoulder of the Knight Panther who had been shot by the mysterious sharpshooter on the Urskoy

Prospekt just before he died from the rampaging infection that Sofia had been unable to halt.

'Show me where this happened,' said Kaspar.

II

Pjotr Ivanovich Losov, chief advisor to the Tzarina of Kislev, scratched nervously at the parchments before him, signing orders, authorising promotions and dating proclamations. But his mind was unfocussed and eventually he stood the quill in the inkwell before him and leaned back in his chair.

He knew now that the attack on Chekatilo's brothel had failed to kill the crook and that Kajetan had somehow survived the assassin's attempt to prevent his handover to the *Chekist*. Losov felt a sheen of perspiration across his body, despite the chill of his private chambers, and rubbed a hand across his thin, ascetic features. His robes of office were scarlet, wound at the collar and trims with gold thread and decorated with black fur and silver tassels. Normally it gave him a sense of security to be so dressed, but he felt acutely vulnerable just now.

What if Chekatilo and the ambassador were to join forces? She said they would not, that the ambassador's hatred for the Kislevite would blind him to the idea of co-operation, but Losov was not so sure. She also believed she had him wrapped around her little finger, that he danced to her tune, but Losov did not think that von Velten was a man who could be so easily manipulated.

Who could have predicted that he would not kill Kajetan? After the violation of his physician, they had felt confident that either Kajetan would kill the ambassador and then be cut down by the Knights Panther, or that von Velten would be forced to kill the swordsman. Either way, it was a problem solved. But when the ambassador had returned with Kajetan alive, it had thrown them into a panic.

It did now appear their alarm had been unfounded, however, Kajetan now little more than a catatonic wretch awaiting death. She was content to simply have Kajetan watched now, saying that his continued descent into madness might yet prove useful to the Dark Gods.

If only Teugenheim had not been such a bloody libertine and got himself sent back to the Empire in disgrace. The man had been a weak-willed fool and easy to control, but von Velten was a different kettle of fish, disrupting plans that had been years in the making with his unthinking blunderings.

Well, at least Pavel Korovic was probably out of the picture. That thought alone gave him comfort; that the fat bastard he had had kill Andrej Vilkova would, if not already dead, be dying an extremely painful death. He wondered if von Velten knew of Korovic's murky past and briefly pondered how he might allow it to reach the ambassador's ears without incriminating himself.

He smiled, feeling sure the ambassador would enjoy hearing that particular nugget of information.

III

SOFIA SAT ON the edge of Pavel's bed, gripping his wrist and feeling the weak, thready beat of his pulse. She had managed to prevent the cold from killing him, but shook her head, knowing that the big man was not out of danger yet.

Colour had returned to his face, but he was still desperately fevered, needing rest and nourishment if he were to regain his strength. She had stitched the cuts and bites across his flesh, sitting up all night to drain the infected wounds of pus and evil humours, and applying ointments that she hoped would kill whatever filth had got into his blood. She had seen too much death recently and was damned if she would lose Pavel. The ambassador had asked her to look after this man and she would not let him down, not for anything.

She felt her eyelids drooping, more tired than she could ever remember. The last few weeks had passed in a blur, the nightmare streets of the city where the plague had taken hold haunting her dreams when she was able to snatch a few fitful hours of rest.

Hundreds had already died and the contagion was spreading. The other physicians did not want to believe that their quarantine and so-called cures were failing to halt the spread of the disease. Starting in the poorer quarters of the city adjacent to the Goromadny Prospekt, the plague had, at first, spread in a highly unusual manner, appearing in areas of the city nowhere near the initial outbreak. Worse, the epidemic seemed to change with each passing day, manifesting symptoms amongst its victims of a dozen different contagions.

While studying in Altdorf, she had read the journals of those physicians who had attempted to fight off the great plague that had swept the Empire in the twelfth century, learning the patterns in which such epidemics typically spread. At first the outbreak in Kislev had defied all that she had learned, appearing to move like a wayward traveller through the city and alter its effects before settling on a final epicentre. If only they could find the source and nature of the contagion they might stand a chance of defeating it.

But she was tired, so very tired, and could think of nothing but how good it would be to fall asleep curled up beneath soft, warm bedsheets.

Sofia cried out as she felt a hand on her shoulder, realising she had fallen asleep for a moment. She shook herself awake and smiled weakly as she saw Kaspar standing over her.

'You startled me,' she said.

'Sorry, I didn't mean to.'

'What time is it?' asked Sofia, rubbing her eyes.

'It's morning,' said Kaspar. 'How is he?'

Sofia brushed a strand of lank, auburn hair from her forehead and said, 'He is better, but is far from well, Kaspar.'

'Will he live? Honestly?'

'Honestly, I do not know,' admitted Sofia. 'I am trying all I can, but there is only so much I can do for him.'

'You should get some sleep,' said Kaspar. 'You look dead on your feet.'

'I cannot sleep,' said Sofia, rather more sharply than she intended, 'there is too much to do. I have to go out, there are more cases of the plague every day and we can't seem to stop it.'

'You need sleep,' pressed Kaspar. 'You will be of no use to anyone if you make a mistake through tiredness.'

'And how many more will die because I am sleeping and unable to care for them?' demanded Sofia, immediately regretting the words. Kaspar seemed not to notice and put his hand back on her shoulder. Without thinking, she reached up and took his hand.

'You can't save them all, Sofia. No matter how hard you try.'

'I know,' she said, 'but it hurts. Every one you lose hurts.'

'Aye, I understand,' agreed Kaspar. 'I felt the same every time I walked the field before a battle. Knowing that no matter what I did, many of my soldiers would die. There is nothing so much like a god on earth as a general on a battlefield, Sofia. With a word I was condemning men to death and nothing I could do would prevent that.'

Sofia nodded, finally noticing the utilitarian clothes Kaspar was clothed in: plain riding britches and a several layers of quilted jerkins. He carried a small pot helmet under one arm and instead of his usual rapier, wore a short, stabbing sword buckled at his waist next to his ubiquitous pistols.

'Where are you going dressed like that?' she asked.

'Below the city, into the sewers.'

'Whatever for?'

'Because I think that we might find something that will explain what the hell is happening to this city. Too much is going on that doesn't make sense, and I think we might get some answers down there.'

'Are you going with Chekatilo? I heard what happened last night.'

'Aye,' nodded Kaspar.

'Do you trust him? Because you shouldn't.'

'No, I don't, but I think he's right, there are forces working against us and I need to know more.'

Seeing that Kaspar would not be dissuaded from this course of action, Sofia simply nodded and said, 'Please be careful, Kaspar.'

'I will,' he promised and leaned down to kiss her cheek.

Neither of them saw Anastasia watching from the hallway.

IV

REJAK WEDGED THE tapered end of the iron bar beneath the rim of the sewer cover and pushed down, levering it from the cobbles of the Goromadny Prospekt. As the heavy bronze cover rose, Kurt Bremen reached down and wedged his fingers beneath it, dragging it away from the opening. A foul stench wafted up from below and Kaspar was glad of the camphor-doused scarf Sofia had given him before leaving the embassy.

He pulled the scarf over his mouth and nose as Bremen finally lifted the sewer cover clear and stared down into the darkness.

'Sigmar's oath, it smells worse than an orc down there.'

'What you expect? It's a sewer,' sneered Rejak, getting down on his haunches and swinging his leg onto the rusted ladder. He wore faded leather riding clothes with a pair of long-bladed daggers sheathed at his waist. In addition to his weapons, he carried a clinking canvas satchel slung over one shoulder and a pair of hooded lanterns over the other. Bremen ignored him and followed the assassin into the sewers with a grimace of distaste. The knight had relinquished his normal plate armour and instead wore a plain iron breastplate over a padded leather jerkin. Kaspar could see how much it irked the Knight Panther to be out of his armour.

As Bremen disappeared below the level of the street, Kaspar and Chekatilo shared an uneasy glance. There was no love lost between them and the idea of descending into the labyrinthine darkness below Kislev with someone who would quite happily see him dead was clearly not an appealing prospect for either man.

'After you,' said Kaspar.

'The ambassador is too kind,' grumbled Chekatilo, lowering himself to the sewer entrance. He clambered onto the ladder and Kaspar feared for a moment that the giant Kislevite crook's girth would be too great to fit through the hole in the ground. Taking a deep breath and sucking in his prodigious gut, Chekatilo was able to squeeze through and, as his head vanished into the darkness, Kaspar followed him down.

THE INKY BLACKNESS was utterly impenetrable beyond the diffuse cone of light that descended from the world above. A glistening tunnel stretched off into the darkness, its continuing course lost to sight. Once Kaspar stepped from the ladder, Rejak knelt at its base and removed a tinderbox, striking sparks with the flint and blowing the tinder to life to light the oil-soaked wicks of the two lanterns.

He handed one lamp to Bremen, keeping the other for himself, and the yellow light cast its warm glow around the dripping echoes of the sewer tunnel. The wet brickwork threw back glittering reflections of light, pinpoints of brightness that rippled on the surface of the sluggish river of effluent that ran down the centre of the sewer tunnel.

'Now what?' asked Kurt Bremen, panning the light from his lantern around the tunnel.

Rejak examined the mud around the base of the ladder, saying, 'Is good. Ground has frozen, so tracks still here.'

'What can you tell?' asked Kaspar.

'Tracks of a man come from that way,' said Rejak, pointing northwards along the length of the tunnel. 'Lot of space between each track, so man was running to ladder.'

'Like a man running from rats that walk like men,' pointed out Chekatilo.

'Running from something, perhaps, but let's wait and see what we find before leaping to wild conclusions,' said Kaspar.

Chekatilo shrugged and set off after Rejak, who started up the tunnel, keeping his eyes locked to the frozen muddy ground. Kaspar followed Chekatilo, with Kurt Bremen bringing up the rear.

The curved roof of the tunnel was just low enough to force him to stoop and Kaspar knew that he would suffer for this expedition on the morrow. The ground was hard and rutted, the imprint of the ratcatcher's tracks clearly visible, and Kaspar wondered what exactly had happened down here to drive the man Chekatilo had brought him to such a state of lunacy.

The tunnel echoed with the steady drip of moisture, the noise of their footsteps and the sound of their breathing. Kaspar's breath misted before him and he shivered in the oppressive gloom that the lamps did little to dispel. Even with the scarf he wore wrapped around his mouth and nose, the stench from the dark water that ran beside them was horrendous.

The four men made slow progress along the curving brickwork tunnel, Rejak stopping every now and then to more carefully examine a track in the frozen mud. Kaspar began to regret his decision to come down here; there was nothing here in the sewers except the stench and the cold.

He pulled the scarf from his face, grimacing as the full force of the sewer stench hit him, ready to call a halt to this foolhardy expedition, when Rejak spoke, his voice magnified in the dim light of the tunnel. 'Something strange.'

'What is it?' asked Kaspar.

'Look,' said Rejak, pointing to where a sprawling pile of debris, bricks and mud lay on the ledge that ran alongside the effluent, leaving a gaping black hole in the wall.

'Some bricks and stone, what of it?' said Kaspar.

'You not see?' said Rejak. 'Bricks been knocked *into* tunnel. Someone broke down wall and tunnelled in here.'

'Why would someone need to tunnel into the sewers?' asked Kurt Bremen.

'Perhaps because they could not travel on the streets above,' suggested Chekatilo.

Kaspar knelt beside the rubble as Rejak shone the light of his lantern into the hole in the wall. The tunnel was wide and high, several yards in diameter, and disappeared into darkness. Kaspar had the sudden sensation that the passage led to a place of terrible nightmares.

Rejak joined him and said, 'More tracks. Two sets, smaller, not human.'

'Not human?'

'No, see. These tracks barefoot and only four toes. Clawed too. Two sets come out, but only one goes back.'

'What do you think made them?'

Rejak shrugged, running his fingers around the edges of the tracks. 'I do not know, but whatever they were, they carried something heavy with them. Tracks coming into tunnel very deep, but one that goes back not so deep.'

Kaspar could see no difference between the tracks, but trusted that Rejak knew what he was talking about. The assassin moved off to continue following the tracks and Kaspar's knee began to ache from crouching, but as he made to stand up, he saw the frozen corpse of a huge rat lying partially buried in the rubble.

'Wait a moment,' said Kaspar, lifting broken bricks from the dead rat and pulling its stiff and frozen body free of the debris. Its spine had been broken, presumably by the tunnel wall when it had collapsed, and a thin line of blood had frozen around its jaws.

'You find something?' asked Chekatilo.

'Maybe,' said Kaspar. 'Kurt, bring the lamp closer.'

Bremen stood behind Kaspar and held his lantern close to the dead rat. Kaspar turned its furry body over, unsurprised to see a triangular brand mark imprinted on its back.

'What is that?' asked Chekatilo. 'A scar?'

Kaspar shook his head. 'No, I don't think so. I saw this same mark on a rat I found in the remains of your brothel. I think it is some kind of brand or something.'

Chekatilo nodded as Kaspar dropped the rat. 'Still think this a fool's errand?'

'I'm not sure what to think just now,' admitted Kaspar, standing and brushing his gloves against his britches; touching the rat had made him feel unclean.

They set off once more, the tunnel curving and soon widening into a domed chamber with a vaulted ceiling and a wide pool of lapping sewage at its centre. The smooth enamelled tiles of the ceiling threw the light from their lamps around the echoing space and Kaspar could see submerged sewage pipes just below the surface of the water. A circular ledge some six feet wide ran around the circumference of the chamber and Kaspar admired the scale of engineering skill that had built these tunnels, proud that it had been one of his countrymen who had designed them.

The group made its way around the edge of the chamber, Rejak following the tracks to a point on its far side. Here, he stopped, kneeling to better examine a patch of ground where a number of differing tracks converged.

'We need some more light,' said Kurt Bremen, squinting at the tracks.

'Not a problem,' said Rejak, opening the clinking canvas satchel he carried and removing thin lengths of timber with their ends tightly wrapped in cloth. Kaspar could smell the acrid reek of lamp oil on the cloth as he took the torch from Rejak and lit it from the flame of Bremen's lamp.

Flickering flames illuminated the chamber and Kaspar took some reassurance from the simple act of having a flame in the darkness. Rejak returned his attention to the tracks as the last of the torches were lit.

'They met someone. Two people,' he said. 'A man and a woman.'

'How can you tell?' asked Kaspar. To him, the tracks were little more than a jumble of impressions in the mud that could mean anything.

'Woman's feet much smaller, not as deep as man's and she wears woman's shoe,' explained Rejak. 'They brought cart or dray with them, see?'

That at least Kaspar could read from the tracks: parallel grooves in the frozen filth running towards an arched opening in the chamber's wall. A brickwork tunnel curved away into the darkness beyond the archway, but even with his burning torch, Kaspar could not see more than a few yards along its length.

'Why would someone in a sewer need a cart?' he wondered.

'Whatever the ones who broke into tunnel were carrying must have been taken away on the cart. Perhaps coffin Nikolai spoke of,' said Chekatilo. 'That explain why tracks that went back into tunnel not as deep. They brought it here, but not leave with it.'

'But who did they bring it for?' wondered Kaspar.

Bremen walked over to the archway, shining the light from his lantern into the tunnel beyond. He bent to examine the cart tracks and said, 'The cart they used has a cracked rim on one of the wheels on its left side, look. See, every revolution it leaves a "v" shaped impression in the mud.'

Rejak nodded. 'Yha, true enough.'

Kaspar shivered, the cold, dark and dampness of the sewers beginning to unnerve him. He held the warmth of his torch close to his body and cast his gaze around the chamber as Rejak and Bremen sought to unlock more secrets from the tracks.

'See, Empire man. Vassily told you more going on than we know,' said Chekatilo, joining him at the edge of the rippling pool that filled the chamber. Dark shapes bobbed in the water and Kaspar looked away, confident that he did not want to see anything that might be drifting in a sewer.

'Just because you may have been right about finding something down here, does not make us friends, Chekatilo. There is still to be a reckoning between us.'

'I know that, Empire man,' promised Chekatilo, the flames from his torch making his features dance. 'Debts to be honoured.'

'What are you talking about?'

'Who do you think got you the map of the boyarins' territories that allowed you to hunt Sasha Kajetan?' asked Chekatilo. 'You think Rejak just found it on street and thought to give it to you? I did this favour for you and will soon ask you to repay that debt.'

'I knew that it had come from you,' said Kaspar. 'But one thing I never understood was how you knew I needed it.'

Chekatilo laughed. 'Thank your fool of a friend, Korovic, for that.'

'Pavel? Why?'

'He came to me and told me you had been to see that snake, Losov. Said you needed to find Boyarin Kajetan's lands quickly, but that he had thrown you out of his office.'

'He wouldn't believe that Sasha was the Butcherman,' said Kaspar.

'Pavel begged me to help you, said you would be in my debt if I did.'

Kaspar's jaw tightened and he shook his head at Pavel's foolishness. It was typical behaviour for him, doing what he thought was for the best, but leaving someone else to pay the price for his good deeds. And to be indebted to a man like Chekatilo...

Who knew what he would demand in return for the aid he had given.

But misguided though Pavel may have been, Kaspar knew that without the map Chekatilo had provided, they would not have been able to bring Sasha Kajetan to justice.

Before Kaspar could ask what price Chekatilo would demand of him he heard a faint scratching noise, barely audible above the noise of the sewer and just at the edge of hearing. He glanced over his shoulder to Rejak and Bremen, who had ventured down the passageway through the archway to examine the cart tracks, but they seemed oblivious to the noise.

A prickling sensation worked its way up his spine as he turned back and saw the dark shapes he had noticed earlier in the water drifting towards them at the edge of the pool. Almost immediately Kaspar saw that the water's current was flowing out of the chamber and that the dark shapes were moving against it.

The scratching noise was getting louder too; he was sure of it.

'We need to get out of here,' he said. 'Right now.'

Chekatilo gave him a puzzled glance then followed the direction of his stare, his eyes widening as he saw what the ambassador was looking at.

'Ursun's blood,' he hissed, backing away from the edge and shouting. 'Rejak!'

Kaspar backed away with him and drew his sword as the scratching noise suddenly swelled in volume and hundreds of enormous black-furred rats swarmed into the chamber, pouring from almost every passageway and climbing from the water with lethally sharp fangs bared for attack.

V

SASHA KAJETAN THRASHED at his bindings, screaming himself hoarse. He could feel their scratching, clawing presence in his mind, their Chaos-tainted blood calling to his own polluted vital fluid. He could sense their hunger and their malice as a physical thing that echoed in his trueself and filled him with dark thoughts of murder and mayhem.

He knew he would not be able to resist the trueself's embrace for much longer and all that was once human of him would be swallowed by its lethal madness.

The door to his cell opened and the hooded gaoler came in, his cudgel raised.

'Time you shut your mouth, you murderous bastard.'

'You don't understand,' yelled Kajetan. 'Death is abroad this night, I cannot stay here!'

'I said be quiet!' shouted the gaoler, hammering the sole of his hobnail boot into Kajetan's face. The swordsman's head slammed into the wall and he felt blood and teeth fly from his jaw.

'Please!' wailed Kajetan, spitting a phlegmy wad of bloody spittle.

He pulled himself upright and had a last fleeting image of the gaoler's cudgel before it slammed into his skull and sent him spinning into unconsciousness.

VI

KASPAR DREW HIS sword as the rats poured into the chamber, fear dumping a hot jolt of adrenaline into his system. The surface of the pool thrashed with swimming rats, their bristle-haired fur black and shining in the lamplight as they sped through the water towards their prey.

'Sigmar's hammer,' hissed Kurt Bremen, drawing his sword and rushing to Kaspar's side. Chekatilo and Rejak hurriedly backed away from the passageway the cart tracks disappeared into as they heard the frantic scratching of hundreds of claws and the shrill squealing of yet more rats from its darkened depths.

Kaspar held his sword and burning torch before him, ready to defend himself, but the rats seemed content simply to watch them, gathering their numbers before closing for the kill.

'Why don't they attack?' whispered Kaspar, as though volume alone might trigger an assault.

'I not know,' said Chekatilo, as something pale and bloated moved sluggishly through the undulating mass of vermin. They parted before the passage of this creature and as it emerged from the mass of rats, Kaspar saw with disgust that it was a large, albino-haired rat with long, distended fangs and bloated belly. The rat looked up at them and hissed, the lamplight reflecting as tiny red pinpricks from its slitted eyes.

As the rat stared at them, Kaspar was struck by the dreadful intelligence he saw there, realising that it was somehow appraising them. Its pointed snout twitched, sniffing the air. Kaspar heard a clink of glass behind him and risked a hurried glance over his shoulder. Rejak rummaged through the canvas satchel once more, removing a handful of glass vials filled with a translucent liquid.

'What are you doing?' hissed Kaspar.

Rejak looked up and grinned. 'After rats attack brothel, I decide I will be prepared if I see many rats again.'

Kaspar nervously licked his lips, unsure as to what Rejak meant, but said nothing, watching the monstrous white rat as it cocked its head to one side as though listening to a sound only it could hear.

'When I shout "run", you run like all the daemons of Chaos were after you. Back the way we came, you understand?' said Rejak.

The white rat hissed again and the rats surged forwards in a heaving, snapping mass, Rejak threw the vials of liquid at the nearest rodents. Chekatilo hurled his torch as the vials shattered and a sheet of flame erupted in the midst of the rats. They squealed and dashed away from the blazing oil, burning rats screeching and rolling in agony as they died.

'Run!' shouted Rejak, sprinting through the gap that had opened in the mass of rats and leaping over the flames. Kaspar bolted after the assassin, swinging his sword at a rodent that leapt towards him with its fangs bared. The blade chopped into its body and sent it tumbling as Kaspar hurdled the flames unleashed by Rejak's vials of oil.

He landed badly, his knee twisting under him, but managed to keep his footing as Chekatilo and Bremen ran along behind him, the rats swarming after them.

Kaspar heard another vial of oil shatter ahead.

Chekatilo shouted, 'Ambassador! Hurry!'

Kaspar turned into the tunnel they had come from, jolts of pain shooting up his leg as his twisted knee flared painfully with each stride. He passed Rejak, who had lit another torch as a boiling mass of rats surged into the tunnel after them. Kaspar heard a whoosh of flames and the tunnel was suddenly illuminated with dancing flames. More rats were dying, but uncounted others were bypassing the flames by leaping into the effluent and swimming past the flaming barrier.

'Hurry!' shouted Rejak. 'Fire will give us time, but not much.'

Chekatilo moved fast for such a big man and overtook Kaspar, whose knee was now an agonised knot of fire. His pace slowed and he knew he could not carry on for much longer. He heard the click, click, click of clawed feet racing towards him and forced himself onwards, fighting to ignore the pain from his knee.

Kurt Bremen helped Kaspar as the rats swarmed forwards, their speed and tenacity incredible. Their squeals were deafening, magnified by the water and close confines of the tunnel. Kaspar heard a loud squeal, far too close, and felt a heavy weight land on his back. He stumbled, pitching forward and was only saved from falling flat out by Bremen's hand.

He twisted wildly, slamming his back against the wall of the tunnel in an attempt to dislodge the rat. He heard it squeal in pain then screamed as he felt its razor-sharp teeth bite into his neck. Its powerful jaws bit again before Kurt Bremen spun him around and hacked the rat in two with one stroke of his long blade.

Even in the midst of this horror, Kaspar was amazed at Kurt Bremen's precise swordsmanship, and pressed onwards, pressing his hand to his bleeding neck. The Knight Panther followed the ambassador, jogging backwards and watching for any other rats that might have managed to get past the flames. Blood spilled around Kaspar's fingers and he knew he was lucky the rat hadn't bitten through the main artery in his neck.

Kaspar ran on blindly, following the bobbing light of Rejak's lamp that glowed like a beacon ahead. He didn't know how far they had to go before reaching safety, but prayed that it would be soon.

He heard Kurt Bremen yell in pain and turned to see the knight struggling with a horde of biting and clawing rats. Three clawed at his legs, while another dragged its long incisors down the metal of the knight's breastplate. He swung the lantern and stabbed with his sword, but the rats were too quick, darting away from the deadly point of the weapon.

Kaspar drew his pistols and leaned against the tunnel wall for support, taking careful aim at the struggling knight. His first shot blew the rat clawing at Bremen's chest apart, his second hurling another into the sewage. The rats paused in their attack, frightened by the sudden noise, and the knight gave them no chance to recover, stamping down on one and skewering the other with his sword.

'Good shooting,' he panted, limping as fast as he could along the tunnel. Beyond the lantern's glow, Kaspar could see a writhing mass of black-furred bodies as they swarmed along the tunnel towards them and realised Rejak's fiery barrier must have finally gone out.

He jammed his pistols into his belt, struggling onwards with Bremen and hearing the scrabble of claws and snap of sharpened teeth growing louder and louder as they ran. They rounded a bend in the tunnel and Kaspar shouted, 'There!' as he saw the cone of daylight that descended from the sewer opening on the Goromadny

Prospekt. Chekatilo was nowhere in sight, but Rejak remained at the bottom of the ladder.

'Must hurry!' shouted Rejak and Kaspar had never more wanted to punch him.

He reached the ladder, his chest heaving and his knee throbbing in pain, but began climbing as quickly as he could towards the light and safety. He gritted his teeth against the pain, feeling more blood pulse from the wound in his neck.

As he reached the top, Chekatilo's thick hands reached down and pulled him through the sewer opening. He took a great gulp of fresh air, like a drowning man breaking the surface of the ocean, and rolled away from the opening. Snow soaked through his clothes in seconds and he felt icy chill seep into his bones, but he was too glad to be out of the sewers to care.

Rejak quickly followed, vaulting through the opening in the ground and grabbing hold of the bronze sewer cover. Kurt Bremen came next, the knight bleeding from a score of bites.

'Hurry!' he cried. 'Sigmar help me, but they're climbing the ladder!'

He stumbled over to Rejak and helped him drag the cover over.

Between them, they manhandled the heavy plate over the sewer entrance and dropped it in place with a loud clang, falling back in fear-induced exhaustion.

The four men backed away from the sewer cover, weapons poised, but whatever nightmarish intelligence the rats possessed, it did not stretch to passing through heavy bronze. Long seconds passed in silence before all four men let out a collective breath and gradually lowered their weapons.

'I hate rats,' said Kaspar finally, sagging against Kurt Bremen as the pain in his knee and neck returned with renewed ferocity.

Kurt Bremen took the weight of Kaspar's injured knee, though he too was badly hurt.

'We need to get back to the embassy,' said the knight. 'Get Madame Valencik to look at that bite and get some ice on your knee.'

Kaspar nodded and said, 'Chekatilo, where is that rat-catcher you brought to the embassy?'.

'Back in the Lubjanko,' said Chekatilo. 'Best place for him.'

'Meet us there in two hours, I need to speak to him.'

'What for?'

'I want to know if he saw who was in that sewer,' said Kaspar. 'He might be our only chance of finding out what the hell is going on here and I need you to translate for me.'

CHAPTER FIVE

I

WITH KURT BREMEN's help, Kaspar made it back to the embassy, though his knee was an agonised mass of pain by the time they passed through the iron gates of its courtyard. The embassy guards helped the knight carry the ambassador inside, calling for Madame Valencik as they lifted him into the receiving room.

Sofia hurried into the receiving room as the guards laid him on a long couch, tying her long hair into a ponytail and rubbing her red-rimmed eyes. Even through the pain of his knee and the bite on his neck, Kaspar was struck by how tired Sofia looked.

She knelt by his side as Kurt Bremen carefully removed his boot and gently rolled up the leg of his britches. A basin of water and cloths were brought and Sofia began cleaning the wound at his neck.

'You stupid old fool,' said Sofia, dabbing water on the cut. 'This is no way for a man of your age to behave.'

'I am beginning to agree with you…' he hissed as she moved on to prod at the swollen bruising on his kneecap.

'And a man of your standing, running around in sewers,' she said, shaking her head. She beckoned one of the embassy guards over and despatched him to get some ice and wrap it in a towel.

'Turn your head,' she said, returning her attention to Kaspar. 'What happened anyway?'

'I jumped and landed awkwardly.'

'No, I mean to your neck.'

'A rat bit me. A big one.'

Sofia nodded and removed a jar of a white, oily cream from her satchel and scooped a handful onto her fingers. Kaspar smelled its strong odour and winced at Sofia spread it liberally over the bite on his neck.

'What it that? It stings like hell.'

'Camphor mixed with white wax and castor oil,' explained Sofia. 'It should help fight any infection the rat's bite might have carried and will numb the area a little.'

With the bite cleaned, she applied a folded bandage and bound it in place with another, which she wrapped around him and tied off behind his neck.

Kaspar grunted in pain as she began massaging his knee, working her fingers deep into his flesh and kneading the ligaments beneath. The guard she had commanded to retrieve ice returned and she placed the freezing bundle of cloth atop Kaspar's knee.

'Let us hope that the cold will bring down the swelling,' said Sofia, turning from the ambassador to begin seeing to the wounds suffered by Kurt Bremen.

'By Sigmar, I hope so,' said Kaspar.

'And did you find anything?' asked Sofia without turning. 'Was it worth all the trouble to go down there after all?'

'Yes, Kaspar, did you find anything?' said Anastasia, appearing at the entrance to the receiving room, her arms folded across her chest and dark hair bound up in a severe bun.

Kaspar nodded, wary at the mocking tone he heard in Anastasia's question.

'I think so, yes,' he answered. 'Tracks and rats. Lots of rats.'

'Tracks of what?'

'People and a cart by the look of them. I think someone had tunnelled into the sewers to deliver something to someone. The ratcatcher Chekatilo found in the Lubjanko said he saw people and a coffin, but I don't know how reliable a witness he is.'

'If he came from Chekatilo, then I would say highly unreliable,' snapped Anastasia.

'I'm not so sure,' said Kaspar, angry that Anastasia was once again dismissing his theories so quickly. 'I don't think he would make such things up.'

'Last night you said the man was a lunatic,' said Anastasia. 'You said he spoke of rats that walked like men? Seriously, have you ever heard of anything so ridiculous?'

'There are beasts that walk on two legs in the depths of the forests and in the far north,' pointed out Sofia. 'Perhaps it was one of those monsters he saw?'

'Oh, you would take his side, wouldn't you?' sneered Anastasia.

'What is that supposed to mean?' demanded Sofia.

'You know fine well. Don't think I haven't seen the way you fawn all over him. I know what you want.'

Kaspar could feel this confrontation spinning out of control and said, 'I agree that it does sound far-fetched, but I think he did see something down there. And as soon as the swelling on my knee goes down, I shall go to the Lubjanko and find out what.'

'It is a fool's errand,' said Anastasia.

'Perhaps,' snapped Kaspar, 'but I will go anyway.'

'I cannot believe you are trusting Chekatilo,' said Anastasia, shaking her head incredulously. 'After all that's happened you'd take his side over mine.'

'Sides? What are you talking about, woman? This is not a matter of sides, it is a matter of getting to the bottom of what has been happening in this damned city for the past few months.'

'Then I think you are a gullible fool, Kaspar,' cried Anastasia. 'I think you are being taken in by a fat crook who wants nothing more than to take advantage of your stupidity!'

Kaspar's lips pursed in anger. He was unused to being spoken to in this manner and felt his temper fraying rapidly.

'Damn it, Ana, why must you always ridicule what I think?' shouted Kaspar. 'I have many faults, but I flatter myself that I do not count stupidity among them. Chekatilo is involved in this, yes, but I do not believe he is behind what is happening. There is conspiracy afoot in Kislev and I mean to get to the bottom of it.'

'Then you will do it alone,' said Anastasia, spinning on her heel and storming from the room. A heavy silence fell and Kaspar felt every eye in the room upon him.

'Nobody say a word,' he cautioned, simmering in anger.

II

THE LUBJANKO WAS just as grim and foreboding as Kaspar remembered it, the high, spike-topped walls and windowless façade warning away those who would dare to approach. Pillars of smoke billowed into the sky from behind the building, but even the warmth generated from the death pyres was not enough to entice the refugee population of Kislev to draw near this dreaded building.

The Lubjanko was now home to many of those struck down with the plague, the lower halls of the former hospital now given over to the business of death, the wails of the dying and afflicted echoing within its dark walls as though the building itself were screaming.

Kaspar and Bremen rode towards the Lubjanko, their horses plodding through the deep snow that lay thick and undisturbed – further proof that no one came this way. Since leaving the embassy, Kaspar had said nothing, still angry at the confrontation in the embassy's receiving room. Anastasia had infuriated him and, despite the many things he enjoyed about her, he knew that there would be no reconciliation this time. His instincts told him that events in Kislev were rapidly approaching a critical point, and he could not be distracted by those who would continually pour scorn on his thoughts.

After Anastasia had left he had endured another hour of ice on his knee until the swelling had gone down to a level where he could put his weight upon it again. Then he had changed into fresh, dry clothing and gathered up his weapons once more.

Sofia had advised him to rest some more before heading to the Lubjanko, but upon seeing Kaspar's resolve, settled for applying a cold compress to his knee and making him swear to be careful. In deference to Sofia's advice, he travelled on his horse, though he could still feel the ache in his joint even as he rode.

Kossars with black armbands and gauze facemasks stood at the gateway of the Lubjanko, an entrance with no gates that symbolised its initial purpose of caring for all who came within its walls. They allowed the ambassador past without comment, resting on the hafts of their long axes and gathered around burning braziers.

'This is a terrible place,' said Kurt Bremen, staring up at the featureless walls.

Kaspar nodded, turning in the saddle as he heard footsteps crunching through the snow behind them. Chekatilo and Rejak approached them, wrapped in furs and struggling through the deep snow with difficulty.

'Well met, ambassador,' said Chekatilo. 'You have recovered enough?'

'Enough,' agreed Kaspar. 'Let us get inside. I have no wish to tarry in this awful place longer than necessary.'

Chekatilo nodded and approached the heavy doors that led within. Twin statues of Shallya flanked the doors, with a Kislevite translation of one of her prayers carved above. Kaspar and Bremen dismounted, tying their horses to the hitching rail beside the door.

'Should I see if one of those soldiers will watch our horses?' said Bremen.

Kaspar shook his head. 'No, I do not think that will be necessary. Even though food is scarce, I have the feeling that few horse thieves would risk coming near this dreadful place.'

Bremen shrugged as Chekatilo hammered on the door and the four men gathered on the icy steps. Kaspar's knee hurt, but it was bearable, though he felt the cold seep into his body as they waited for someone to respond to the knocking.

'Damn this,' he said finally, pushing open the door without waiting for an answer. Kaspar stepped into the gloomy halls of the Lubjanko, the stone flagged hall he found himself within, cold and empty. A set of wide stairs led up to his left and a set of double doors marked with a painted white cross led deeper inside.

'Where will we find this ratcatcher, Chekatilo?' he asked.

'Upstairs. White cross means lower chambers are kept for those who will soon be dead from plague. Not so much work to carry them to the pyres if they kept here.'

Kaspar nodded and set off up the stairs, feeling his knee twinge with each step. Bremen, Chekatilo and Rejak followed him quickly, each sensing his dark mood. The stairwell was lit by the occasional lamp, doglegging several times before emerging onto a landing. Screams, hacking coughs and weeping could be heard from behind a nearby doorway and Kaspar pushed it open as Chekatilo nodded.

The long hall appeared to run the width of the building, the walls lined with wooden cots upon which desperate unfortunates rested in various stages of madness or catatonia. What little space was not filled with beds was occupied by sorry specimens of humanity curled up on blankets as they waited to die or go mad with cold and hunger.

Hundreds of people filled the hall, their demented wailings echoing from the high ceiling like a chorus of the damned. Black robed priests of Morr made their way up and down the aisles between the people who had been dumped here, speaking words of comfort to those who would listen or signalling the ragged orderlies to bring a shroud to wrap another body in.

The babble of lunatic voices was disorienting, hundreds of human beings reduced to such wretched misery by war, suffering and poverty. Kaspar felt his anger turn to sorrow as he took in the scale of human anguish he saw around him.

This was the result of wars, he knew. Men might tell grand tales of the glory of battle and the eternal struggle for freedom, indeed he himself was guilty of such sentiments, having spoken of these things before battle was joined to rouse the courage of his soldiers. But Kaspar knew that such talk was easy when the battle was long over, when the terror, bloodshed and suffering was nothing but a half-remembered nightmare, and he felt a deep wave of loathing wash through him.

Amidst such thoughts, he saw a hugely fat man standing beside a bed containing a supine young man. The man snapped his fingers to summon the orderlies before drawing his finger across his throat. The meaning was clear and Kaspar found this callous display of inhumanity utterly unforgivable.

As he moved onto the next bed, the fat man noticed Kaspar and his companions and limped towards them, his ruddy features clouded with anger. He unleashed a torrent of Kislevite, and Kaspar fought the urge to smash his fist into the man's ugly features.

Seeing Kaspar did not understand, he switched to heavily accented Reikspiel.

'Who you and what you be doing here?' he demanded.

'Dimitrji...' said Chekatilo. 'It is good to see you too.'

The man appeared to notice the fat crook for the first time and sneered. 'Vassily? What you here for?'

'I want to see Nikolai again,' said Chekatilo.

'Pah! That madman!' snapped Dimitrji. 'I have priest of Morr give him much laudanum to keep him quiet. His ravings set others off and place become madhouse.'

'I thought it already was.'

'You know what I mean,' growled Dimitrji, his flushed features red with a lifetime's abuse of *kvas*.

'Where can I find him?' pressed Chekatilo.

'In storeroom at end of hall,' said Dimitrji, waving his hand vaguely towards the far end of the scream-filled hall. 'I keep him apart from others.'

'Your compassion does you credit,' chuckled Chekatilo.

Dimitrji sneered and limped off, leaving them to make their way through the hall. They stood aside respectfully for the shaven-headed priests of Morr, stately and dignified in their long black robes and silver amulets bearing the symbol of their god, the gateway that separated the kingdoms of the living and the dead.

The Lubjanko was truly a place of horror. Kaspar saw all manner of disfigurements, both physical and mental in the forms of the inmates sequestered here. Those cursed by deformities from birth, mutilated by war, ravaged by sickness or left with broken minds following some nightmarish trauma; all were equal within the walls of the Lubjanko.

So touched by the scale of suffering he saw, Kaspar didn't notice the hooded priest of Morr coming the other way until he ran into him.

'I'm sorry–' began Kaspar, but the stoop-shouldered figure ignored him, walking quickly in the opposite direction, his plain black robes swathing him from head to toe. Kaspar shrugged, his nose wrinkling at the rank smell that came from the priest, but supposed that working in such a terrible place did not leave much time for personal hygiene. Something about the priest seemed out of place, but Kaspar could not say what and put the encounter from his mind as they reached the door to the storeroom Dimitrji had indicated.

He pushed open the door and immediately saw that they had made a wasted journey.

Nikolai Pysanka lay on a simple cot-bed with his throat pumping a jet of blood onto the floor. His slack, dead features were twisted in an expression of pure terror, as though his last sight had been of his greatest fear made flesh. There was no need to check if he was still alive; no man could live with his throat opened like that.

'By Sigmar!' swore Bremen, rushing to the corpse. 'How could anyone have known?'

Rejak stepped over the spreading pool of blood and said, 'This done not long ago. Blood still flowing from him.'

'Whatever Nikolai knew, he takes to Morr's kingdom with him,' said Chekatilo.

'That's it!' exclaimed Kaspar and bolted from the storeroom. He ran back to the wide hall full of human detritus and quickly scanned the room. There! Bremen, Chekatilo and Rejak joined him, looking quizzically at the ambassador as he shouted, 'You! In the black robes, stop!'

Kaspar set off in the direction of the stairs

Various priests of Morr looked up from their labours at the sound of Kaspar's shout, but he ignored them, running as fast as his injured knee allowed towards the man he had bumped into; the man who did not wear a pendant with the gateway symbol of Morr.

The figure ignored him and Kaspar drew his pistol, pulling back the flint with a loud click. He aimed just above the figure's head and shouted again. 'Stop! Stop now or I fire!'

The black robed figure was almost at the door that led to the stairs and Kaspar had no choice but to pull the trigger. The pistol boomed, the noise deafening, and the din in the hall rose as the inmates, frightened by the gunshot, erupted in a heightened cacophony of shrieks and wails. Madmen surged from their beds, cripples diving to the floor as nightmare memories of battle returned to haunt them.

The figure at the end of the hall spun, inhumanly quick, and Kaspar saw its hands dart beneath its robes. He jammed his pistol into his belt and ducked towards the cover of a stone column as he drew his second pistol and a blur of silver steel flashed through the air towards him.

He heard a series of clangs and risked a glance around the column, seeing three razor-edged triangular throwing stars embedded in the stone. He felt hands upon him and turned to see a filthy man dressed in a soiled smock pawing at his shoulders.

'Yha, novesya matka, tovarich!' yelled the man, spittle flying from his cracked lips.

Kaspar pushed the man away as Rejak and Bremen pounded past him, heading after the figure in black as it dashed through the door to the stairs.

Kaspar ran after them, fighting his way through the mad press of bodies that filled the hall. Screaming lunatics surrounded him, yelling insensible babble. Madness shone from every face as he fought to break free and pursue the ratcatcher's murderer. Hands tore at him, broken nails drawing blood from his cheeks as they clawed at his eyes. He felt himself being borne to the ground and lashed out with his fist and elbows as they began tearing at his clothes.

'Get off me!' he yelled, but either they did not understand him or paid him no mind if they did. A bare foot hammered his groin and the breath was driven from him, his body jack-knifing in pain.

Then suddenly it was over as Kurt Bremen returned and fought his way through the crowd of attacking madmen. His fists and feet cleared a path and the others fell back, terrified at this fearsome warrior in their midst.

'Ambassador! Grab my hand!' shouted Bremen. Kaspar reached up and Bremen hauled him to his feet, dragging him towards the stairs.

'Did you catch him?' managed Kaspar at last.

'Rejak is going after him.'

Kaspar and Bremen barged through the door and hurried downstairs in time to find Chekatilo's assassin lying at the foot of the stairs, his left arm hanging uselessly at his side. The man's face was deathly pale and blood matted the furs he wore.

'Rejak!' shouted Kaspar. 'Where is he?'

'Outside,' said Rejak slowly. 'Ursun save me, but he was quick. Fastest bladesman I ever see. He make me look like child. A heartbeat slower and my guts be all over floor.'

Kaspar had seen Rejak's speed with a blade and felt a chill race up his spine at the thought of an opponent faster than him. The only man faster with a blade that Kaspar knew of was securely locked away.

Bremen pulled open the Lubjanko's main door and raced outside into the snow.

Kaspar knelt by the wounded swordsman and tried to assess the damage. He was no surgeon, but knew that Rejak was lucky to be alive. Blood soaked his stomach and britches where a blade had cut him across the belly. A fingerbreadth deeper and Rejak would have died, not that Kaspar would have shed any tears for him.

'You are lucky to be alive,' said Kaspar as Chekatilo finally reached the bottom of the stairs. Chekatilo glanced at Rejak's injury and said, 'Will he die?'

'I'm not sure. I don't think so,' said Kaspar, 'but he needs a physician or he will.'

Chekatilo nodded, his breathing ragged and uneven. 'I not built for running.'

'You are not built for anything, Chekatilo,' said Kaspar bitterly.

'No sign of him,' said Bremen, returning to the entrance hall, frustrated at their failure to capture the killer.

'Damn,' swore Kaspar. 'Now we are back to square one.'

His heart sank as he knew that their best chance to unravel the truth had just been snatched from beneath their very noses.

III

THERE SEEMED LITTLE point in any further action that day so Kaspar and Bremen left the Lubjanko to return to the embassy, leaving Chekatilo to requisition a genuine priest of Morr to tend to Rejak's wounds until a priestess of Shallya could be brought.

Rejak's survival was a matter of supreme indifference to Kaspar, but the thought of how easily the man had been bested by the black-robed killer unsettled him greatly. Were their unknown foes so highly skilled? The only man of such skill Kaspar had seen was Sasha Kajetan, and he wondered if the swordsman would know of anyone else in Kislev with similar gifts. He wondered if there was enough of Kajetan's mind left to ask.

Kislev was quiet as the afternoon drew on, the low sun bright in a sky of azure blue, the day seeming so much brighter than it had earlier on. Kaspar wondered if this were really were true or whether it was simply the joy of leaving such a dark hellhole that made it seem so.

They rode back to the embassy in silence. He dismounted and handed the reins of his horse to one of the Knights Panthers' lance carriers, feeling a real sense of hopelessness.

He was not equipped to deal with such matters. Understanding the nature of warfare and how best to motivate his troops; those things he understood, but intrigue and mysteries were matters he felt were beyond him. The thought depressed him, but as he limped into the embassy and saw Sofia smiling at him, he felt his spirits lift.

He saw her notice the weariness in his face and said, 'What happened?'

Kaspar shook his head. 'I'll tell you later, but right now I need a drink.'

She stepped close and took his arm. 'Are you alright? Are you hurt?'

'No, I am fine, I am just... tired,' said Kaspar. 'Very tired.'

Sofia saw the exhaustion in his eyes and knew not to press the point. 'Very well. I have some news that might cheer you.'

'That would be a nice change. What is it?'

'It looks as though Pavel's fever has broken,' said Sofia. 'I think he is over the worst of his ordeal. If he can stay off the *kvas*, he may actually live to see the new year.'

Kaspar looked up. 'Is he awake?'

Sofia nodded and Kaspar set off upstairs to Pavel's room, where he found his old comrade sitting up in bed blowing on a bowl of hot soup. Pavel was still a terrible sight, covered in stitches and bandages and Kaspar forced himself to smile as he entered the room.

Pavel looked up and grimaced. 'I look that bad?'

'You've looked better,' answered Kaspar. 'But I'll wager the other man looks worse.'

'Ha! If by other man you mean rats and a broken window, then yha, they look worse.'

'What happened?' asked Kaspar, pulling up a chair and sitting beside the bed. 'How much do you remember?'

'Pavel not remember much after the rats. By Olric that was bad. Hundreds of rats, they came from everywhere at once. Biting, clawing and killing. I never see anything like it in all my days. They kill everyone...'

'What happened to you after that?'

'I... I am not sure. I was very drunk already when I get there and had begun to drink more when it all happen. To get away from the rats, I jump through window and cut myself badly.'

'You will have some fine scars, it's true,' said Kaspar.

'Perhaps they make Pavel more handsome,' laughed Pavel, grimacing as the stitches in his face pulled tight.

'Maybe,' said Kaspar, doubtfully, 'you never know what some people find attractive.'

'Yha, Pavel will be dangerously handsome with scars, but to be honest, I not know what happened after the rats. I wandered through streets and collapsed. All I remember is terrible dream about falling and then thinking that I had to get back here. I not know how long I was away or how I find my way back. Next thing I knew I was back here with Madame Valencik cleaning my wounds.'

'Well, I'm glad you are on the mend, Pavel.'

Pavel nodded and took a mouthful of soup. 'Sofia tell me that you and Chekatilo working together now. He is dangerous man, you sure that is wise?'

The question was asked lightly, but Kaspar could sense the tension behind it.

'He told me you went to see him, Pavel,' said the ambassador. 'That you asked him to help me find Kajetan.'

'Kaspar, I–' began Pavel, but Kaspar cut him off.

'I know you went to him for all the right reasons, but you once said that Chekatilo was not a man to be indebted to, and that's just where you have put me. Haven't you?'

Pavel hung his head and did not reply.

'Haven't you?' barked Kaspar.

'Yha,' said Pavel at last.

'I told you before that I cannot afford to be looking two ways at once and, now more than ever, that still holds true. I have excused your foolishness in the past because I know you acted with good intentions, but no more, Pavel. If I find that you have done anything else stupid, then, by Sigmar, you and I are finished as friends. I will throw you out on your arse and you can drink yourself to death for all I care. Do we understand each other?'

Pavel nodded, and Kaspar could see the remorse etched across his features. He did not enjoy saying these things, but knew he had no choice. If Pavel were to remain here, then he would need to learn that he could not continue to behave in such a manner.

He turned and left the room without another word, leaving Pavel to his misery.

IV

THE DAYS DRAGGED on with no end in sight to the winter, though some who claimed a sense for such things, spoke of a coming thaw with the break of the new year. The days passed slowly and painfully, with Kaspar enduring agonising days of Sofia massaging his injured knee and exercise to reduce the swelling. He was past the age when such injuries could be shrugged off so easily and Sofia predicted that his knee would be weak for the remainder of his days.

Pavel also recovered his strength slowly, though he kept a remarkably low profile around the embassy. Sofia ensured that he kept off the *kvas* and as the weeks passed, the big Kislevite's strength gradually returned.

The year turned from 2521 to 2522 with little fanfare, the city too beaten down to celebrate Verena's sacred day. Though plague continued to kill scores every day, it appeared that the outbreak had at last been contained. Scant comfort to those quarantined within the affected areas, but a source of great relief to everyone else.

A number of Kislevite boyarin gave rousing speeches to the soldiers on the first day of Nachexen, promising them a year of battle and victories. Kaspar himself was called upon to make a number of speeches to the Empire regiments camped beyond the walls of the city when riders from Talabheim delivered missives that informed him that the armies of Talabecland and Stirland were on the march to Kislev.

Perhaps it was the hope of reinforcements, or perhaps it was the lengthening days and the breath of the new year, but a tangible sense of optimism began to permeate the Kislevite capital.

* * *

V

HE HAD NEARLY forty thousand warriors, and more were arriving every day. High Zar Aelfric Cyenwulf of the Iron Wolves watched with satisfaction as yet more riders rode in from the cold steppe of the north to join his army, their ragged skull totems raised as high as their ululating war cries. Victory bred victory and the tribes of the north – the Kul, the Hung and the Vargs, as well as Kyazak raiders – were flocking to his banner, eager to share in his future successes. Individual warbands of fearsome champions came too, and his army grew.

The warriors he had assembled to fight for him were the fiercest he could have wished for. No other army of the north had won so many battles or conquered so many tribes. No other army had provoked such fear and loathing in its victims, or slaughtered so many of its vanquished.

Hundreds of horsemen and thousands of warriors on foot gathered on the snow-covered landscape below him, too many to be seen at once. Whole wings of his army were scattered, a day's ride or more from here, spread out across the steppe until the order was given to march south. Men and monsters fought for the High Zar, malformed trolls from the high mountains, bestial monstrosities gifted by the touch of the Dark Gods and mindless things so twisted and mutated that they defied any easy description.

It was an army raised not for conquest, but destruction.

The people of the southern lands knew a terror of him and his armies, and the High Zar knew that such tales would do more to defeat his foes than axe or sword.

The High Zar was a giant of a warrior, broad shouldered and powerful, carrying his horned, wolf-faced helm in the crook of his arm as he stood atop the craggy foothills of the mountains and allowed his army to see him. His cloak billowed behind him in the wind, the iridescent plates of his heavy armour gleaming in the late winter sun.

He raised his tattooed arms, the many trophy rings wrapping his muscles glinting as they caught the light. He held his mighty pallasz above his head, hefting the fearsomely heavy weapon as though it weighed nothing at all. He towered above the eight handpicked warriors who accompanied him, a mighty champion of Chaos, favoured son of Tchar and soon to be destroyer of nations.

Silver hair, with a streak of pure black at either temple, rippled in the wind and framed a scarred face that had known only victory. He smiled, exposing teeth that had been filed to sharp points.

The spring thaw was upon the land and his shaman, Kar Odacen, had promised him that the snows were already receding. Come the morning, they would march south, following the line of the World's Edge Mountains and skirting Praag before turning westwards towards the great scar on the landscape known as Urszebya.

Ursun's Teeth.

'Many warriors,' said a voice that sounded like glaciers colliding, and the smile fell from the High Zar's face.

He felt his skin crawl and the hairs on his arms crackle with the arrival of the Old One as it climbed the rocks behind him. The ground shook with its weight and sapphire sparks began dancing around the gold-fluted edges of Cyenwulf's armour at its presence. He licked his suddenly dry lips before replying.

'Aye, many warriors. We take war to the south on the morrow.'

Wisps of dark, flickering smoke curled around his body as the beast that had awoken from beneath the mountains stepped forwards, its heavy tread shaking the mountain. The High Zar dared not look too closely at it; he had seen the fate of those who had done so, and had no wish to end his days a burned out husk of dead flesh.

'I do not remember this world,' it said. 'I remember the destruction of the Great Gateway and the world in turmoil, but all this… all this was young then. I have slept for so long that I do not remember it any more.'

'It is ours for the taking,' promised Cyenwulf.

'Yes…' rumbled the creature, the smoke that concealed its dark majesty pulsing with cerulean lightning, and the High Zar breathed a sigh of relief as it turned and climbed back down the mountainside.

VI

WHEN KASPAR HAD been told that Vassily Chekatilo was downstairs, he had assumed that the Kislevite had come with further news of the unseen enemy who had thus far eluded them. But now, sitting in his study with Chekatilo lounging beside the fire, he wished he had never allowed the smug bastard within the walls of the embassy. Many days had passed since the events at the Lubjanko and Kaspar had put off speaking to Chekatilo for as long as he could.

'You cannot possibly expect me to do this,' said Kaspar, his lips pursed in a thin line.

Chekatilo simply nodded. 'I do indeed, ambassador.'

'I won't.'

'I think you will, it is in your interests to do so,' said Chekatilo ominously. 'Remember, you were only too willing to put yourself in my debt when your precious Sofia was missing, when Sasha Kajetan was torturing her in his death attic. You begged me to help.'

'But we got Sofia back without your help,' pointed out Kaspar.

'Aye, that you did, but without my help you not have caught Kajetan, eh?'

'No,' admitted Kaspar, 'but I never asked you to do that. It was Pavel who came to you. I owe you nothing.'

Chekatilo laughed. 'You think that matter, Empire man? If a man owes me money and he dies, do I not demand the money from his woman? And if she dies, do I not then demand it from his son? It the same thing, the debt passes. You owe me and I remember you giving me your word on this. Said it was iron, once given, never broken.'

Kaspar got up from behind his desk and turned his back on Chekatilo, staring through the window over the rooftops of Kislev. The snows were retreating and the first rains had turned the streets into slushy quagmires, dampening the optimism the new year had brought to the city.

Armies were on the march, he knew. Forward riders from the vanguard of the army of Talabecland had already arrived, bringing news of the arrival of nearly seven thousand fighting men under General Clemenz Spitzaner, a man Kaspar knew well and did not particularly relish meeting once more. He wondered briefly if the years had dimmed the man's bitterness, but supposed he would find out soon enough.

'Ambassador?' said Chekatilo, startling him from his reverie.

'What you are asking me to do violates every duty and oath I took when I accepted this posting to your miserable country,' said Kaspar, facing Chekatilo once more.

'So? Such things not a problem for your predecessor.'

'I don't suppose they were, but Teugenheim was a coward and I will not be blackmailed in the way he was.'

'I am not blackmailing you, Empire man,' said Chekatilo. 'I only ask you to honour your debt to me. I am leaving Kislev for Marienburg and need to travel very far. Through your land – and land at war is a dangerous, suspicious place. As Empire ambassador, you can sign documents that will allow me to pass… what is the phrase? Ah, yha, "without let or hindrance" through Empire. Teugenheim also tell me that as ambassador you entitled to soldiers from Empire regiments to protect you on journeys.'

'I know all this,' snapped Kaspar.

'I know,' smiled Chekatilo. 'You will authorise men from your soldiers to see me safely to Marienburg. After all, they sit outside of walls of Kislev and do nothing anyway, it not like they do anything useful.'

'But they will be called upon soon,' said Kaspar. 'It may have escaped your selfish notice, but war is coming to your land and these men will soon risk their lives defending it.'

'Pah, is of no matter, I not ask them to come here. I think many of them would be glad of chance to get out of Kislev before war.'

'You may have no sense of honour, running from your country like a cowardly rat, Chekatilo, but I do and I will be damned if I will sign any travel documents or assign you any of my nation's soldiers to do so.'

'You refusing your debt to me?' said Chekatilo darkly.

'You're damn right I am.'

'I not ask politely again, Empire man. You *will* give me what I ask for.'

'Over my dead body,' growled Kaspar.

'If not yours, then someone else's perhaps,' promised Chekatilo, rising from the chair and taking his leave.

VII

PAVEL TRUDGED THROUGH the slush of the Goromadny Prospekt, keeping his head bowed against the drizzling rain that greyed the sky and washed the colour from the world. He knew he should not be out in this kind of weather – Sofia had warned him as much – but he could not stay in the embassy. Not with the constant reminders of his shame at having let the ambassador down all around him in the accusing stares of his knights and guards.

He wished that he had a bottle of *kvas*, but was also glad that he did not. The past weeks had been a constant battle between his craving for the powerful spirit and a desire to not let his oldest friend down again. If he was honest, he knew he was probably too weak to win that battle, but hoped to eke out what little remained of their friendship before he inevitably failed once more.

'You are a stupid old fool,' he said to himself.

'You'll get no argument from me on that score,' said a cold voice from the street corner ahead of him. His heart sank as he recognised the voice and looked up into the flinty eyes of Chekatilo's killer, Rejak.

Rejak lounged on the corner of a redbrick building, his left arm held in a sling that was bound tightly to his body. Pavel could also see a thickness at the man's waist where the cut across his stomach had been heavily bandaged.

'Rejak,' said Pavel guardedly. 'I heard you were dead. What do you want?'

'No greeting for an old friend? And no, I'm not dead, sorry to disappoint you.'

'We were never friends, Rejak, even then. You are a cold blooded killer.'

Rejak laughed. 'And you are not? I seem to remember it was you who cracked open Andrej Vilkova's skull. I only held him down for you.'

Pavel closed his eyes, feeling the familiar guilt as he thought back to that dark night of murder. He took a deep breath to clear his head and said, 'I see someone taught you a lesson in swordplay. Almost emptied your belly to the floor, I heard.'

Rejak's eyes flared. 'It won't happen a second time,' he snarled. 'When I see that tricksy bastard again, I'll take his damned head off.'

Pavel laughed, tapping Rejak's injured arm. 'Best hope not to meet him too soon, eh?'

'I could still best you right now,' snapped Rejak.

'I don't doubt it, but that's not what you're here for is it?'

Rejak smiled, regaining his composure, and said, 'No, you're right, it's not.'

'Then what is it? Hurry up and tell me so I can get out of this bloody rain.'

'Chekatilo wants to see you.'

'Why?'

'He needs you to do something for him.'

'What?'

'Ask him yourself. I'm taking you to him.'

'What if I don't want to see him?' said Pavel, though he knew it was pointless.

'That doesn't matter. He wants to see you and I won't ask you again,' grinned Rejak, lifting aside his cloak with his good arm to show the hilt of his sword.

Pavel sighed in resignation, knowing that to follow Rejak was to damn himself completely, but knowing he was too pathetic to refuse and suffer the consequences.

Rejak smiled, seeing the defeat in Pavel's eyes, and turned to walk up the street.

Pavel followed him.

CHAPTER SIX

I

WITH ITS GOLDEN, eagle-topped banner poles shining in the sun, brightly patterned standards flapping in the stiff breeze and gaudily caparisoned knights, the army of Talabecland was a vibrant sight as nearly seven thousand men marched in good order along the rutted roadway towards Kislev. Kaspar's heart swelled with admiration to watch such an overt display of martial might, proud to see such fine men of his nation coming to the aid of their ally.

He and Kurt Bremen sat atop their steeds to one side of the main road at the foot of the *Gora Geroyev*, wrapped in thick fur cloaks. Officially, he was here in his capacity as Imperial ambassador to greet the army's general and welcome him to Kislev, but Kaspar knew Clemenz Spitzaner from the days he had carried his own general's baton and was in no hurry to renew that acquaintance.

No, Kaspar had come for the spectacle.

Densely packed blocks of pikemen in long tabards of red and gold marched behind halberdiers in padded, cross-coloured surcoats who carried their long-hafted weapons proudly, the blades gleaming like a forest of mirrors. Kaspar watched the different regiments as they passed in a riot of colours, golds, reds, whites and blues; swordsmen in feather-peaked sallets bearing iron-rimmed shields on their back: arquebusiers wrapped in long tunics and bristling with silver cartridge cases; archers in cockaded tricorne hats with bows wrapped in oilcloth; warriors in gleaming hauberks and scarlet puff-breeches who carried heavy greatswords over their shoulders.

Regiment after regiment of the state infantry of Talabecland marched to the beat of the drummer boys, who played rousing martial tunes accompanied by the horns of the following regiments.

Cavalry riding fine, grain-fed Empire steeds rode alongside the infantry, their mounts of obvious quality and a sure sign of wealth. The young riders wore light, flexible breastplates of toughened leather and plumed helmets, their long barrelled carbines holstered from looped thongs fastened to the saddle horn. Fast, deadly and brave to the point of recklessness, many an enemy had cause to regret underestimating these lightly armoured cavalrymen.

But the glory of the army was the knights in gleaming plate armour riding monstrous horses, fully seventeen hands or more. Great, northern-bred warhorses, these snorting, stamping beasts carried the Knights of the White Wolf; fearsome, bearded warriors, who matched their mounts' wild appearance.

Wrapped in shaggy wolf pelts and disdaining to carry a shield, they carried heavy cavalry hammers and shared raucous jokes with one another as they rode.

'That is no way for a Templar to behave,' said Kurt Bremen, shaking his head.

Kaspar chuckled, well aware of the rivalry that existed between the Templars of Ulric and Sigmar. He smiled, finally catching sight of the black and gold banner tops of the Nuln artillery train. Straining oxen and shouting teamsters with whips guided the massive cannons and bombards along the road, sweating teams of muscled men pushing the monstrously heavy bronze guns when their carriage wheels became stuck in the mud. Wagon after wagon followed the artillery, laden with shot, shell, black powder, handspikes and rammers.

'Ah, it does the heart proud to see the guns here, Kurt. The Imperial Gunnery school still produces the best guns in the world, no matter what the dwarfs might say.'

'You can keep your guns, Kaspar,' said Bremen with a smile. 'Give me an Averland steed and a sturdy lance any day.'

'Warfare is moving on, Kurt,' said Kaspar. 'The things the School of Engineers are producing now are frightening in their potential. Pistols that do not need to be loaded again until a revolving mechanism is expended, black powder rockets that can reach further than the heaviest cannon, though they can't hit anything worth a damn, and armoured machines that can carry a cannon across the battlefield.'

'Aye, soon a soldier himself will be incidental.'

'I fear you might be right, Kurt,' said Kaspar sadly. 'Sigmar save us from such times. I fear for what wars we might make when we no longer have to fight the foe face-to-face. How much easier will it be to kill when we can do it from leagues away and don't have to feel the enemy's blood on our hands or look into his eyes as he dies?'

'All too easy I suspect,' replied Bremen.

Such melancholy thoughts soured Kaspar's enjoyment of watching the spectacle of his countrymen's arrival in Kislev and he felt his mood worsen as he saw the unmistakable banner of its general approaching: a scarlet griffon rampant on a golden background, surrounded by a laurel wreath and decorated with numerous scrolls and trailing prayer pennants.

'Shit, here comes the man himself,' sighed Kaspar.

'You know the general?' asked Bremen.

Kaspar nodded. 'He was an officer on my staff that I could never quite shake loose. Unfortunately, his family had money and I was obliged to keep him around. A competent enough soldier, but there is no humility to the man, no sense that he owes it to his soldiers to try and bring as many of them back alive as he can. Show him a battle and he will hurl men at it until it is won, regardless of the cost.'

'From that, I take it there is no love lost between you?'

'Not much,' Kaspar chuckled. 'When I retired from the army, Spitzaner assumed that, as ranking officer, he would take over, but there was no way I was going to let him have it. Instead I promoted an officer named Hoffman, a good man with a brave heart and uncanny sense for good ground.'

'That can't have been easy to bear, a more junior officer being promoted over him.'

'No, but I was damned if I was going to let "Killer Clemenz" have my regiment. Thank Sigmar, the countess-elector's father, who was the Count of Nuln back then, agreed with me and Spitzaner left, purchasing a commission in a Talabecland regiment.'

'Where he has obviously prospered if he is now a general,' pointed out Bremen.

'Or, more likely, his money has greased his ascent up the promotions ladder.'

Further discussion was prevented by the arrival of Spitzaner and his coterie of horsemen: his officers, his priests, his bookkeepers, his historical recorders, his personal valets, a pair of men in long frock coats with the Imperial seal of Karl-Franz pinned to their lapels and a group of fork-bearded men with long swords who looked like they knew how to use them. As well as his banner bearer, General Clemenz Spitzaner travelled with his own trumpeter, who blew a series of rising notes on his brass bugle as the group of horsemen approached Kaspar and Bremen.

Spitzaner was a man in his early forties, but appeared much younger, thanks to a life free of the vice and loose living that so typified much of the Empire's nobility. His thin face was sallow and angular, as though his bones pressed too tightly against his skin and his eyes were a pale shade of green. The general wore a scarlet greatcoat with gold braid looped across one shoulder and a golden-fringed pelisse of emerald green velvet draped across the other. His riding britches were a spotless cream and his knee-length boots a brilliant, lustrous black.

Kaspar could tell that Spitzaner had known who he was going to meet at Kislev by the general's attire. Any other man would have ridden in practical furs and quilted jerkin, but not Spitzaner; he had a point to make. Kaspar wondered how long he had forced the army to wait, just outside of view of Kislev, while he changed into this ridiculous finery.

The general's group halted in a jingle of trace and bridle and Kaspar put on his best smile of welcome.

'My compliments to you, General Spitzaner. As ambassador to Kislev I bid you welcome to the north,' said Kaspar, turning to indicate the knight by his side. 'Allow me to introduce Kurt Bremen, he is the leader of my detachment of Knights Panther.'

Spitzaner bowed to Bremen before nodding curtly to Kaspar and saying, 'It has been a long time, von Velten.'

'Aye, it has that,' said Kaspar. 'I believe it was the countess-elector's ball of 2512 we last spoke.'

He saw Spitzaner's jaw clench and could not resist twisting the knife a little further.

'And how is Marshal Hoffman? Do you keep in touch?' he said.

'No,' snapped Spitzaner. 'Marshal Hoffman and I do not correspond.'

'Ah, so often that is the way when brother officers are promoted over one another. I, on the other hand, still receive letters from him every now and then. One of my most gifted protégés, I always thought. No doubt you will be pleased to know he prospers.'

'Indeed, but be that as it may,' said Spitzaner, a little too loudly. 'He is not here and I am. I am general of this regiment and you would do well to accord me the respect that my rank demands.'

'Of course, general, no disrespect was intended,' said Kaspar.

Spitzaner looked unconvinced, but did not press the point, casting his gaze out over the unkempt soldiers camped around the city walls and seeing scattered Empire standards planted in the hard ground.

'There are Imperial soldiers here already?'

'Aye,' said Kaspar. 'Remnants of the regiments scattered after the massacre at Zhedevka. Perhaps three thousand men.'

'Are they quality?' asked Spitzaner.

Kaspar bit back an angry retort and said, 'They are men of the Empire, general.'

'And who commands them?'

'A captain named Goscik, a good man. He has kept the soldiers together and in readiness for the fighting season.'

'A captain commands three thousand men?' said Spitzaner, outraged.

'He is the highest ranking and most competent officer who survived the battle.'

'Intolerable! I shall assign a more senior officer from my staff once we have established ourselves in this dreadful country. I would be grateful if you could show us to out billets, it has been a long and arduous ride from the Empire.'

'So I see,' said Kaspar, admiring Spitzaner's gleaming uniform.

Spitzaner ignored Kaspar's barb and turned in his saddle to wave forward the two men who bore the Emperor's seal in their lapels.

'This is Johan Michlenstadt and Claus Bautner, emissaries from the Emperor,' said Spitzaner by way of introduction. 'Their safe passage to Kislev was entrusted to me by the Reiksmarshall himself.'

Kaspar nodded a greeting to the two men, wondering how desperate Kurt Helborg must have been to trust Spitzaner with keeping these men alive. 'A pleasure to make your acquaintance, gentlemen.'

'Likewise, Ambassador von Velten,' said Michlenstadt.

'Yes, General Spitzaner has told us a great deal about you, though I am sure he exaggerates sometimes,' said Bautner.

Kaspar caught the man's ironic tone and warmed to Bautner immediately. He could well imagine the poison Spitzaner would have been spreading about his former general, and was pleased to meet someone who could see through it.

'I am sure the general does me proud with his tales,' said Kaspar graciously, 'but I am intrigued as to what manner of mission you would be upon that the Reiksmarshall himself would take such interest in it.'

'A matter of gravest urgency,' said Michlenstadt. 'It is imperative that we see the Ice Queen at the earliest opportunity.'

'Yes,' continued Bautner. 'We bring missives from the Emperor himself and must deliver them to the Tzarina's own hand.'

'That might not be so easy,' said Kaspar, faintly amused by the two emissaries' habit of finishing each other's sentences. 'The Tzarina is not an easy woman to see.'

'It is vitally important,' said Michlenstadt.

'Yes,' nodded Bautner. 'The fate of the world depends upon it.'

II

ICICLES DROOPED FROM the cellar's roof, the steady drip, drip of moisture on the top of the bronze coffin echoing loudly in the icy room. The pale blue of the ice that covered the walls and floor was shot through with black and green veins, poisonous corruption that had spread quickly from the miasma that surrounded the coffin and infected everything around it with deadly, mutating sickness.

The plague that stalked the streets above and killed scores daily was ample demonstration of the power of what lay within the coffin, its pestilent makers having excelled themselves in its creation. Perhaps too much so, she thought as she idly paced in a circle around the coffin, her breath feathering before her in the chill air. The force within was a living thing now – its power to corrupt growing with every passing day – and it had taken potent wards to keep its malice in check lest its eagerness to writhe and mutate unmask her before she was ready to unleash it.

The tiny corpses lying frozen in the corner of the cellar gave testimony to the amount of innocent blood it had taken to subdue its malice, but fortunately Losov could obtain an almost limitless supply of such nameless, faceless victims from the Lubjanko.

When it came time to break those wards and allow that malice its full, unchecked rein, she would relish the spectacle of painful death and mutation that would swiftly follow. The arrival of the Empire force, two days ago, had filled her with elation then disappointment. She had been told that the armies of both Talabecland and Stirland would be coming to Kislev, but now it seemed as though the Stirland force was marching west to link with the forces of Boyarin Kurkosk.

With so many men camped outside the city wall, she could feel the pulsing, deathly desire of the corruption locked within the coffin to be released, to wreak its misery upon so many living things, to reduce them to foetid piles of mutated flesh and bone. She suspected that the Stirland army would come to Kislev eventually, and knew that she could inflict much greater suffering were she to bide her time.

She ran her delicate fingers along the rusted top of the coffin, feeling its power and its desire to inflict horrific change. But she was touched by the Dark Gods' favour and was resistant to its evil.

'Soon,' she whispered. 'Curb your wrath for but a little longer and you shall be the unmaking of more life than you know.'

She turned on her heel, more pressing business now occupying her thoughts.

Sasha Kajetan.

She knew that the swordsman had now descended to the point where his madness was complete and his obsession with the ambassador had consumed him utterly.

It was time to set her handsome prince on the hunt once more.

III

'DAMN IT, HOW much longer must we wait?' snapped Clemenz Spitzaner, pacing up and down before the great portrait of the Khan Queen Miska in the Hall of Heroes. The interior of the Tzarina's Winter Palace was just as impressive as Kaspar remembered, the walls of solid ice glittering in the light of a thousand candles hung from shimmering chandeliers. Columns of black ice, veined with subtle golden threads rose to the great, vaulted ceiling with its mosaic depicting the coronation of Igor the Terrible.

'You'll wear a rut in that rug, general,' said Kaspar, standing with his hands laced behind his back. Though he hated its ostentation, he wore his formal attire for the audience the Tzarina had finally deigned to give them: a cockaded hat with a long blue feather, a long embroidered coat with a waistcoat held shut by engraved silver buttons and elegant britches tucked into polished black riding boots. Spitzaner and his staff officers wore their colourful and ridiculously impractical dress uniforms, laden with gold braid, lace trims and bronze epaulettes.

Both emissaries of the Emperor wore sober dark dress, their only concession to decoration the gold and scarlet sashes they wore bound about their waists and the Imperial seals pinned to their lapels. Bautner stared in wonder at his surroundings, while Michlenstadt picked small pieces of lint from his coat.

'You are the ambassador,' said Spitzaner angrily. 'Shouldn't you be able to procure us an audience with Tzarina quicker than this? My army has been camped beyond the walls of her damned city for five days now. Does she not want our help?'

'The Tzarina makes her own decisions as to who she sees and when,' explained Kaspar. 'Her advisor, Pjotr Losov is… shall we say, not the most cooperative of men when it comes to facilitating audiences.'

'Sigmar damn her, but this tries my patience,' grumbled Spitzaner.

'I do not believe we have any choice but to wait,' said Michlenstadt amiably.

'Yes,' said Bautner. 'None of us can force a monarch to move to the beat of any drum but their own. We must await her pleasure, for we have strict instructions to deliver our missives to her hand and her hand alone.'

Kaspar forced himself to ignore the impatient pacing of Spitzaner – the man had been nothing but an arrogant ass and pain in the backside the last few days – and moved further down the length of the hall, halting before the portrait of the other infamous Khan Queen, Anastasia. The woman in the picture was depicted riding her war-chariot, arms aloft as the heavens raged above her. Tall and beautiful, this Anastasia had a fierceness to her features that the Anastasia he knew did not, a ferocity that echoed the harshness of the land that had borne her. She was a living, breathing representation of all that made the Kislevites such a hardy race of passionate warriors.

Thinking of Anastasia brought a familiar melancholy to him as he thought of how they had become estranged.

Part of him wanted to reach out to her and make amends for the harsh words that had passed between them, but he knew that too much time had passed for him to know how to make such an approach. Sadness touched him at his limitations, but he knew himself well enough to know that it was too late for him to change and that the easiest way to bear that sadness was to lock it away in the deepest corner of his being.

The chiming of the clock above the beaten golden double doors shook Kaspar from his thoughts and he turned back to the main hall as Spitzaner and his gaudily dressed officers arranged themselves before the doors, a strict hierarchy observed in their positioning.

Bautner and Michlenstadt stood slightly behind and to the left of Spitzaner, who, naturally, took centre stage for the promised audience. As the ninth chime struck, the doors to the inner apartments swung open and the Tzarina Katarin, Ice Queen of Kislev entered the Hall of Heroes.

Once again Kaspar was struck by the sheer primal force of her beauty. The Ice Queen's sculpted features were regal and piercing, as though carved from the coldest glacier with eyes like chips of blue diamond. She inspired awe and Kaspar remembered the fear and wonder that had passed through her subjects when he had last seen her move amongst them. A long, glittering gown of ivory trailed behind her, layered with ice-flecked silk and strings of pearls. Her hair was a fierce white, the colour of a winter's morning, threaded with rippling ice-blue streaks and braided with strings of emeralds beneath her glittering crown of ice. Kaspar saw she was armed with the mighty war-blade of the khan queens, Fearfrost, and could feel the bow-wave of chill that preceded her.

Unusually, she came without her normal array of flunkies, hangers-on and family members. Instead, four bare-chested warriors with shaven heads and long topknots and drooping moustaches followed her, bearing a heavy golden throne between them. Each carried a pair of curved sabres across his back and had a long, thin bladed knife sheathed in a fold of flesh on their flat stomachs.

Warriors from Sasha Kajetan's former regiment, thought Kaspar, recognising their skin-crawling habit of scabbarding blades within their flesh. A show of bravado, a rite of passage or a tradition? Kaspar didn't know which and had no desire to ask.

The temperature continued to drop as the Ice Queen approached, and a ghostly mist rose around their ankles. Kaspar heard a soft tinkling, as of ice forming, and the scent of cold, hard, northern forests swelled to fill the air. He heard muffled gasps of unease from the men of the Empire as they bowed to her, a chill wind carrying the bitter cold of the oblast snaking around them. Every one of them would have heard the Tzarina's reputation as a powerful sorceress, but none of them had expected to feel such power so closely.

Kaspar smiled to himself as he bowed. For all her intelligence, the Ice Queen was not subtle in the demonstrations of her power, and Kaspar was struck by how much he actually liked her. Her guards placed the throne behind the Tzarina and she arranged herself artfully upon it, the warriors taking up position either side of her, their arms folded and their posture aggressive.

'Ambassador von Velten,' said the Ice Queen, her voice unexpectedly warm. 'It is good to see you again. We have missed you at the palace.'

Kaspar bowed again graciously. 'It is an honour to be here again, your majesty.'

'And how is that temper of yours?' she asked playfully.

'As bad as ever,' smiled Kaspar.

'Good,' nodded the Ice Queen, inclining her head. 'And who is this you have brought to see me? Other men of ill-temper?'

'I fear not,' said Kaspar, turning to introduce his companions. 'This is General Clemenz Spitzaner of Nuln, your majesty. He commands the army camped beyond your walls.'

'An honour, your majesty,' said Spitzaner, bowing elaborately and sweeping his feathered hat in an overblown gesture of greeting.

'Quite,' said the Ice Queen, her eyes sliding from the colourful martinet.

Kaspar continued his introductions, saying, 'And these are the envoys from your brother monarch to the south, the most noble Emperor Karl-Franz. Emissaries, Michlenstadt and Bautner.'

Kaspar saw a flash of anger cross Spitzaner's face at being so easily dismissed from the Ice Queen's notice, but wisely the general said nothing.

Emissary Michlenstadt stepped forward as the Ice Queen said, 'I am told you come with news of great import for me?'

'Indeed we do, your majesty,' said Michlenstadt, striding forward and reaching within his coat's inside pocket. He had taken only a few steps when the warriors behind the Tzarina had their blades drawn and were holding them at the emissary's throat.

'What?' gasped Michlenstadt, his face ashen as he pulled a wax-sealed letter from his coat. The nearest warrior grunted and snatched the letter from his hand, turning and passing it to the Tzarina.

'Sigmar protect us,' whispered Bautner as the shaking Michlenstadt backed away from the fierce warriors.

'Forgive their ardour,' said the Ice Queen. 'Protecting my life is a duty these men take very seriously, and they take a dim view of folk they do not know approaching me.'

'Quite alright,' gasped Michlenstadt, though Kaspar could see the man was visibly shaken. 'Their devotion does you credit.'

The warriors returned their blades to their sheaths and stepped back behind the throne, though Kaspar was in no doubt that the Ice Queen was fully capable of protecting herself should the need arise. She broke the seal on the letter and unfolded the parchment, quickly scanning the words written there.

'Emissary Michlenstadt,' said the Ice Queen without looking up.

'Your majesty?'

'Explain this to me, if you would.'

'I am not sure I understand, your majesty,' said Michlenstadt, sharing a confused glance with Bautner. 'I helped draft the Emperor's letter myself and strove for clarity in every word.'

'Indulge me,' said the Tzarina, and Kaspar could sense the cold undercurrent to her words. 'Pretend I am some simple girl-queen you wish to impress with your fine words. Tell me what this letter asks of me.'

'It is an invitation to journey to Altdorf and join with those who would stand against the forces of darkness that threaten to destroy us all,' said Michlenstadt. 'The Emperor has decreed that on the Spring Equinox, there shall be a great Conclave of Light, a gathering of the great and mighty where the fate of the world shall be decided.'

'You think its fate is yours to decide?' laughed the Tzarina. 'Then you are a fool. So like men to believe that the world is theirs to save or destroy as they choose.'

Both emissaries stared at each other in confusion, unable to have anticipated this reaction.

'This world will turn regardless of what you and your Conclave of Light decides. What matters now is not talk, but action. Armies pillage my land, kill my people and sack my cities. My warriors fight and die, and your Emperor would have me leave my land in its hour of greatest need?'

'He seeks only to defeat the greater menace that threatens us all,' protested Michlenstadt.

'Yes,' agreed Bautner. 'As free peoples we must all stand together or we shall surely perish separately.'

'A convenient sentiment now that there are armies despoiling your own land,' said the Tzarina, turning towards Kaspar, and he felt the chill of her gaze upon him, his skin prickling to goosebumps beneath his clothes.

'Ambassador von Velten,' began the Ice Queen, 'you say nothing here?'

Kaspar knew he would need to choose his next words with great care, seeing the emissaries' desperate eyes upon him.

'I leave such games of state for those best suited to them, your majesty.'

The Tzarina scowled, 'You are the Emperor's ambassador to Kislev are you not?'

'I am,' agreed Kaspar.

'And as his ambassador, you speak here with his voice do you not?'

'I do, yes,' said Kaspar, seeing the trap she had laid for him, but unable now to remove his head from the snare.

'So tell me, ambassador, what would your Emperor do were the situations reversed, if the Empire were ravaged by war and he was called to abandon his land while enemies killed his people and burned their homes?'

Kaspar hesitated before speaking, though he knew the answer to the Tzarina's question clearly enough.

'He would refuse to go, your majesty,' said Kaspar, hearing outraged intakes of breath from Spitzaner and the Emperor's emissaries. 'Karl-Franz is a man of honour, a warrior king, and he would never abandon his people while his heart still beat.'

The Tzarina nodded, smiling as though she had known exactly what answer Kaspar would give. She rose from her throne and addressed the two Imperial emissaries directly.

'You may take word to your Emperor that I thank him for his invitation, but that, regretfully, I must decline. I have a land to save and I cannot leave it while the tribes of the north make war upon us. I shall send my most trusted envoys with you on your return to Altdorf and they shall speak with my voice at this conclave.'

The Tzarina bowed gracefully to the men of the Empire before turning away and gracefully departing the hall through the golden doors from whence she had come, her warriors following closely behind her. As the doors shut, a detachment of bronze armoured knights threw open the entrance that led to the vestibule of the Winter Palace, standing guard to either side.

Thus dismissed, Kaspar and his fellow countrymen marched dejectedly from the Hall of Heroes under the unchanging gaze of the Tzars and Khan Queens of Kislev.

IV

KASPAR SHOOK HIS head as the squire came forward to take Magnus's reins, dismounting and leading the horse around the side of the embassy to stable the horse himself. He could see the guards who had accompanied him to the palace groan at the thought of not getting inside the warmth of the embassy and said, 'You men go on. I won't be long.'

The guards gratefully retreated into the embassy, leaving Kaspar to open the frost-limed stable door and lead his horse inside. He was cold and tired, but his nerves were wound too tightly for him to think of sleep just yet. He bent down, wincing as his knee cracked, and undid the girth around Magnus's belly, removing the heavy leather saddle and slinging it across a nearby rail.

He fed the horse a few handfuls of grain then took out a stiffened wire brush and began giving the horse's coat a thorough rub down, combing his mane and working out the stresses of the day with every stroke.

Though he knew he could not have given the Tzarina any other answer, he wondered if the Emperor would see it that way when Michlenstadt and Bautner returned to the capital and informed him of her refusal to attend his conclave. Spitzaner and the emissaries had been furious with him upon leaving the Winter Palace.

'Sigmar damn you, von Velten!' Spitzaner had shouted, his normally pale features ruddy with outrage. 'Do you know what you have done?'

'I said nothing the Tzarina did not already know,' pointed out Kaspar.

'That's not the point,' said Michlenstadt, trying to keep his voice even.

'No,' agreed Bautner, shaking his head. 'An ambassador is not simply the Emperor's voice at another court, but a means of enacting his will. You should not have said what you did, ambassador, it was highly inappropriate.'

'You mean I should have lied?'

Bautner sighed, as though being forced to explain something straightforward to a simpleton. 'These are dark times we live in, ambassador, and sometimes the values we cherish in peacetime must, shall we say, bend in times of strife. If the idea of lying is offensive to you, perhaps you could simply have omitted to mention certain truths that might have influenced the Tzarina's decision.'

'Omission of the truth? Since when is that not lying?' asked Kaspar.

'In the affairs of courtly politics it can be an important distinction sometimes,' said Michlenstadt.

'She would not have gone to Altdorf regardless of what I said.'

'We do not know that for sure, von Velten,' snapped Spitzaner. 'Make no mistake, the Emperor will hear of what happened here tonight.'

'Of that I have no doubt,' said Kaspar, already weary of Spitzaner's voice.

The general and the emissaries had ridden back to their billets in the city without another word, escorted by their halberd-wielding soldiers, leaving Kaspar and his guards to ride through Geroyev Square towards the embassy.

The night had been cold, but without the sharpness that had characterised it throughout the winter and it was plain to see that, while winter had not yet released its grip on Kislev, it was definitely in retreat.

Kaspar had worked up a sweat while grooming Magnus and felt its chill on his skin as he finished the task of stabling his mount for the night. He threw a thick, brightly patterned blanket over the horse's back to keep him warm overnight and left the stables, careful to drop the latch as he left.

He trudged across the slushy ground towards the servants' door at the rear of the embassy, deciding that he could use some food and a drink of *kvas*. Kaspar pushed open the door, surprising the few servants gathered there playing cards with his arrival. They hurried to make themselves look busy, but Kaspar bade them return to their game, removing his boots and cloak and handing them to his manservant.

Wanting a light supper to take to bed, he cursed softly as he remembered that there was no *kvas* in the embassy; Sofia having made sure that every drop of the spirit had been poured into the gutters to keep Pavel from temptation.

Kaspar shrugged. Probably for the best anyway; the last thing he needed at the moment was alcohol. He might have put the final nail in his ambassadorial career tonight, but he was damned if he was going to face any repercussions of what had happened with a hangover. He cut some slices of bread, cheese and ham and prepared a sweet tisane before picking up a candle and climbing the back stairs to the upper floor of the embassy and his bedroom.

The servants' corridors were dimly lit by tallow candles that flickered in the draft from below, but they were quiet and, for that, Kaspar was grateful. He had no wish for conversation tonight and just hoped he would be able to snatch a few hours of sleep before first light.

He pushed open the servants' door to his bedroom and set his supper down on the table beside his bed. He could see a bulge in its centre where a bronze bedwarmer filled with heated coals had been placed and angled the candle he'd taken from the kitchen to light the lamps at the side of his bed.

Something registered at the corner of his vision and he paused, cocking his head to one side as he heard a rustle of papers and a soft thump from his study next door. He lifted the candle away from the lamp, leaving it unlit and gripped the butt of his pistol with his free hand. There should be no one in his study at this time of night and his mind filled with dark possibilities as to who might be within.

Treading carefully so as not to alert the intruder, Kaspar approached the door to the study, his anger building with each soft step. He knew he should go back downstairs and alert his guards to this trespasser, but his already dark mood was filling him with the desire to hurt the bastard himself. He eased the flint back on his pistol, seeing a flicker of light and shadow beneath the bottom of the door.

He held his pistol before him, took a deep breath and kicked open the study door.

'Don't move!' he shouted, quickly entering the room. 'I am armed.'

He saw a bulky figure standing behind his desk and was about to repeat his warning when he recognised the man rifling through the contents of his desk.

Pavel. It was bloody Pavel.

V

SASHA KAJETAN GROANED as he shifted his weight, the chains around his wrist digging into the raw flesh of his wrists. His world had shrunk to the point where all he knew now was pain and hunger and he welcomed it. The trueself had eroded all but the last remnants of his sanity and all that remained in his mind were thoughts of violence and death.

He knew his longing for atonement would never come now and silently prayed for death from whatever deities might not yet have abandoned him. But death would not take him. It seemed even the kingdom of Morr was to be denied him. He could not blame the guardian of the kingdom of the dead; after all, who would want such a wretched soul as his?

He had accepted now that this was his lot – an eternity of suffering and starvation in this gaol with nothing but the steady drip of water and mange-ridden rats for company.

One such specimen sat on its haunches at the doorway, where it had pushed itself through a gap between the rusted iron door and the crumbling brickwork. It scrabbled at the hole it had come through with its claws, digging away the sodden brickwork for some unguessable purpose.

He watched the rat for a while, losing track of time as he became transfixed by its diligent labours. Eventually, it completed its task and turned to face him, squealing at him as if trying to impart some message. He gave the appearance of ignoring it and the animal drew closer, squealing with greater urgency.

His foot lashed out. The rat darted aside, but not fast enough as the heel of the swordsman's foot caught it in the centre of its spine and broke its back. He grinned crookedly as the rat twitched and died. He might now be a broken, shell of a human being, but he was still quick. He dragged the dead rat towards him with his feet, leaning down to sink his teeth into its furry belly.

Sasha felt thin bones snap under his rotten teeth and tasted the rodent's warm blood fill his mouth like a tonic. He swallowed a gristly lump of meat, biting off another chunk as he suddenly became aware of being watched, turning his head to see a bloated white rat squeeze its bulk through the widened hole in the brickwork. Its fangs were long and curved, like the daggers of the steppe nomads, and its small, slitted eyes glittered an unhealthy red.

He watched the rat for several seconds, blood dripping from his chin, as it looked him up and down as though appraising him. Its lips curled back from its fangs and it gave a long, squealing bray, unlike any sound Sasha would have expected a rat to make.

Was this some kind of sign? He had felt the rats above him before, plotting and planning, but until now they had been content to merely watch him. Did they now have greater designs in mind for him?

Dimly, he heard the clang of an iron door and, seconds later, saw a soft glow from beneath his cell door. Fear fluttered in his breast as he heard the rattle of keys and the cell door was flung open. The white rat scurried from the cell, but it was forgotten in an instant as Sasha saw the glowing shape that filled the doorway.

She stood before him in all her remembered glory, beautiful, auburn haired and full of love for him. She wore a long green gown, the shimmering fabric and pale nimbus of light haloing her head hurting his eyes.

'Matka…' he whispered, weeping tears of shame, love and happiness as his matka opened her arms to him. Sasha sobbed like a child, the trueself surging to the forefront of his consciousness at the sight of her. He reached for her, but was prevented from touching her by the shackles that bound him to the wall.

As if in answer to that thought, the gaoler stumbled into the cell, blubbering uncontrollably as he was hurled to the floor by a stooped figure swathed in black robes and carrying a short, curved sword.

'Free him,' said his matka.

The gaoler nodded hurriedly, fumbling for the key in terror. At last he found the correct key and unlocked the fetters that bound Sasha. The swordsman slumped to the ground, his wrists raw and bleeding and skin covered with festering sores.

His matka knelt beside him, cupping his head in her wonderfully soft hands. He couldn't see her face properly, her features blurred and indistinct as the light swum around her head.

'It's me, my handsome prince,' she said.

'Matka…' he hissed, his throat parched and constricted.

'Yes. I've come for you.'

'So sorry,' he managed, pushing himself upright.

His matka wiped a finger across his jaw, flicking the rat's blood at the brickwork walls of the cell. She shook her head. 'Wouldn't you rather have something else? Something better than the blood of vermin?'

The robed figure with the sword darted forward, grabbing the gaoler by the neck and, tearing his glass-lensed hood off, slashed his sword across the man's throat. Blood fountained from the wound, arterial spray gushing like a hose over Sasha's face.

Hot blood, straight from a beating heart filled the swordsman's mouth and he drank it greedily, feeling his matka's hands upon him as he swallowed and swallowed. He felt her hands warm him, a pleasant heat and arousal radiating outwards from where she touched him.

Fresh vigour seeped into his body and he felt forgotten strength flow through his atrophied muscles as he drank and his matka somehow restored his life. He snarled, feeling the trueself's lust for death grow. He reached out and took hold of the twitching gaoler, biting and tearing in a frenzy at the flesh of the man's neck.

'Yes,' said his matka. 'Feed, grow strong. Tchar has need of you.'

Sasha hurled aside the mutilated corpse and pushed himself to his feet, hot, angry energy coursing around his body.

'Not too fast, my love,' cautioned his matka, as he steadied himself against the wall of his cell, 'it will take time for your strength to return in full.'

He nodded, watching as the gaoler's killer wiped his sword on his victim's undershirt. The hands clasping the sword's hilt were furred and clawed and, as though sensing his scrutiny, it turned towards him, hissing in challenge.

Sasha stared into the beady black eyes beneath the hood and wondered if this – thing – was also a minion of the bloated albino-furred rat.

He turned his back on the verminous killer, following his matka from the cell and along the corridor towards an open iron door that led to some stairs. A body lay at the foot of the stairs, a triangular piece of metal embedded in its neck.

'Come, Sasha,' said his matka, 'I have such things for you to do…'

The trueself nodded, hearing the little boy that had once been Sasha Kajetan screaming from the depths of his tortured soul.

CHAPTER SEVEN

I

KASPAR LOWERED THE pistol as the two men faced one another over the top of his desk. A lamp sat on its corner, casting a fitful illumination around them, but leaving the rest of the room in shadow. Pavel said nothing, clutching a sheaf of papers in one hand and a wooden handled seal-stamp in the other.

'What the hell do you think you're doing, Pavel?' asked Kaspar, lowering the flint and jamming his pistol through his belt.

'Please,' begged Pavel. 'Let me do this and go. You never see me again.'

'I asked you a question, damn it.'

Pavel circled the desk and said, 'I can explain this.'

'You bloody well better,' snapped Kaspar. He closed with Pavel and snatched the papers and stamp from his old comrade's hands. Pavel bit his bottom lip as Kaspar moved towards the lamp, examining what had been taken from his desk. The seal was his personal crest, ringed by the spread wings of the Imperial eagle, while the documents were letters of transit, letters that would allow the bearer to traverse the length and breadth of the Empire without let or hindrance.

He recognised the documents for what they were and his heart sank as he realised who Pavel must have been stealing them for. He sat down heavily in his chair, dropping the items and rubbing the heels of his palms across his scalp.

'Damn it all to hell,' he whispered to himself.

'Kaspar, please–' began Pavel.

'Shut up!' roared Kaspar. 'I do not want to hear it, Pavel. Everything that comes out of your mouth now is nothing but dung! It has been so long since I heard you speak the truth I have forgotten what it sounds like.'

'I know,' said Pavel. 'I stupid fool. But I sorry.'

'Don't tell me you are sorry, you miserable piece of shit, don't you dare tell me you're sorry! You were stealing these for Chekatilo, weren't you? Answer me! Weren't you?'

Pavel slumped into one of the chairs beside the fireplace, his face wreathed in dark shadows as he moved away from the lantern.

'Yha, I was stealing them for Chekatilo.'

Kaspar felt his anger at Pavel reach new heights, heights he did not believe it was possible to reach. Was there no limit to Pavel's betrayal?

'Why, Pavel, why? Help me understand why you did this, because I cannot fathom it. What would make you turn your back on your friend to do this for such a loathsome piece of scum like Chekatilo?'

'It because I am your friend that I do this,' said Pavel.

'What? You steal from me because you're my friend?' snapped Kaspar. 'Well I suppose I should count myself lucky I am not one of your enemies, for I would hate to see what you do to them.'

'I mean it,' barked Pavel.

'Talk sense, man.'

'Chekatilo sends Rejak for me, tells me I am to steal these things from you.'

'And you said yes?' asked Kaspar. 'Why?'

Pavel shook his head. 'I cannot say.'

'You bloody well will say,' promised Kaspar. 'I want to know what that bastard said to make you betray me.'

Pavel surged from the chair and planted his hands on Kaspar's desk and shouted, 'I cannot tell you!'

Kaspar rose from his chair and faced Pavel, his anger hot and raw. 'Either tell me or get out of here now. I warned you what would happen the next time you did anything stupid, did I not?'

'Aye, but, please, Kaspar. I cannot tell you, it was before you came here. Chekatilo knows things of me, bad things, secret things. Trust me, I cannot tell you.'

'Trust you?' laughed Kaspar coming from behind the desk and jabbing his finger against Pavel's chest. 'Trust you? Am I hearing you right? You are asking me to trust you?'

'Yha,' nodded Pavel.

'Oh well, then I suppose I should, eh? Now that you have led one ambassador astray, put me in debt to Chekatilo and then tried to steal from me, I suppose I should. What could I possibly have to lose?'

Pavel's face darkened and he said, 'You always so perfect, Empire man? You never make mistakes?'

'Mistakes?' snapped Kaspar. 'Mistakes, yes, but betray my friends? Never. What kind of mistake would make you betray me, Pavel? Tell me. We fought together for years, saved each other's lives more times than I can count. Tell me the truth, damn you!'

Pavel shook his head. 'You not want the truth.'

'Yes,' shouted Kaspar, getting right in Pavel's face. 'I do, so damn well tell me!'

Pavel pushed the ambassador away and turned his back on him. A great sob burst from the burly Kislevite and he said, 'I murdered Andrej Vilkova, Anastasia's husband. Rejak and me killed him. We caught him outside Chekatilo's brothel and beat him to death. There! You happy now?'

Kaspar felt his senses go numb and a sick feeling spread from the pit of his stomach to his furthest extremities. He put a hand out to lean on the desk, his mind a whirlwind of confused thoughts.

'Oh, no, Pavel, no...' hissed Kaspar, the breath tight in his chest. 'You didn't, please tell me you didn't.'

Pavel returned to his seat and hung his head in his hands. 'I so sorry, Kaspar. Chekatilo has held this over my head since that night. He said he would tell you if I not do this for him and I not want you to find out about what I did, what a pathetic, snivelling piece of scum Pavel Korovic is.'

Kaspar could not answer Pavel, still reeling from the shock of discovering that one of his oldest friends was revealed as a murderer, no better than Sasha Kajetan. He felt tears of betrayal course down his face, horrified that a man he had trusted his life to on so many occasions was nothing but a common killer.

Pavel stood and put his hand on Kaspar's shoulder.

'Don't touch me,' roared Kaspar, throwing off Pavel's hand and backing away from him. He could barely stand to look at him.

Anastasia...

By Sigmar, all these years thinking that some street thug had murdered her husband, and all the time the killer was sitting in the Empire embassy, friend to her new lover. As he attempted to comprehend the scale of Pavel's crime, a soft knock came at the main door of the study and one of the embassy guards entered.

'Sorry to disturb you, sir. Heard shouting and wondered if everything was alright?'

Kaspar did not trust his voice yet, so simply nodded and raised his hand. The guard, sensing the mood within the room, said, 'Very good, sir,' and withdrew.

Silence descended on the study, uncomfortably stretching until Kaspar felt like his heart would burst. He wiped his face with his sleeve and managed to say, 'Why?'

'Why what?' asked Pavel.

'Why was he killed, damn it?'

Pavel shrugged, defeated, and said, 'I not know. All I know is Losov came to Chekatilo and paid him to have Andrej Vilkova killed.'

Kaspar rubbed a hand across his jaw, his brow furrowing as he realised he recognised the name Pavel had mentioned.

'Losov? Pjotr Losov? The Tzarina's advisor? Are you telling me that he paid Chekatilo to have Anastasia's husband murdered?'

'Yha, I heard him. I think that why Chekatilo have me do it.'

'That son of a bitch,' swore Kaspar, now realising the source of the enmity between Pavel and Losov. 'Why the hell would he do that?'

'I not know,' said Pavel.

'I wasn't talking to you,' said Kaspar, his jaw clenched and his fingers beating a nervous tattoo on his desktop. 'Damn you, but I should hand you over to the *Chekist.*'

'Yha, probably you should,' agreed Pavel.

'No,' said Kaspar, shaking his head. 'I won't. You have saved my life too many times for me to send you to those bastards, but…'

'But what?'

'But you and I are finished,' said Kaspar. 'Get the hell out of my embassy. Now.'

Pavel rose from the seat and said, 'For what it worth–'

'Stop,' said Kaspar, his voice little more than a whisper. 'Just go. Please, just go.'

Pavel nodded sadly and walked to the door. He turned as though about to say something, but thought the better of it and left without another word.

As the door shut, Kaspar put his head in his hands and wept openly for the first time since he had buried his wife.

* * *

II

MORNING BROUGHT A cold rain from the east. Kaspar sat behind his desk as weak sunlight spilled in through the window behind him. He had not slept since Pavel had left, his emotions too raw, too near the surface for him to close his eyes. Each time he tried, he would picture Anastasia's face and the pain would surface again. Part of him wanted to tell her of her husband's murder, to lay to rest the ghost of his death, but to renew a friendship on such news was not a possibility.

He missed her, but felt powerless to do anything about it. She had made her feelings plain and there was nothing he could do to alter them. He was too set in his ways and she in hers for either of them to change and though he craved her company, he knew that they would soon go through the same dance again should they renew their relationship. He would always care for her, but could not allow himself to do more than that.

And Pavel…

He cursed Kislev, cursed its people, its language, its customs, its… everything. He felt an intense wave of bitterness rise in him, wishing he had never set foot in this godforsaken country again. It had brought him nothing but pain and misadventure.

He rubbed his tired eyes, knowing he was reacting with his heart and not his head, but unable to curb the bile he felt. He knew his eyes must be swollen and bloodshot from tears and lack of sleep, so he stood and ran a hand across his scalp, making his way towards his bedroom.

As he rose from behind his desk, he glanced through the window, seeing a lone horseman ride hard for the embassy, jerking his horse to a sliding halt at the gates. The man wore black armour and an all-enclosing helm of dark iron, but Kaspar immediately recognised him as Vladimir Pashenko, head of the *Chekist*. He swore silently to himself. Today of all days, he could do without this. But he had a duty to his position here and reluctantly straightened his clothing, still the formal regalia he had worn to the Winter Palace the previous evening.

He watched Pashenko push through the gate and march purposefully towards the embassy door. His haste and obvious anger told Kaspar that something serious had happened and he wondered what calamity would drive the normally emotionless Pashenko to such heights of agitation.

The door below slammed shut and he heard heavy footfalls ascend the main stairs, hurried steps following them along with blustering protests. Kaspar seated himself behind his desk again and waited for Pashenko to enter, which he did seconds later, hurling the door open and striding straight towards Kaspar. His helmet was held under the crook of his arm, but he threw it on a chair as he approached.

'Ursun damn you, von Velten!' shouted Pashenko, his face purple with rage.

Of all the things Kaspar might have expected Pashenko to say, this was not one of them. He raised his hands and said, 'What is going on? Why are you here?'

'I'll tell you why,' snapped Pashenko, his accent slipping towards his native Kislevite. 'Because thirteen of my men are dead, that's why!'

'What? How?'

'That *Svolich*.'

Kaspar felt a chill seize him and raised a hand to his temple, feeling the onset of a pounding headache. He shook his head free of his tiredness and faced the angry Pashenko once more.

'Kajetan?' he said. 'I don't understand. How could he kill thirteen of your men?'

'No,' said Pashenko, shaking his head and pacing the room like a caged animal. 'Not Sasha, someone else. Someone else.'

'Pashenko, slow down, you're not making any sense. Tell me what has happened.'

The head of the *Chekist* took a deep breath, forcing himself to be calm. Kaspar could see that Pashenko had not slept for some time either by the look of him. His normally clean-shaven cheeks were stubbled and hollow, his long hair wild and unkempt.

'This does not happen to the *Chekist*,' he said. 'We are feared and that is how we are able to do our job. People fear us and they do not violate our laws because of that. That is the way it is supposed to be anyway. But now…'

Kaspar could not bring himself to feel sorry for Pashenko, knowing the brutal methods his *Chekist* employed and having seen the horror of the gaol beneath their grim building on the Urskoy Prospekt. But the pain of losing men under your command was something he was all too familiar with, so in that at least they had a common bond.

'I am still not sure what happened,' continued Pashenko, 'but it looks as though two people walked into our building and slaughtered their way towards the cells.'

'Two people killed thirteen of your men? Who were they?'

'I do not know, but it was only one.'

'One what?'

'Only one person killed my men, a man who wore black robes and a hood. And who was quicker than a snake by all accounts.'

'I think I know of this man,' said Kaspar. 'He attacked us in the Lubjanko.'

'The Lubjanko? What took you to that wretched place?'

'It is a long story,' said Kaspar, not wanting to go into the details of his earlier co-operation with Vassily Chekatilo in front of the *Chekist*. 'But I have seen his speed, it is incredible, inhuman almost. Who was the other person?'

'A woman, but no one I've spoken to can give me a good description of her.'

'Why not?'

Pashenko shrugged and Kaspar could see the deaths of his men and the apparent ease with which they had been killed had hit Pashenko hard.

'It is strange,' said Pashenko. 'I have spoken to the survivors of the attack and every one of them gives me a different description of her. And not just little things that I could put down to simple errors, but major differences. Some saw a young woman, others an older woman. To some she was blonde, to others dark haired and yet others saw her as auburn haired. Some saw a thin woman, while others say she was heavyset. But all of them agree that she was beautiful, that they could no more raise a blade against her than stop their own hearts from beating.'

'How do you think she was able to confuse so many people?'

'I do not know, but all of them said she had a... a radiance to her, as though her skin had a light burning beneath it. It reeks of sorcery to me.'

Kaspar felt his skin crawl, remembering Sofia describing something similar while she had been held within Sasha Kajetan's death attic, a magical light that had spoken with a woman's voice. She had not been able to see the face of the speaker, but taken together with the hooded assassin, it was surely too great a coincidence that these events could not be linked. How far back did everything go? The Butcherman, Sasha, the black robed killer, the rats? Was it all connected?

Something in Pashenko's words tugged at a faint memory, but it was not until Sofia appeared in the doorway of his study, her hair worn down around her neck, that it hit him.

'Is it true?' asked Sofia, her arms wrapped about herself. 'Has Sasha escaped from your gaol?'

Pashenko nodded. 'Yha, last night.'

'Did he kill anyone?'

'Probably. The gaoler had his throat torn out, most likely by someone's teeth, and it looks like some of his flesh was eaten. It is the same as the Butcherman killings. It could only have been Kajetan.'

Kaspar leaned forwards. 'You said that some of the people who saw this woman saw her as auburn haired?'

'Yes, but lots of other colours too.'

Kaspar moved from behind his desk towards Sofia, reaching up to lift a handful of her long, auburn hair.

'I think this is partly what stayed Kajetan's hand when he held Sofia prisoner,' he said. 'His madness saw her as his matka, his mother reborn. And when I saw the skeleton he had dug up on the grounds of his family's land, the skull had scraps of auburn hair still attached to it. Whatever magicks this woman was able to conjure, it was for one purpose and one purpose alone – to make Sasha Kajetan believe his mother had come back to him.'

'Everything he did, he did for her,' said Sofia. 'Every murder was for her.'

'And now he is free, ambassador,' hissed Pashenko, 'and it will be your fault when he kills again.'

'Mine?'

'Yha, Kajetan *should* have been hanged weeks ago, but no, the ambassador wants to keep him alive to learn what made him a monster. And like a fool I agree, I think that this new Empire man is clever and may be right. Now look where your curiosity had led us.'

Kaspar wanted to argue, but knew that Pashenko was right: Kajetan should have been executed long ago.

'Well, what is being done to find him?' asked Kaspar. 'And what can I do to help?'

'Nothing. On both counts.'

'Nothing? You are not making any effort to catch him?'

'I have no men to spare, and the city is so crowded I could search for years and never find him. And I think that whoever has him now will be keeping him well hidden, don't you? No, I will not waste more of my men's lives in hunting Kajetan down. If he is truly mad then he will surface again when he kills, and sooner or later we will catch him.'

Pashenko turned to retrieve his helmet and turned, bowing stiffly to Kaspar and Sofia.

'But there will be more deaths, of that I am sure. I just wanted you to know that,' he said and marched from the study.

Sofia shivered and Kaspar put his arm around her. 'You shouldn't worry, Sofia. I don't think Kajetan will come for you again. He has his matka now.'

She shook her head.

'I'm not worried about him coming after me,' she said at last. 'I'm worried about him coming after you.'

III

As THE NEW moon rose on the thirteenth night of Nachexen, riders entered the city from the west. Ungol horsemen of wild appearance, they had ridden hard from the western oblast to bring great news, news they shouted from their horses as they galloped through the city streets towards the Winter Palace.

Cheers followed the riders, all of whom looked on the verge of collapse, who were kept in the saddle by sheer joy. The news soon spread through the city, Boyarin Kurkosk's Sanyza pulk and the army of Stirland had fought and destroyed a great mass of northmen led by a chieftain named Okkodai Tarsus at Krasicyno, putting it to flight and killing thousands of the tribesmen.

It was the first tangible victory for the allied armies and when he woke to the news, Kaspar had a real sense of history unfolding before him. This was a time of great moment and heroes were being forged daily on the fields of battle. Another horde of tribesmen, many times the number of the allied armies, was said to be marching back from the Empire to destroy Kurkosk's army and both the army of Talabecland and the Kislev pulk were being called to battle at a place called Mazhorod.

In the days that followed the news, the city had seethed with activity as warriors were mustered and the Kislevite pulks, camped along the Urskoy within a day's march of the city, were finally drawn together to head westwards.

Kaspar watched the preparations for march from the snow-capped ramparts of the city wall with thousands of the city's populace who had turned out in the icy chill to cheer their brave warriors. It did Kaspar's heart a world of good to see such an ebullient display of optimism shining from every face around him.

He watched the preparations below with a mixture of pride and regret. The greater part of him wanted to ride alongside these brave men of Talabecland, but without a field rank – something he knew Spitzaner would never grant him – he would simply be an observer. The thought of being powerless to intervene in whatever battles these men would soon have to fight was an intolerable prospect.

Spitzaner had made it perfectly clear that he did not want Kaspar to accompany his army and Kaspar could not blame him. It would undermine Spitzaner's authority were Kaspar, his former commanding officer who many knew had passed him over for promotion, to be there, and Kaspar had reluctantly accepted that he must remain in Kislev. The Emperor's emissaries, Michlenstadt and Bautner, travelled with the general, accompanied by the envoys of the Tzarina who would journey to Altdorf in her stead.

For all his faults, Clemenz Spitzaner knew how to get an army ready to move with commendable speed. The general had been angry to have missed the great battle at Krasicyno and was determined not to miss this chance for glory. His soldiers were drawn up in their regiments along the roadway, thousands of men formed in column of march, with their weapons high and their colours flapping in the cold wind.

The general himself rode up and down the line of men, inspecting his soldiers with the eye of a man who knows people are watching.

Soldiers shivered and stamped their feet in the snow to ward off the cold as they awaited the order to march, fife and drum keeping the men entertained with martial tunes as black-robed Kislevite priests pronounced blessings upon them. But Kaspar's attention was not for the army of his countrymen, but the magnificent spectacle of the Kislev pulk.

The Kislev pulk was a wondrous thing to behold. Kaspar had thought the army of Talabecland had been a colourful sight when it had arrived, but it was as nothing compared to the glory of a Kislevite army bedecked in all its finery.

Glorious red horsemen with eagle-feathered back banners and shining, fur-edged helmets gathered at the foot of the *Gora Geroyev*, their scarlet and gold banners streaming behind them as they galloped westwards. He felt a stab of sadness as he remembered going into battle alongside such warriors and the memory of Pavel leading them in a magnificent charge. He missed his comrade, and had not seen him since throwing him from the embassy, but he could not undo what had been done.

The lighter cavalry was followed by their more heavily armoured brethren, colourfully caparisoned knights in bronze armour who carried long lances and an enormous banner embroidered with a bear rampant. Swirling hordes of ragged but magnificent-looking archers on horseback whooped and hollered, the long scalp-locks whipping around them as they rode marking them as Ungols.

Singing blocks of Kossars marched down the frozen roadway from the city gates, their strong voices easily carrying to the people on the walls. Each block wore a riot of colourful shirts and cloaks, baggy troos held at the waist by scarlet sashes and pointed iron helmets fringed with mail. Each man carried a long, heavy-bladed axe and Kaspar saw a great many carried powerful bows slung across their backs. Some carried shields, but it seemed that carrying something that could kill northmen was more important than a shield to most.

Every single group of men carried either a wolf-headed standard, colourful banner or trophy rack bedecked with wolf tails, skulls and captured weapons and the barbaric splendour of the army was a truly breathtaking sight.

But greatest of all was the Tzarina herself.

Positioned at the head of her army, she was ready to take the fight to these northern barbarians who dared invade her land. Riding atop a tall, high-sided sled of shimmering icy brilliance, she watched her warriors prepare for march with an aloof gaze. A team of silver horses whose flanks shimmered with hoarfrost and whose breath was the winter wind were hitched to the front of the sled. The Tzarina's crown of ice glittered at her brow and her azure gown sparkled in the afternoon sun. Fearfrost was sheathed at her side and she wore a cloak woven from swirling crystals of ice and snow.

A team of bare-chested warriors carried her banner, a monstrous, rippling thing of sapphire and crimson, and her soldiers cheered with their love for her as they gathered.

The shouts of the soldiers and spectators died away at some unseen signal, the drummer boys and pipers quieting their instruments as a series of mournful peals were rung from the bells of the Reliquary of Saint Alexei. The pulk dropped to one knee, each man whispering a prayer to the gods that they would be victorious as the bells tolled across the silence of the steppe.

As the last echoes of the bells faded, the Ice Queen drew her mighty war-blade and the armies of the Empire and Kislev marched westwards to war.

Kaspar watched them go and prayed that Sigmar would watch over them.

IV

THE FROZEN EYES of the children stared unblinkingly at him, refusing to avert their dead, accusing gaze from him. Sasha Kajetan sat on a cold, damp floor of earth with his back to an icy cellar wall, hugging his knees tightly to his chest. The dead children with the slashed throats in the corner of the room were his only company and all they did was accuse him.

Had he killed them? He could not remember having slaughtered them, but memory meant nothing when it came to his murderous nature.

His breath misted before him and he wondered when his matka would return. She had led him to this icy cellar and commanded him to wait. And as he had done since he was old enough to walk, he had obeyed her.

But this was a terrible place, even the trueself retreating from the uppermost reaches of his consciousness at the pure, undiluted malice that seeped from the thing held within the locked bronze coffin that sat in the centre of the room.

The scale of its desire to do harm exceeded even that of the trueself and he knew it was an unnatural creation that, but for the darkness within his own soul, would have killed him the instant he had set foot in this room.

Sasha could feel his strength growing with each passing day he spent in the gloom of the cellar, the fragments of his rational mind that remained realising that it returned with unnatural speed, but grateful for whatever his matka was doing to hasten his recovery.

He would need all his strength if he were to fulfil the purpose of his continued existence, and he allowed himself a tight smile as he thought once more of Ambassador von Velten.

CHAPTER EIGHT

I

THE DRUMS OF war beat out the pace of march, vast kettledrums mounted on brazen war-altars and struck by grossly swollen men covered in writhing tattoos and little else. Skulled totems raised on the backs of the war-altars were branded with the marks of the Dark Gods, shaggy, bestial creatures capering behind them braying their praise to their infernal masters.

High Zar Aelfric Cyenwulf rode at the head of forty thousand warriors, an army of northern tribesmen that had never known defeat, and watched the lightening sky to the east as the first signs of the sunrise spilled over the snow-capped peaks of the World's Edge Mountains. The new year was barely weeks old and foaming rivers spilled down the flanks of the dark mountains, cold and hard with melted ice water as the breathlessly young spring took hold.

He and his dark knights, giant warriors mounted on midnight black steeds barded with blooded mail, halted on the crown of an upthrust crag of black rock. Their giant horses had coal-red eyes, wide chests and huge, rippling muscles, each beast at least twenty hands high, the only mounts in the world capable of carrying the High Zar's armoured knights of Chaos.

The High Zar scanned the ground before him, spotting the route his army must take through the foothills of the mountains without difficulty; his forward scouts having travelled this way earlier the previous year to find the best route for his army to travel. Soon their course would lead them westwards towards the southernmost tributary of the Tobol and the valley of Urszebya.

They had bypassed Praag over a week ago without incident, his Kyazak outriders capturing and skinning itinerant rotas of Ungol scouts that approached too incautiously. Cyenwulf knew it was inevitable that word of his army's route would soon reach the south, but the longer he could delay it the better.

He twisted in the saddle of his huge black mare, watching his horde of dark armoured warriors, beasts, monsters and heavy chariots as it emerged from a deep cut in the foothills. What force in the world could stand against such an army? He longed for battle again, the enforced preparations over the winter chafing at his warrior's soul that hungered for the screams of his enemies, the lamentations of their womenfolk and the glory of Chaos that would be his when they swept aside the armies of the southlanders.

A hoarse cheer went up from the army as the concealing darkness of the Old One came into sight through the cut in the ground. Cyenwulf saw that the lightning sheathed darkness surrounding it seemed somehow thinner, less substantial, as though the further it travelled from its mountain lair, the less concealment it could summon. Massive-thewed reptilian limbs, with claws as large as a man's arm, and a wild mane of shaggy black fur were all he could make out through the thinning smoke, but he now knew that the stories of the Old One's strength and power were not misplaced.

The bestial ones of his army abased themselves before the creature, howling in praise of its terrible majesty and waving their crude iron axes as it passed. Cyenwulf had seen that his own warriors were now worshipping this creature as a sign of the dark gods' favour, offering the skinned, still-living bodies of prisoners for it to devour.

The Old One was a blessing, but, as was typical for the blessings of Tchar, it came with a price. With the Old One's presence they could not lose, but as its worship spread throughout his army, he could feel its fighting discipline diminish.

Some groups of fierce norsemen had already descended into blood madness and slaughtered one another that it might glance their way. Other tribes were turning to cannibalism, which, in itself, was not that unusual, but these killers were preying on warriors from other tribes and such slaughter could only lead to devastating blood-feuds.

Such bloody displays of devotion were growing daily and Cyenwulf knew that he had to bring his army to battle soon or risk it becoming a thrashing, mindless mob.

II

CHEKATILO DRAINED THE last of his *kvas*, hurling the glass into the roaring fire, where the residue of the spirit flared briefly with a bright flame. His temper had deteriorated as the weeks had passed and spring took hold of Kislev, even the great victory of the allies at Mazhorod not quelling his desire to leave the city.

Yesterday, forward riders of the Tzarina's personal guard had brought news that the combined armies of Kislev and the Empire had met the army of a Kurgan war leader named Surtha Lenk at the river crossing of Mazhorod and destroyed it utterly. Boyarin Kurkosk remained in the west to hunt down the last elements of Lenk's army, but the armies of Stirland and Talabecland had buried their dead before marching east towards

Kislev with the Tzarina to fight a host of northmen rumoured to be following the course of the World's Edge Mountains. It was said the allied armies were a day from Kislev's walls.

Chekatilo needed to be away from Kislev, a growing sense of being suffocated in this doomed city growing with each day. But without the ambassador's travel documents and Imperial seal, it would be a risky venture at best to travel through Kislev and the Empire towards Marienburg. The odds were against him arriving as anything other than a pauper, and that was *not* going to happen.

Rejak poured him another *kvas* in a fresh glass and said, 'You'd best not break this one, it's the last of them.'

Chekatilo grunted in acknowledgement. Rejak took a swig from the bottle as he paced the room, the fire casting a flickering glow on the bare timber walls. Chekatilo's valuables were packed into a train of covered wagons ready to be driven to the Empire once he had what he needed from the ambassador.

It still galled him that von Velten had refused to honour his debt. Such things simply did not happen. Not to him.

'You're sure there's still no word from Korovic? It's been weeks,' said Chekatilo.

'None at all,' confirmed Rejak. 'I don't expect any either, I think he's probably fled the city already. And even if he hasn't, he's not going to do it. He won't betray the ambassador.'

'You underestimate Korovic's weakness, Rejak,' said Chekatilo.

'You should have let me kill him long ago.'

'Perhaps,' agreed Chekatilo, 'but I owed Drostya and could not do that, but the time has passed for observing such niceties.'

Rejak grinned. 'I can kill Korovic then?'

Chekatilo nodded. 'Of course, but I think von Velten needs to learn the meaning of pain first. I think then he will begin to regret his decision to throw his debt back at me.'

'What do you have in mind?' asked Rejak eagerly.

'I have been too forgiving with the ambassador,' mused Chekatilo. 'I think that I quite liked him, but it is of no matter. I have killed men I liked before.'

'You want me to kill von Velten?'

'No,' said Chekatilo, shaking his head and sipping his *kvas*. 'I want him to suffer, Rejak. A foolish sense of honour has kept me from treating him the way I would anyone else, but that ends now. Tomorrow night I will speak to Ambassador von Velten again and tell him to give me what I want.'

'What makes you think he will agree this time?'

'Because before I go, I want you to go to the home of that woman he cares for, Anastasia Vilkova, the one the soldiers call the White Lady of Kislev.'

'And do what?'

Chekatilo shrugged. 'Rape her, torture her, kill her; it is of no matter to me. You saw how desperate von Velten was to get his physician back, so imagine how much more terror he will feel when I tell him that you have Anastasia Vilkova prisoner. He will have no choice but to give me what I want. By the time he discovers she is already dead, it will make no difference.'

Rejak nodded, already anticipating the terrible things he was going to do to Anastasia Vilkova.

III

THE BANQUETING HALL of the Winter Palace was the centre of the formal ensemble of parade halls in the Tzarina's fastness. Like the Gallery of Heroes, the walls were fashioned from smooth ice with central doors that led onto a terrace overlooking the gardens below. From where he sat, Kaspar guessed that the room was set for about four hundred diners with service stations along the wall, one for each table. The table settings included all the glassware required for the meal, flawlessly etched and enamelled with the Tzarina's monogram and Kislevite bear. The excited buzz of conversation filled the hall, officers and soldiers animatedly telling tales of the battles won and battles yet to be fought.

The allied army had arrived at Kislev that morning, amid celebrations so riotous that Kaspar had thought the war already won. Cheering crowds lined the road to the city to welcome home their victorious Tzarina, hanging garlands of spring flowers around the necks of the returning soldiers. The men were weary and hungry, having marched almost non-stop to reach Kislev as quickly as they could. Kaspar just hoped they had enough time to rest, because if the rumours of Aelfric Cyenwulf's horde were to be believed, then the chieftain of the Iron Wolves came with a force much larger than anyone had expected.

With a speed Kaspar found incredible, the Tzarina had announced a victory banquet at the Winter Palace and, as ambassador, he had received his gilt-edged invitation that very afternoon. It seemed inappropriate to feast while so many people went hungry in the streets of the city, but as Pavel had pointed out many months ago, etiquette demanded that the Ice Queen's invitations take precedence over all other previous engagements, even duty to the dead.

As Kaspar and Sofia had made their way to their table, he had stepped from the path of a red uniformed lancer, whose faded tunic strained to contain his prodigious gut, before realising with a start that the man was Pavel.

'Pavel? Why are you here?' Kaspar had asked.

His old friend had shuffled nervously from foot to foot before saying. 'I rejoin old regiment now that war has come. Many die at Mazhorod and they need every man who can fight. Because I fight for them before they make me *towarzysz*.'

Kaspar nodded, saying, 'Good, good.'

'It means "comrade",' explained Sofia, seeing Kaspar's confusion. 'It is a leader of a cavalry troop.'

'I see,' said Kaspar. The thought of his old comrade going into battle without him gave him a dark feeling of premonition and they moved on.

'One day you will need to tell me what happened between the two of you,' said Sofia.

'Perhaps one day,' agreed Kaspar as they finally arrived at their designated table and sat in time for a short prayer of thanks from a priest at the top table.

Set with huge, solid silver candelabras, he and Sofia had been seated with several junior officers of the Stirland army and as the evening progressed, the conversation was lively and interesting. Whoever had decided upon the seating plan for this victory banquet obviously knew of his antipathy towards Spitzaner, who, along with the boyarins of the Kislev pulk and General Arnulf Pavian, commander of the army of Stirland, sat at the top table with the Ice Queen herself. Standing behind the Tzarina was Pjotr Losov, and Kaspar had to fight the urge to do something he knew he would regret.

He had brought Sofia because he hated to attend such occasions alone, knowing that while the commanders of the army might celebrate victory, the men who had won it were usually not enjoying the rewards of their courage. She looked stunning in a velvet gown of deep crimson, her auburn hair worn high on her head, exposing her long neck and shoulders. A smooth blue stone wrapped in a web of silver wire hung around her neck on a thin chain and Kaspar smiled, glad to have her with him.

Sensing his scrutiny, she looked up from a conversation she was having with a dark haired man wearing an ostentatious uniform of puffed blue silk and silver, with a white sash worn diagonally across his medal-strewn chest. His skin was swarthy and his moustache waxed in an elaborate upward curl. Sofia smiled back at him and said, 'Have you met General Albertalli, Kaspar? He leads the Tilean mercenary regiments that fought with General Pavian at Krasicyno and led a charge that broke the Kurgan line at Mazhorod.'

'No, I have not,' said Kaspar graciously, extending his hand for the Tilean to shake. 'A pleasure, sir.'

The man shook Kaspar's hand enthusiastically, saying, 'I am knowing you, sir. I read all about you. You never lost a battle.'

Kaspar tried to hide his pleasure at meeting someone who knew of his career in the army, but blushed as he caught Sofia smiling at his obvious pride.

'That is correct, sir. Thank you for mentioning it. My compliments on the victories at Krasicyno and Mazhorod.'

The Tilean bowed and said, 'Hard days, much blood shed to win them.'

'I do not doubt it,' agreed Kaspar. 'What were they like, the Kurgans I mean?'

Albertalli sucked in a great breath and shook his head. 'Bastards to a man. Big, tough men that fight like daemons, with swords as long as a tall man. Packs of wild hounds, and warriors on the biggest horses I ever see. No one want to say it, but we were damn lucky at Mazhorod. Fought on a river, should have been easy, yes? But the river freeze solid in an instant and Kurgans were all over us. Hard, bloody fighting that day, but we killed many men and it is they who run from us, yes?'

Kaspar and Albertalli fell deep into conversation concerning the Kurgans, their tactics and how the various generals had led their men on the day. Kaspar was surprised to learn that Spitzaner had actually done well, leading his soldiers competently and solidly.

The two men only paused in their discussion when a gong sounded and the victory dinner itself was served. It proved to be a lavish affair, consisting of seven courses of the finest quality accompanied by an equally impressive array of wines from the Morceaux Valley in Bretonnia and the hills around Luccini – a subject Kaspar saw was close to Albertalli's heart as he expounded on how the Tilean wines were clearly the superior.

As the evening progressed, Kaspar was quick to discover that there were unwritten rules to a Kislevite dinner, as his plate of roast veal was whisked away virtually untouched.

Before he could protest, Sofia explained that should a diner set down their knife and fork, it was the signal to the attending servants to remove his plate. It appeared that each course was rigidly timed, and an hour later, as the last plates were being cleared away, Kaspar found himself amazed at the sheer logistics of serving, feeding and clearing a seven course meal for four hundred people in under an hour.

With the dinner over, the speeches began and, despite himself, Kaspar felt himself getting caught up in the spirit of the evening. First the Empire generals spoke and Kaspar recalled similar speeches he himself had given. The boyarins spoke next and the difference was incredible. Where the men of the Empire spoke of duty and honour, the Kislevites filled the hall with hot-blooded passion, shouting and gesticulating wildly as they spoke.

Sofia translated parts, but Kaspar understood enough from the fierce zeal of the boyarins to know that they filled the assembled soldiers' souls with piss and vinegar. Rousing cheers and toasts were made and glasses smashed on the floor amid much yelling and punching of the air.

The soldiers filled the hall with their glorious cheering and Kaspar laughed as Sofia took his hand, utterly convinced that they would win this war.

IV

THE CRESCENT MOON slid behind a low cloud, wreathing the walls of the palace in momentary darkness. But it was long enough for the dark robed figure to nimbly slip over the spike topped wall and drop lightly into the palace grounds.

Hugging the shadows, the figure stealthily made its way through the Winter Gardens towards the palace.

Moonlight spilled around glittering, diamond-like flowers and trees of this winter forest of frosted grass. A gravel pathway wound its way between a host of exquisite sculptures of ice – carved trees, exotic birds and legendary beasts. The moonlight bathed everything in a monochrome brilliance, the silence and sense of isolation a physical thing within this icy wilderness of dragons, eagles and bone chilling cold.

The black robed figure halted suddenly, blending so completely with a pool of shadow that even the most dedicated of observers would have had trouble spotting its existence.

A pair of patrolling knights in bronze armour crunched along the pathway, their hands on their sword pommels. The silver bears on their helmets caught the moonlight and, without knowing it, the knights passed within yards of the intruder.

But lives can often hang on the slightest turn of fate and it was at that moment that the moon chose to emerge from behind another cloud, dispelling the shadows along this section of the pathway and bathing the robed figure in light.

One knight managed to shape words of warning before a silver steel slash opened his throat, the killer's blade expertly finding the gap between his helmet and gorget. The other guard had his sword partially drawn when the intruder's sword flashed again and the knight's head fell to the path and rolled into the glittering undergrowth.

Pausing only to clean his blade, the figure moved off again into the shadows.

The lights of the palace were just ahead.

V

KASPAR EXCHANGED PLEASANTRIES with Albertalli as they filed into the timber-panelled West Hall, where great oak beams ran the width of the hall and a vast fire set below a great stone mantle filled the room with warmth and the aroma of fresh-cut wood. Hundreds of candles lined the walls between the tall windows, together with innumerable shields and suits of bronze armour. Faded battle flags hung from the beams and the hardwood floors echoed to the jangle of sabres and spurs as the senior officers retired to plan their strategy against Aelfric Cyenwulf's horde with the Ice Queen.

The womenfolk and junior officers remained within the Banqueting Hall, finishing off the wine from dinner and speculating upon what was going on in the other hall. Under normal circumstances, Kaspar should have remained in the Banqueting Hall as well, but the Tzarina herself had sent a functionary to instruct him to attend upon her with the other commanders.

Sofia had remained behind, chatting with some dashingly attired lancers and Kaspar had been surprised to feel a pang of jealousy. There was no doubt he liked Sofia immensely, and he wondered whether their relationship had become something more than mere friendship after her abduction by Sasha Kajetan. He didn't know, but looked forward to the prospect of finding out.

The assembled officers and boyarin gradually fell to silence as the Ice Queen entered the hall together with her fierce, shaven headed guards and Pjotr Losov, who closed the doors to the Banqueting Hall behind him before vanishing into the background.

The Ice Queen marched to the centre of the hall as the boyarin formed a circle around her, kept at a respectful distance from their queen by her guards.

Without preamble, the Ice Queen said, 'The horde of Aelfric Cyenwulf draws near and it is time to take the war to him.'

The boyarins cheered loudly and the Empire officers clapped courteously. Now that he was closer, Kaspar could see the commander of the Stirland army more clearly, curious as to what kind of man he was. General Pavia was a slighter figure than Kaspar had first expected, not tall, but with a commanding presence to him that he immediately liked.

'He is cunning, this Cyenwulf,' continued the Tzarina when the cheering had died down. 'He comes with greater ambition than simple pillage.'

'Is of no matter, my Queen!' shouted a red uniformed boyarin of lancers. 'For we shall still send him back north without his balls, won't we, comrades?' Roars of affirmation and laughter followed the man's boast and Kaspar saw the Ice Queen fight to hold back a scowl. He remembered the Tzarina once talking of her father's boyarin, calling them an insufferable band of brutes, but men who had been the most loyal, steadfast warriors anyone could wish for. In that respect, the boyarin surrounding her seemed no different from those of her father, but he could see their raucousness did not sit well with her icy demeanour.

'I am sure we will, Boyarin Wrodzik,' said the Tzarina over the laughter, 'but this barbarian strikes for a place at the very heart of Kislev, he makes for Urszebya.'

The laughter faded quickly, replaced with a deadly earnestness and Kaspar was suddenly confused. What was Urszebya? After a moment's thought he hazarded a guess that it translated as Ursun's Teeth, but what was that but an earthy soldier's curse?

Satisfied that her words had had the desired effect, the Tzarina continued. 'This Cyenwulf knows what makes us who we are. Kislev is land and land is Kislev.'

'Kislev is land and land is Kislev,' repeated the boyarin in unison.

'The valley of Urszebya, the wound where Great Ursun took a bite from our land and left us his stone fangs is under threat and our enemies plan its desecration. Their cursed shamans would use dark magicks to pervert the spirit of the land, to corrupt the primal, elemental power of Kislev with Chaos and blight our great land forever.'

The boyarin roared a denial and Kaspar could see they were horrified by the notion of this valley's desecration.

'There is power there, my boyarin, power that must not be taken by the forces of the Dark Gods. It falls to us to stop him.'

The Ice Queen's eyes swept the assembled boyarin with a fierce pride and Kaspar shivered as her gaze fell upon him. She nodded slowly and said, 'The land has called every one of you to this place, to this time, and cries out for all those with the soul of Kislevite to rally to her defence. Will you answer her call?'

The hall rang to the sound of a hundred throats shouting that they would.

VI

It DID NOT take long for the corpses of the two knights to be discovered. The security of the Tzarina was a duty taken very seriously by her protectors and within minutes of the killings, a second pair of knights found them lying in wide pools of rapidly cooling blood and raised the alarm.

But by then it was already too late.

VII

STANDING NEAR THE windows of the West Hall, Kaspar heard the sound of hand bells over the cheering and wondered briefly what they signified. But as the urgent ringing continued, a growing sense of unease crept over him. Few of the boyarins had heard the bells and, surrounded by roaring warriors, none of the Tzarina's guards had heard it either.

His suspicion that something was amiss grew to a certainty as he looked through the window into the darkness and saw knights bearing lit torches and drawn swords running through the grounds of the Winter Gardens.

Kaspar turned from the window and began pushing his way through the cheering boyarin, many of whom were

already three sheets to the wind and mistook his efforts
to be drunken enthusiasm for the coming war. Ruddy-
faced Kislevites gripped him by the shoulders and kissed
both his cheeks with shouted northern oaths as he struggled to get through them to the Tzarina.

'Get off me, you oaf!' he yelled as a heavyset man
gripped him in a tight embrace and shouted something
at a nearby boyarin. The man released him and Kaspar
pushed his way forwards once more. The Ice Queen's
guards saw him coming and the frantic look in his eyes,
the ringing of the alarm finally penetrating the slowly
diminishing cheering.

'Your majesty–' shouted Kaspar as a window smashed
inwards, glass shards falling to the floor as a spinning
brass sphere bounced on the wooden floor and rolled
across the rugs towards the assembled soldiers. Smaller
than a cannonball, it wobbled slightly as it came to a halt
before Arnulf Pavia.

'What the hell?' said the Stirland general.

'No!' shouted Kaspar, trying to force his way towards
Pavia. He didn't know exactly what the sphere was, but
knew enough to recognise trouble when he saw it. The
general looked up in puzzlement and that was the last
Kaspar ever saw of him as a shrieking darkness exploded
outwards from the sphere.

Fell winds howled around the West Hall, extinguishing
every candle in a single bellow, and the wails of the
accursed filled the room with cacophonous screaming.
Gibbering voices, plucked straight from the abode of the
damned, rang within every skull and a terrifying, aching
dread filled the soul as the lingering echoes of some vile
otherworld seeped from the evil corona of energy that
burned darkly in the centre of the hall.

Kaspar felt the innards of his soul ravaged by unseen
claws of ice and cried out in pain as an aching cold of the
spirit, far deeper than anything natural could ever be,
stabbed through him. The fire below the stone mantel-
piece dimmed as swirling shadows writhed around him,

exposing him to the sheer vastness of the universe and his own insignificance within it. He tried to crawl away, but his limbs were leaden, powerless and he knew that this was his death, a meaningless speck in an uncaring universe.

Hands gripped him and he felt himself being dragged away from the nightmare vortex. He opened his eyes, the aching dark sliding from his soul, and he gasped at the dreadfulness of what he had felt. He rolled onto his side, heaving for breath as the swirling blackness in the centre of the room began shrinking away to nothing, closing the window to the horrifying realm beyond. The fire roared back to life as he pushed himself to his knees with a grimace and turned to thank his rescuer.

He recognised the flushed, firelit features of Pavel Korovic and gripped his old friend's shoulder tightly. 'Thank you,' he said.

'Is of no matter,' said Pavel, his face ashen and Kaspar could tell he too had felt the awful madness that lay within the darkness. He turned back to the centre of the room, seeing nothing but a shallow crater of splintered floorboards and fragmented foundations where the brass sphere had exploded. Of General Pavia and his senior officers, there was no sign.

Screams filled the room where men lay in pieces, entire limbs shorn from their bodies where the deadly energy of Chaos had touched them: boyarin with half their heads gone or missing the front of their ribcages lay around the circumference of the crater, blood spattered around their hewn corpses.

Kaspar looked for the Tzarina and saw her and her guards backing towards the main doors to the hall. Blood streamed from a deep cut on her temple and she was supported by one of her boyarin. An Empire captain of arquebusiers lay screaming before Kaspar, his legs severed from his body just below the pelvis by the lethal explosion.

Shouts of outrage and confusion began, but before anyone could do more than pick themselves up off the floor, Kaspar saw a dark shape ghost through the window, a solid darkness against the moonlit sky beyond.

'Watch out!' he yelled to the Tzarina's guards, pointing at the window.

Two of the bare chested warriors leapt towards the figure, the third remaining with their queen. Their swords were golden blurs as they attacked, sparks flying from the blindingly swift impacts. The figure in black swayed aside from a blow Kaspar felt sure would cleave him in two, rolling beneath his opponent's guard and with his sword flicking out. The first guard collapsed, his guts looping around his knees as he was expertly disembowelled and the second desperately parried, edging backwards from the terrifying speed of his opponent and employing every shred of his skill just to survive.

Kaspar desperately wished to help the man, but knew he would be dead in a heartbeat were he to face this black-robed killer. He had no weapons of his own, his lack of a military rank preventing him from bearing arms in the presence of the Tzarina. He crawled as fast as he could to the fireplace, realising that his only hope of helping lay with giving the Tzarina's guards a fighting chance in this unequal struggle.

The second guard was down, the assassin's blade deep in his chest and Kaspar watched as the Tzarina's last guard yelled a fierce oath and leapt to the attack. The boyarin were finally overcoming their confusion and panic, cries of alarm sounding as they saw the danger to their queen. They were arming themselves, but Kaspar knew that by then it would be too late and the Tzarina would be dead.

He reached into the fire and dragged out a blazing brand, feeling the flames burn his skin, but gritting his teeth against the pain. He surged to his feet as the assassin spun beneath a beheading stroke and opened the Tzarina's warrior from groin to sternum with his sword.

Kaspar had seconds at best. As the killer fought to free his blade from his victim, Kaspar hurled the fiery missile at his back.

Fat orange sparks flared where it hit and the black robed figure shrieked as its robes caught light.

'Kaspar, down!' shouted a voice he recognised as Pavel's.

He ducked as something flashed over his head and saw a glass bottle shatter upon the murderer. Flames engulfed the killer, spreading wildly over his body and transforming him into a blazing torch. He lurched around the room like a drunk, ablaze from head to toe, and his shrieking squeals rose to new heights, sounding for all the world like a wounded animal.

The doors to the hall burst open and more warriors burst in, men with spears and long muskets. The black powder weapons boomed and the blazing figure was blasted from its feet, landing in a thrashing heap in the centre of the crater its mysterious sphere had blown.

The warriors with spears ran to the blazing body and stabbed it repeatedly with the iron tips of their weapons until at last it was still.

Kaspar rolled onto his back and said, '*Kvas*?'

Pavel nodded as the flames consumed the killer's flesh and filled the room with its sickening stench.

'I not have any need for it any more,' said Pavel, offering his hand to Kaspar.

'Good,' said Kaspar, accepting Pavel's hand and climbing to his feet.

He saw that the Tzarina was no longer in danger, her warriors gathered about her as the boyarin took stock of their losses and shouted great oaths of vengeance to Ursun, Dazh and Tor.

Kaspar limped over to where the shaken boyarin gathered around the smouldering corpse, spitting on its charred remains. Much of the flesh had been seared from its body and the charred remains were twisted and deformed, but the skull was strangely elongated and possessed more than a passing resemblance to...

Kaspar turned away from the corpse, unwilling to believe that what he had seen could be real. It was a man, deformed and obviously disfigured, but a man. It surely could not have been anything else, surely...

The boyarin parted as the Tzarina walked stiffly to the edge of the crater in the floor. Her face was a mask of controlled rage, glittering blood coating one side of her face and a mist of sparkling ice crystals forming in the air around her. As the crystals fell to the floor around her and shattered musically on the floor, Kaspar and her boyarin backed away from a fury that burned the air with its frozen heat.

'Get me Losov,' she said.

CHAPTER NINE

I

FINDING PJOTR LOSOV took longer than expected, but eventually he was brought before the Tzarina, his face lined with concern and worry. The West Hall was no longer the bloodbath it had been half an hour ago, the bodies of the dead having been removed and the wounded taken to the Banqueting Hall, where Sofia and other hastily gathered physicians were caring for them as best they could.

The Ice Queen stood with the mighty sword Fearfrost drawn, holding it by the pommel so that the tip of its shimmering blue blade rested on the floor. The dead assassin's sword lay on the floor in front of her.

Kaspar sat on a wooden bench near the fire and sipped a mug of *kvas*, his nerves still unsettled after the horror of the killer's attack. He could not rid his memory of the sight of the charred, deformed corpse and, most of all, the hideous, crawling sense of insignificance and misery he had experienced while lying next to whatever damned realm the killer's brass sphere had opened a gateway to.

'My queen,' said Losov, dropping to his knees before her, 'you are hurt!'

'I will live, Pjotr, it–'

'Oh, it gladdens my heart to see you,' interrupted Losov. 'When I heard that there had been an attack I feared the worst and set out to double the guards on the gates. Ursun bless us, but I am so glad you are alive.'

'Spare me your lies, Pjotr,' said the Tzarina, her voice like a dagger of pure ice. 'It is your own hide you should be more concerned with now.'

'Lies? I don't understand.'

'Come now, Pjotr… did you really think you could have betrayed me for all this time without me knowing?' asked the Tzarina, a mist of sparkling cold forming around her.

'Betrayed you? I swear I am loyal!' protested Losov.

The Tzarina shook her head. 'Stop it, Pjotr, you only diminish yourself further now. You of all people should know that the *Chekist* have eyes everywhere. I know all about your sordid little visits to the Lubjanko and what you do there. Your deviant practices disgust me, and you will pay for all the suffering you have caused. But to think you could fool me for so long, that is just insulting.'

Despite the icy mist that reached out from the Tzarina, Kaspar could see that the kneeling Losov was sweating now and relished the man's discomfort.

'No, no, you are mistaken, my queen!'

'It was useful and amusing for me to keep you around, to listen to your prattle, your pathetic attempts to manipulate me and manipulate you in turn, but now many of my finest warriors are dead or dying and the commander of my allies is vanished. You are no longer useful or amusing, Pjotr.'

Losov spun, seeking supporters around the hall, but finding none. Kaspar saw the fear in his eyes and raised his mug of *kvas* in mocking salute.

'Now all that remains is for you to tell me who you have been collaborating with, for I know a man as foolish as you could not be working without a more cunning master. Tell me, Pjotr, who else is involved in this conspiracy to kill me and destroy my land?'

Kaspar and Pavel listened intently, both eager to hear more of Losov's disgrace. Kaspar desperately wanted to know why Losov had paid to have Anastasia's husband killed, sure that the name the Tzarina would get from the traitor would be his answer.

'It is of no matter now, Pjotr,' continued the Ice Queen when Losov did not answer her question. 'One way or another I *will* find out what I want to know. You have seen the *Chekist's* gaol and you know that there is no man alive who can withstand their tortures. Tell me what I want to know and spare yourself that agony.'

Final desperation flashed in Losov's eyes and Kaspar saw him snatch for the assassin's fallen weapon. Losov surged to his feet, the blade stabbing upwards for the Tzarina's stomach.

Kaspar saw a flash of blue steel and a spurt of red, and Pjotr Losov was falling, his sword arm severed at the elbow and his torso cleft from pelvis to collarbone by the freezing edge of Fearfrost.

The Ice Queen held her sword before her, frozen icicles of blood dripping from the blade.

Boyarin Wrodzik kicked the dismembered body into the crater along with the charred corpse of the black robed assassin and spat on Losov's remains.

'Such is wrath of the Khan Queens and the fate of all traitors,' said the Tzarina.

II

DAWN WAS ALREADY lightening the sky by the time Kaspar and Sofia were able to finally return to the embassy, carried back in one of the Tzarina's lacquered, open topped carriages driven by an uncommunicative driver in a square red cap. They were swathed in furs and though it was nowhere near as cold as it had been in previous months, they huddled close to one another beneath the thick furs for warmth and comfort, the fingers of their hands laced together.

Neither of them had said anything on the way back, still in shock at the bloody events of the night and the cold anger of the Tzarina. Far from the regal, aloof monarch the Tzarina usually appeared to be, her execution of Pjotr Losov had recalled the wild ferocity of the first khan queens, and Kaspar shivered as he remembered how he had shouted at her several months ago.

Surgeons more qualified in battlefield injuries had taken over from Sofia, and she had only reluctantly allowed herself to be led away where she could clean her bloody hands and change from her gore-smeared dress.

Seventeen men had lost their lives in the attack. Clemenz Spitzaner and most of his staff officers had survived the violence, but General Pavia and his senior commanders had not. In the context of the loss of life suffered at Krasicyno and Mazhorod, such numbers were slight; they represented the upper echelons of command in the Stirland army.

Seven boyarin were dead, obliterated like the general by the terrible weapon the robed assassin had used, and six others would never fight again.

Kaspar had immediately volunteered for a field rank. Of course Spitzaner had protested immediately, but Kaspar had seen that the idea appealed to the remaining officers of the Stirland army, his reputation as a fine commander well known to them. Kaspar had arranged a meeting with them in the morning, giving everyone a chance to recover from the night's slaughter before speaking of such weighty matters.

Despite the bloodshed of the evening, the thought of leading men into battle once more gave him a satisfying feeling that he would be able to play a part in the coming war. He could see that Sofia was unhappy with his decision to volunteer for command, but he could not take it back now.

Before leaving the palace, Kaspar had approached Pavel and said, 'I never thanked you properly for pulling me away from that vile darkness. I think I would have died there if not for you.'

'Is of no matter,' said Pavel lightly, but Kaspar could feel the gratitude in his words.

'No,' said Kaspar. 'It is of some matter. You and I have been through much together and I counted you as one of my truest friends, but too much has happened in Kislev for me to forget the things you have done since I saw you last.'

'I know,' said Pavel. 'There nothing can undo what I did, but I wish...'

'Wishes are for songs, Pavel, and neither one of us can sing worth a damn. But know this: if the fates see fit for us to fight alongside one another again, I will do so gladly. I think our friendship has died here, but I will not be your enemy.'

'Very well,' agreed Pavel. 'A man can ask for no more than that.'

Kaspar nodded and offered his hand to Pavel. 'Fight well and try not to get yourself killed,' he said.

'You know me,' grinned the big Kislevite, shaking the ambassador's hand. 'Pavel Korovic too stubborn to die. They will tell tales of my bravery from here to Magritta!'

'I am sure they will. Farewell, Pavel,' said Kaspar as Sofia led him to the carriage that would carry them back to the embassy. The journey passed in silence until the driver halted before the embassy, stepping down from his seat to open the door for them. He accepted a copper coin from Kaspar before climbing back and driving off in a clatter of hooves.

Red and blue liveried guards opened the gates for them and as they walked arm in arm to the embassy, Sofia asked, 'Do you really mean to take a field rank if they offer you one tomorrow?'

Kaspar nodded. 'Yes, I do. I have to.'

'You don't, you know. You have done your duty to the army and there are others who can do it,' said Sofia.

'No, there aren't and you know it,' said Kaspar softly, seeing the worry in Sofia's face. 'Spitzaner cannot command two armies and I am the only other man who has experience of leading such numbers of soldiers.'

'Surely one of the boyarins could command?'

'No, the Empire soldiers would not accept a Kislevite as their general.'

'But you are too old to go into battle,' protested Sofia.

Kaspar chuckled, saying, 'Very well, there you might be correct, but it changes nothing. If they offer me the rank, I will take it, things are moving too fast for me to refuse.'

'What do you mean?'

'Don't you feel it, Sofia? History is unfolding before us,' said Kaspar. 'I remember once the Ice Queen told me that I had the soul of a Kislevite, that the land had called me back here to fight for it and that I had something to do here. "Come the moment, come the man", those were her very words. I didn't understand what she meant then, but I think I am beginning to.'

'Damn you, Kaspar, we had no time,' said Sofia, tears gathering at the corners of her eyes. 'Why did this have to happen now?'

'I don't know,' replied Kaspar, stopping and turning her to face him. 'But it has, and sometimes there are things we have to do, no matter what our heart tells us.'

'And what is your heart telling you to do?'

'This,' said Kaspar, leaning down to kiss Sofia on the mouth.

They kissed until a booming laugh sounded from outside the embassy gates and Vassily Chekatilo said, 'This all very touching, Ambassador von Velten. I think I right when I ask you if you in love with Madame Valencik.'

'Chekatilo,' snarled Kaspar turning to see the fat Kislevite lounging beside the embassy gates in a thick cloak of black fur. 'Get out of here, you bastard.'

Chekatilo chuckled and shook his head. 'No, not this time, Empire man. This time you will listen to me.'

'You and I have nothing to say to one another, Chekatilo.'

'No? I think you wrong. You still owe a debt to me and I here to collect.'

Sofia opened the door to the embassy and more guards appeared, their halberds bright in the first rays of morning sunshine.

'And I will tell you again that I will not give you what you want. I know about what you had Pavel do, so you can forget about getting him to do your dirty work any more. Get it through your thick skull, Chekatilo, I will never help you!' shouted Kaspar. He felt his temper getting the better of him again, but had seen too much pain and suffering tonight to be browbeaten by a common criminal.

'I think you will tonight,' promised Chekatilo.

'And why is that?' asked Kaspar, not liking Chekatilo's catlike grin one bit.

'Because if you do not, Anastasia Vilkova will be dead within the hour.'

III

REJAK YAWNED, FLEXING his shoulders as he watched the house come to life. Servants filled pitchers of water from the well and opened shuttered windows to let the weak morning sunlight in. He cracked his knuckles and rapped his fingers against the iron pommel of his sword with a predatory smile.

He sat resting his back on the wall of the building across the street from Anastasia Vilkova's house, his sword concealed beneath his cloak and features obscured by a furred hood. He did not think that the Vilkova woman knew him or would recognise him, but there was no sense in taking chances.

He knew she was home, having seen her return less than an hour ago. Where she had been he didn't know, probably enjoying a tryst with the ambassador and returning before morning to avoid scandalising her prettified society.

Reasoning that enough time had passed for her to have gotten herself cleaned up and perhaps even undressed, he pushed himself to his feet, wincing as the injuries to his shoulder and stomach pulled tight. He had always healed fast and the weeks since his wounding by the black-robed killer had been hard for him, unused as he was to enforced inactivity. But the wounds had healed well and though he would never be as supple and fast as he once had been, he was still as quick as any man alive he knew of.

Rejak strode across the street, his excitement growing at the thought of violating such a beautiful and respected woman. Normally his conquests were weirdroot whores from Chekatilo's brothels, and the idea of this influential woman beneath him and begging for her life as he took her hurried his steps. He thought of her soft mouth, long dark hair and full breasts and licked his lips. Yes, he would enjoy breaking this bitch.

He entered the grounds of her house, marching up the gravel incline and passing the pathetic specimens of humanity she had granted shelter within her walls. Scores of people camped within her grounds, hardly any of them sparing him a second glance as he made his way to the front door.

The main door was lacquered black wood with a brass knocker at its centre. He gripped his sword handle and rapped the brass ring hard against the door. Best to give the impression of civility, he supposed.

Rejak heard the tumblers of the lock turn and a click as the door eased from the frame. He hammered his boot into the timber, slamming the door back on its hinges and sending the old servant woman behind it sprawling with blood streaming from her face.

Swiftly he crossed the threshold, entering a marble-floored hall and seeing a curved flight of stairs with a brass balustrade rising to the upper floor ahead of him. Twin suits of armour flanked the bottom of the stairs and a family crest bearing two crossed cavalry sabres hung from the adjacent wall. An incongruous door of iron was set on the curve of the stairs, partially obscured by a leafy potted evergreen, but Rejak ignored it as he heard a door slam upstairs. ·

That would be her, reasoned Rejak, shutting the front door then locking it and pocketing the key. He sprinted for the stairs, taking them two at a time. Upon reaching the upper landing he drew his sword and made his way down a long, carpeted hallway. Heavy doors lined one side of the corridor and he began kicking them down one by one.

'Come out, come out, wherever you are!' he yelled.

He saw a flash of colour from ahead of him and grinned as he saw Anastasia in an emerald green nightgown running for another set of stairs at the far end of the corridor.

'Oh, no, pretty one, you won't get away from Rejak that easily,' he shouted, sprinting after her. She was quick, but Rejak was quicker, catching her as she reached the top of the stairs. She spun, lashing out with her fist at the side of the head.

He laughed, catching her wrist and backhanding his sword hand into her chin.

She screamed and fell against the wall, blood streaming down her chin.

'You bastard!' she shouted, aiming a kick for his groin. Rejak twisted out of the way and slapped her hard with his free hand. His excitement was growing and he pressed himself against her, tearing her nightdress from her shoulder. 'Careful there, my beauty. Don't want to hurt me there. Not when I've still got things to do to you.'

To her credit she kept on struggling, even though she must have known it was useless against his superior strength and only served to arouse him more.

'I can see why von Velten likes you,' he hissed in her ear. 'I hope he doesn't mind spoiled meat, because that's all you're going to be soon.'

Rejak pinned her against the wall and pressed a hand to her breast. He squeezed hard, grinning lasciviously as it drew a cry of pain from her. Her chest heaved in terror and he laughed. 'That's it... struggle harder!'

He lowered his head to lick her cheek.

She slammed her forehead into his face and he cried out in pain, releasing her as his hands flew to his face and blood burst from his nose.

'Bitch!' he yelled and hammered his fist into her jaw.

She fell to the floor, but rolled quickly to her feet as he shook his head clear of the headbutt's impact. He turned his bloody face towards her as she lurched along the corridor towards the stairs that led to the main entrance and shouted, 'That's it, you bitch! I'm really going to hurt you now!'

Rejak set off after her, his anger hot and urgent.

He caught her at the top of the stairs, grabbing her by the arm and twisting her around. She spat in his face and he hit her again, sending her crashing downstairs. She tumbled all the way to the bottom, landing awkwardly and he followed her, no longer caring about having her, just about killing her.

She scrambled back from the bottom of the stairs, running to the front door, tugging ineffectually at the brass handle.

Rejak lifted the key from his pocket and grinned. 'Looking for this?'

She edged away from him around the walls, but there was nowhere to go.

'You die now,' he said.

IV

KASPAR RIPPED A halberd from one of his guards and ran to the iron gates of the embassy. Chekatilo backed away towards the gurgling bronze fountain in the centre of the courtyard in front of the embassy, his hands raised in theatrical terror.

'You kill me and she dies,' he promised. 'If Rejak not hear from me in one hour, he is to treat her like whore and then cut her into pieces. He do worse than Butcherman, that one, I think. Loves to kill, too much maybe.'

Kaspar forced himself to stop moving, to lower the halberd and think clearly. He felt his hate for Chekatilo threaten to overwhelm his judgement. He cried out in anguish and threw the halberd aside, taking several deep breaths as he fought for calm.

'What have you done?' he demanded. 'As Sigmar is my witness, if any harm comes to her, no force in the world will stop me from hunting you down and killing you.'

'She not be harmed if you honour debt to me and give me what I want,' said Chekatilo.

'How do I know she is still alive? For all I know, she's already dead.'

Chekatilo looked hurt at Kaspar's accusation. 'I many things, ambassador, but I not a monster. I hurt people because sometimes that the only way to get what I want. So now you will give me what I want or I have Rejak kill her in such painful, degrading way that people will talk of it for years.'

Kaspar wanted to run through the gates and strangle Chekatilo with his bare hands, to choke the life from his miserable, filthy body and spit in his eye as he died. But he could not, and from Chekatilo's smug expression, he could see the bastard knew it too.

'Damn you, but you are wrong, Chekatilo. You *are* a monster,' he said.

Chekatilo shrugged. 'Maybe I am, but I get what I want, yah?'

Kaspar nodded. 'Very well, I will give you what you want,' he said slowly.

Chekatilo laughed as Kaspar turned and entered the embassy.

* * *

V

ANASTASIA EDGED AROUND the hall, her breathing ragged and laboured. Rejak could feel his arousal growing again as he saw the curve of her breasts exposed where he had torn her nightgown.

'Nowhere to go,' he said, wiping blood from his chin.

'No,' she agreed, continuing around the edge of the hall and looking at something beyond his shoulder.

'There isn't, is there?'

'Best not to fight then, eh? Might not hurt as much, but I can't promise.'

He moved left, cutting her off from reaching the stairs as she reached the family crest bearing the two crossed cavalry sabres. She quickly reached up and tore the weapons from their hangings, turning to face him with them held awkwardly before her.

'You think you can use one blade let alone two?' laughed Rejak.

'They're not for me,' said Anastasia, throwing the swords across the room.

The swords sailed over his head and Rejak followed their spinning trajectory until they were plucked from the air by a man standing beside the iron door he had noticed earlier.

The man was thin and wasted, his skin blotchy and scabrous, and Rejak relaxed.

Until the man spun the swords in a blindingly quick web of silver steel and dropped into a fighting crouch. The man's movements were sublime, his every motion honed to perfection, and there was only one man Rejak knew of who could move like that.

His features were sunken and hollow, and only when Rejak looked deep into the man's violet eyes, did he finally recognise him.

Sasha Kajetan.

The *Droyaska*. The Blademaster.

* * *

VI

KASPAR WHIPPED HIS horse to greater speed as he and the Knights Panther rode desperately through the streets of Kislev towards the Magnustrasse and Anastasia's house. The streets were thronged with people and he shouted fearful oaths to try and get them out of his way.

His heart was heavy with black premonition, but there was nothing he could do except ride harder, pushing Magnus to more reckless speeds as they thundered towards the wealthy quarter of the city.

Kaspar prayed he was not riding towards more grief.

VII

REJAK FELT HIS momentary flutter of fear fade as he saw the ruin of the legendary swordsman's form. The man's limbs were thin and wasted, the flesh sagging from his bones, and his ribs were plainly visible through the skin of his chest.

He looked no better than a beggar and Rejak grinned through his mask of blood.

'I have always wanted to fight you,' said Rejak, circling the room with his blade aimed at Kajetan's heart. 'Just to know who was the faster.'

'You hurt my matka,' hissed Kajetan, circling in time with Rejak.

Rejak glanced over at Anastasia in confusion. What in Ursun's name was the swordsman talking about? There was no way she could possibly be Kajetan's mother.

'That's right, my handsome prince,' said Anastasia. 'He did. He hurt me just like your father, the boyarin, did.'

Kajetan screamed, 'No!' and launched himself at Rejak. Their swords clashed and Rejak spun away from the attack, his own weapon sweeping low to cut the swordsman's legs out from under him, but Kajetan was no longer there, somersaulting over the blade and landing lightly on his feet.

'Kill him, my prince!' screamed Anastasia and Kajetan attacked again, his twin swords slashing for Rejak's head. Chekatilo's assassin parried swiftly, launching a deadly riposte and slicing his blade across Kajetan's thigh next to a scar on his leg where he had obviously been recently wounded. The swordsman stumbled and Rejak kicked him in the balls.

Kajetan grunted in pain and dropped to one knee, vomiting across the floor. Rejak jumped back in horror as the black, gristly liquid bubbled and hissed, eating away at the marble flagstones.

Overcoming his revulsion, he closed to deliver the killing strike, slashing his sword at Kajetan's neck. The swordsman rolled beneath the blow, vaulting to his feet in time to block Rejak's return stroke.

Kajetan recovered quickly, his swords drawing blood from Rejak's arm, and the two swordsmen traded blows back and forth across the marble floor of the hall, fighting a duel the likes of which had never been seen before. Kajetan was by far the better bladesman, but his strength was a fraction of its former self and Rejak could see that he was tiring rapidly.

But Rejak was tiring too, his sword arm burning with fatigue and the wound in his belly stabbing hot spikes of pain into his body with each lunge and parry.

The two men warily circled each other once more, exhausted by their furious exertions and knowing that only one of them would walk away from this fight.

Rejak attacked again, a blistering series of slashes and cuts designed to keep an opponent on the back foot. His bladework was faultless, but nothing could penetrate Kajetan's twin sabres and Rejak realised with sick horror that he had no more to give.

Kajetan's blades caught his sword on his last downward stroke and with a twist of the wrist, Rejak's blade was wrenched from his grip, skittering across the floor and coming to rest at the bottom of the stairs.

Rejak leapt backwards, diving across the floor towards his sword.

His hand closed on its leather-bound hilt and he rolled to face his opponent again.

Kajetan was before him, his crossed blades resting either side of Rejak's neck.

'You want to know who is faster?' snarled the swordsman. 'Now you know.'

Kajetan slashed both blades through Rejak's neck and he toppled backwards onto the stairs, his head almost completely severed.

His last sight was of Anastasia Vilkova staring down at him with undiluted hate.

She spat in his eye and said, 'Tchar take your soul.'

VIII

THEY RODE THROUGH the open gateway of Anastasia's home, Kaspar vaulting from the saddle before his horse had stopped moving. He ignored the flare of pain in his knee, running for the black door and drawing both his pistols. The door was locked, but a few heavy kicks from the armoured boot of Kurt Bremen soon smashed it from its hinges.

Kaspar bolted inside, moaning as he saw a body lying at the foot of the stairs in a lake of blood. He ran over and knelt by the body and felt his heart lurch in surprise and relief as he recognised Rejak's dead-eyed features. The man's head hung slack on his shoulders, attached to his body by a few gory scraps of severed muscle and sinew.

Kurt Bremen joined him as the knights fanned out through the house to search for Anastasia.

'I don't understand,' he said. 'What the hell happened here?'

Kaspar did not reply, his eyes falling upon a pair of bloody cavalry sabres lying beside the body and a pool of glistening black liquid in the centre of the marble floor.

He left the body where it lay and bent to examine the black pool and the floor beneath it. The marble flagstone had been eaten away by the stinking substance's corrosive properties and Kaspar knew he had seen something like this only once before.

Below the Urskoy Prospekt as it turned an iron breastplate to molten slag before his very eyes.

'Is that what I think it is?' asked Bremen.

Kaspar nodded. 'I think so.'

Bremen looked back at Rejak's body and the cavalry sabres. 'But that means…'

'Aye. That Sasha Kajetan was here. He killed Rejak.'

'But how?' asked Bremen. 'It doesn't make sense, why would Kajetan be here?'

Kaspar wondered the same and felt a creeping horror overtake him as the significance of Rejak's death and Kajetan's presence in this house settled on him like a sickness. Kajetan had been a broken man, a virtual catatonic, and Kaspar knew that there was only one thing that roused the swordsman to such violence. Matka.

'It does, Kurt. Sigmar, save me, but it does,' said Kaspar sadly; as the veil finally fell from his eyes and he saw how masterfully he had been manipulated.

'Sigmar's blood, do you think Kajetan has Madame Vilkova?'

'No,' said Kaspar, shaking his head. 'And your knights will not find her here either.'

'What do you mean? Where is she?'

'It's been her all along, Kurt. It all makes sense now,' said Kaspar, as much to himself as to the Knight Panther. He sank to his haunches, dropping his pistols as his heart beat wildly at the scale of this treachery.

'What does? Kaspar, you are not making any sense.'

'She has played us all for fools, my friend. The woman no one could describe who freed Kajetan? The woman in the sewer who took delivery of the coffin? Our unseen adversary who knew everything we discovered? The woman who tried to discourage me from even looking in the first place? Losov's collaborator? It was her, it was all her.'

'Anastasia?' said Bremen, incredulous.

Kaspar nodded, cursing himself for a fool. 'Damn it, Kajetan told us as much. "It all was her for", he said. I didn't realise he meant those words literally. It was her directing Kajetan's murders all along. No wonder she tried to have him killed before we could hand him over to the *Chekist.*'

'I can't believe it,' whispered Bremen.

'All the things I told her,' said Kaspar, rubbing his eyes and fighting back the hot flush of shame. 'All the times we lay together in bed and talked of the boyarins, the forces of the Empire, where they were massing, how they would fight and about the men who commanded them. And like a bloody fool I told her everything.'

Kaspar slumped to the floor, holding his head in his hands. 'How could I have been so stupid. Her husband... she had Losov pay to have him killed so she could take his wealth. All this time...'

'I still find this hard to accept, but assuming you are correct, where do you think she and Kajetan are now?'

Kaspar rubbed his face and pushed himself to his feet before bending to retrieve his pistols. 'That's a damn good question,' he said, his anger now beginning to push aside his hurt.

'She must have known that when we found this mess, she would be unmasked,' said Kaspar, heading for the front door and marching towards the scabrous refugees camped throughout the grounds of Anastasia's home.

'Speak to these people, Kurt,' ordered Kaspar. 'Find out if they saw where she went and don't stop asking until you get some damn good answers.'

Kurt Bremen made his way around the refugees, shouting in fragmented Kislevite as Kaspar walked towards the gateway in the wall, confused thoughts spinning around inside his head.

He had ridden here to save Anastasia, but it appeared that she had needed no rescuing, what with the deadliest bodyguard in Kislev to call her own. He wondered if she had ever really cared for him, then chided himself for such selfish thoughts when much deadlier matters were afoot.

He leaned against the gatepost, his eyes idly following the profusion of tracks in the slush that ran through the gate. Most of the slushy mud had been churned by the passage of their own horses, but one patch of ground retained tracks other than theirs; cart tracks...

Cart tracks with a cracked rim on one of the wheels that left a V-shaped impression with every revolution.

It took Kaspar a few seconds to remember where he had seen similar tracks.

In the sewers beneath Kislev.

Made by a cart that had been driven off laden with a strange coffin.

Kurt Bremen approached him. 'They say the White Lady left here not long before we arrived, that she was driving a cart with a long box on the back. No one mentioned anyone else, so I don't believe Kajetan is with her.'

Kaspar felt a terrible fear as he looked up at the sky.

Dawn was hours old and he knew exactly where Anastasia would be heading now.

For months people had seen the White Lady of Kislev drive carts of supplies and food to the armies camped beyond the walls. She was a vision of hope and had been a welcome sight to the soldiers of Kislev and the Empire.

So no one would bat an eyelid to see her driving a cart into their midst today.

'Sigmar save us,' swore Kaspar, running for his horse. 'Everyone mount up!'

'Kaspar, what is it?' shouted Bremen.

'We have to stop her, Kurt!' replied Kaspar, pulling himself into the saddle and guiding Magnus towards the gateway. 'I don't know exactly what it is, but I think that whatever is in that coffin is some kind of terrible weapon. She means to destroy our armies before they can fight!'

IX

SHE WHIPPED THE horses, pushing them as fast as she dared through the breaking morning towards the Urskoy Gate. People huddled at the side of the road waved to her as she passed, recognising her distinctive white cloak edged with snow leopard fur. Anastasia ignored them, too engrossed in reaching the city gate before anyone stopped her.

How could she have been discovered? The man who had come to murder her, who had sent him? The ambassador? Had the fool finally realised how he had been deceived and sent this man in a fit of one of his tempers? No, from her would-be-killer's words she felt sure that Kaspar had not sent him, but who?

Chekatilo? The Ice Queen? Or had it been mere happenstance that had sent a killer to her home – this morning of all mornings – when she was on the brink of fulfilling her destiny to her dark lord?

She allowed herself a tight smile as she remembered that in the works of the Great Tchar, there was no such thing as happenstance. Everything that had happened had unfolded according to his great, unfathomable designs, and no mortal could hope to divine his true purpose.

It angered her that she could have so nearly been undone by such a brutish foe. That an initiate of Tchar such as she had so very nearly been killed by a piece of filth like that...

If she had not already spent much of her power on holding the deadly corruption secure within the bronze coffin, she would have had no need to rely of the protection of Sasha Kajetan.

And it pleased Anastasia to know that her decision to free Kajetan had been proved to be part of Tchar's plan all along, though thinking of the swordsman brought a sharp frown to her face.

When Sasha had killed the other swordsman, he had dropped to his knees beside the corpse and sobbed like a baby. She had put her hand on his shoulder and said, 'There, my handsome prince. You have done your matka a great service and–'

'You are not my matka!' he had screamed, dropping his swords and surging to his feet, his face alight with anguish. His callused hands had gripped her shoulders and she saw with a shock that his normally violet eyes burned with an inner radiance, both orbs flecked with blazing winter fire.

'Oh, please no, not again...' he wailed, sliding to his knees and weeping as he saw the blood spreading from the man he had killed. 'This is not me, this is not me...'

'Sasha,' said Anastasia, 'you need to help me.'

'No!' he screamed, scrambling away from her. 'Get away from me. You are *Blyad*, woman. I see you now.'

'I am your matka!' roared Anastasia. 'And you *will* obey me!'

'My matka is dead!' shouted Kajetan, climbing to his feet and slamming his fists against his temple. 'She died a long time ago.'

Anastasia had stepped forward, but Kajetan had fled deeper into the house and she had no time to hunt him down. Whoever had arranged this morning's violence would soon realise their assassin had failed and wheels would be set in motion that would drive events beyond her control.

There was no time to waste, and so she had immediately gone down to the icy cellar through the iron door in the hallway and awkwardly dragged the coffin up the curling stairs. The coffin was heavy, but eventually she was able to haul it into her house's rear courtyard and lift one end onto the back of a cart. Gasping in exhaustion, she finally loaded her deadly cargo onto the cart and leaned against its iron-rimmed wheel.

When she had her breath back, she led two of her horses from their stalls and hitched them to the trace. One horse was missing from the stalls and she shrugged, guessing that Sasha Kajetan must have taken it.

Where would he go, she wondered, but dismissed the thought as irrelevant? She could not worry about that now. Kajetan was a rogue element best forgotten, and, pausing only to retrieve her white cloak from the house, she set out into the streets of Kislev.

At last she saw the high towers of the city walls ahead of her and turned from the Goromadny Prospekt into the main esplanade of the gateway. The gates were open and she hauled back on the reins as she approached, the armoured men standing with their long axes bared smiling and waving to her as they saw her brilliant white cloak.

Anastasia forced herself to smile back as they wished her a good morning, hearing herself mouth banal pleasantries in reply as she passed beneath the shadow of the gateway to emerge onto the crest of the hill upon which Kislev sprawled.

The cart rumbled across the timber bridge over the moat and she turned off the main roadway onto the rutted tracks that led towards the encampments of the allied armies. Hundreds of morning cookfires and thousands of tents filled the steppe plain before Kislev and she felt a thrilling excitement build inside her at the thought of the charnel house this place would soon become.

Nearly twenty-five thousand soldiers and perhaps another ten thousand refugees were camped around the base of the *Gora Geroyev*, the Hill of Heroes.

Soon it would be known as the Hill of the Dead.

The track angled downwards and she leaned back on her seat, hearing the good-natured shouts of welcome from hundreds of soldiers' throats as they recognised her. The sounds of the camp surrounded her, the clatter of pots as cooks prepared food for the hungry soldiers, the wailing of children, the barking of dogs and the whinny of horses.

Soon there would be nothing but the silence of the grave.

An ad hoc square had been cleared at the base of the hill, where generals and boyarin gave speeches to rouse their soldiers, and it was at this spot she finally halted the cart.

Anastasia pulled on the reins and climbed down to the mud, digging a rusted bronze key from her cloak and making her way to the back of the cart.

She slid the key into the first padlock that secured the coffin shut. As the key turned, the padlock crumbled to umber dust and a breath of corruption, like the death rattle of a thousand corpses, sighed from the coffin.

Taking an instant to savour the moment, Anastasia smiled as the sun finally began breaking through the early morning clouds and burning away the low ground mist.

It was going to be a beautiful day.

X

KASPAR DRAGGED ON the reins, swerving to avoid a burly Kossar waving his axe as they approached the gates. He and the Knights Panther had ridden their horses almost into the ground as they raced through the streets of Kislev. Kaspar prayed they would be in time to avert whatever terror Anastasia planned to unleash.

The Kossars waved at them to stop, but Kaspar had neither the time nor the inclination to waste his breath on them now. He rode past the Kislevite soldiers, galloping hard for the open gateway, his knights following close behind with wild yells at the confused Kislevites.

They rode out onto the cold, windswept expanse of the *Gora Geroyev* and Kaspar stood tall in the stirrups, desperately seeking any sign of where Anastasia might have gone. He turned the air blue with his oaths, unable to see her and felt a terrible powerlessness.

Kaspar kicked back his spurs and rode over to a group of red and gold liveried arquebusiers who sat beside a flickering cookfire brewing some soldiers' harsh-tasting tea.

'The White Lady of Kislev! Have you seen her?' he shouted.

'Aye,' replied a Talabecland sergeant, pointing to the base of the hill. 'The good lady headed down that way, sir.'

'How long ago?' demanded Kaspar, wheeling his horse.

'A few minutes ago, no more.'

Kaspar nodded his thanks and raked back his spurs, risking life and limb as he thundered downhill, barely avoiding pockets of soldiers, camp followers and rocks in his mad rush. He shouted at people to get out of his way and left angry yells and curses in his wake as the knights followed him, their passage made easier by the ambassador's frenetic ride.

He reined in Magnus and again stood high in the stirrups, twisting left and right.

Kaspar's heart raced as he finally saw her, a few hundred yards away, her white cloak a beacon amidst the muddiness of the campsite. She stood at the back of a small cart, a coffin of bronze glinting in the sunlight.

'Kurt!' he yelled, pointing to the bottom of the hill. 'With me!'

He whipped Magnus hard and leaned low in the saddle as he guided his mount through the crowded camp towards Anastasia.

She turned as he drew near, hearing the thunder of horsemen approaching her, and Kaspar was left in no doubt that she had been the architect of his woes as she smiled at him with a predatory coquettishness.

'I knew you would come,' she said as he dismounted from his panting horse.

'Whatever that thing is,' begged Kaspar, pointing to the rusted coffin, 'I beg you not to open it.'

There were only two padlocks securing it shut and Kaspar could feel a terrifying threat emanating from within.

'Begging, Kaspar?' laughed Anastasia. 'I thought that was beneath you. You were always so proud, but I think maybe that was what made you so easy to manipulate.'

'Anastasia,' said Kaspar as the Knights Panther dismounted and a crowd of curious onlookers began gathering around the unfolding drama. 'Don't do it.'

'It is too late, Kaspar. This is corrupting entropy given physical form and such a beauteous thing cannot be kept confined for long, it must be allowed free rein to do what it was created to do.'

'Why, Anastasia? Why are you doing this?'

Anastasia smiled at him. 'These are the last days, Kaspar. Don't you feel it? The Lord of the End Times walks the earth and this world is ready to fall to Chaos. If you knew what awaits these lands at the hands of Lord Archaon, you would drop to your knees and beg me to open this coffin.'

'You would kill everyone here, Anastasia?' asked Kaspar. 'There are thousands of people here. Innocents. Women and children. Are you really such a monster?'

'I would kill everyone here a dozen times over for Tchar!' laughed Anastasia and turned her back on him, slipping a key into the coffin's penultimate padlock.

Kaspar dragged out his pistols and aimed them at her back.

She cocked her head as she heard the click of the flintlocks.

'Anastasia, please! Don't do this.'

Kaspar saw her turn the key and the padlock crumbled to powder. Seething horror seeped from the coffin lid and the crowds surrounding them began muttering in fear as they felt the malign power strain at its confinement.

'Stop. Please stop this,' pleaded Kaspar, the pistols trembling in his hands.

'You cannot do it, can you?' said Anastasia without turning. 'You're not able to murder me in cold blood. It is not in your nature.'

She placed the key in the last lock.

And Kaspar shot her in the back.

Anastasia sagged against the coffin, a neat hole blasted through her cloak.

She gripped onto the cart and struggled to face him, her face twisted in pain and disbelief.

'Kaspar...?' she gasped, and he felt something die inside him as a hateful rose of bright blood welled on her white cloak. She put a hand to her chest, her fingers coming away stained crimson.

Kaspar fell to his knees, tears blurring his vision as Anastasia fought to stay upright.

She reached for the key and Kaspar fired his second pistol into her chest, the bullet slamming her against the side of the cart and pitching her to the ground.

She dropped to the mud, her eyes glazing over in death.

And Kaspar saw that he was too late.

The last padlock fell from the coffin as a fine dust, blowing away in the deathly gust that seethed from the unlocked lid.

CHAPTER TEN

I

LIKE THE SOFT exhalation of a drowned corpse, a low moaning issued from the coffin and wisps of a sparkling mist seeped from the gap between the lid and sides. The coffin rattled and shook with unnatural life. Snaking tendrils of iridescent mist whipped from its corrupt depths as the lid flew open and a sparkling jet of coloured light and vapour fountained from inside.

A Stirland pikeman was the first to die, the spectral light wreathing him in glittering mist that ripped the flesh from his bones as he was turned inside out by its mutating power. His scream turned to a gurgle as the collection of disembodied muscles and organs he had become collapsed in a steaming pile. Another man died as the light enveloped him and he sprouted appendages from every square inch of his flesh: arms, hands, heads and legs bursting forth from his skin in a welter of blood and splintered bone.

Everything the spreading mist of corrupt light touched warped into some new and bizarre form, men reduced to boneless, jelly-like masses of flesh, women bloating into fat, glossy skinned harpies with distended, vestigial wings. The ground itself writhed under its touch, brightly patterned grass and outlandish plants springing forth from the unnaturally fecund earth.

Kaspar backed away in horror from the coffin, now almost obscured by the multi-coloured spume that spread further with every passing second. Screams and cries of terror spread before its mutating power and he cursed himself for not firing sooner.

He and his knights ran for their horses, but Kaspar had no intention of riding away from this hellish power. He knew what he planned would destroy him and just hoped that more people would be able to outpace this daemon-spawned power before it killed every living soul.

The knights climbed into their saddles and Kaspar watched them ride off with heavy heart. They had served him faithfully and he had not had time to tell them how honoured he had been to have them with him in Kislev. The corrupting light was almost upon him and he wondered if he would even be able to reach the coffin and close it before its power turned him into some hellish abomination. Would closing it even stop it?

He didn't know, but he had to try.

Shapes writhed in the misty light and Kaspar gave thanks that he could not see them clearly, their piteous cries of agony tearing at his heart. Monstrous silhouettes thrashed in their agonies and mutated beasts that had once been men gorged themselves on the flesh of the dead.

Kaspar reached his horse and climbed into the saddle, twisting as he heard the beat of hooves coming towards him and someone shout his name. He searched for the source of the shout and saw Sasha Kajetan riding around the colourful light towards him. He grabbed for his pistols before realising that he had fired both of them, and reached for his sword.

Kicking his feet from the stirrups, Kajetan leapt from the saddle and crashed into the ambassador. The two men slammed into the ground, the breath driven from Kaspar's lungs by the impact. He rolled onto his side and tried to pick himself up, but fell as his knee gave out under him.

Kajetan stood above him, and Kaspar could not help but shudder at the ruin of a man he had become. Gone was the fierce, proud swordsman and in his place, a wasted, desperate creature of pain and misery. Kaspar managed to pull himself to his knees with a grunt of pain and unsheathed his blade, saying, 'Stay back, Kajetan,' as the dazzling mist crept forwards.

'Ambassador von Velten...' hissed Kajetan, and Kaspar could see that the swordsman was badly injured. Rejak obviously did not die without a giving a good account of himself.

The swordsman stared at the rainbow-streaked froth that bubbled from the coffin and said, 'I told you there was thing I was yet to do.'

'We don't have time for this, Kajetan. I have to stop this,' said Kaspar, brandishing his sword before him.

'I told you there was thing I was yet to do,' repeated the swordsman, as though Kaspar had not spoken. 'And I told you that it involved you.'

The swordsman looked away from the ambassador as he heard an approaching horseman. 'No time,' he said and reached for Kaspar.

Kaspar roared and thrust with his sword, the blade plunging into Kajetan's belly and ripping from his back. Blood burst from the wound and the swordsman grunted, hammering his fist against the ambassador's jaw. Kaspar dropped, but Kajetan dragged him to his feet and thrust his unresisting body towards the knight who galloped towards him with a roar of fury.

Kurt Bremen had ridden back as soon as he had realised that the ambassador had not fled with them and reined in his horse with his sword raised to strike Kajetan down.

'You!' gasped Kajetan, 'take him and get him out of here!'

Taken aback, Bremen lowered his weapon when he realised what Kajetan was planning. The knight sheathed his blade, taking the ambassador from the swordsman and hauling him up behind the neck of his warhorse. He nodded his thanks towards Kajetan, watching in amazement as the man climbed into the saddle of his own horse, Kaspar's sword still lodged deep in his belly.

'I said go!' shouted Kajetan before riding hard towards the hellish epicentre of the brightly coloured nightmare.

II

THE PAIN THREATENED to overwhelm him, but Sasha held it in check as he rode through the scintillating fog of light. Creatures that had once been human thrashed and mewed piteously all around him; wild fronds of ever-changing plant matter whipping from the ground and a breathless fertility saturating the air itself.

His breath writhed with life as the power of change seized it, flickering like tiny fireflies in front of him. Briefly he wondered what black miracles and dark wonders might be worked with his other bodily fluids: his spit, his blood or his seed.

He could feel his horse stagger beneath him as the corrupting power overtook it. Rippling bulges seethed from the beast's flanks and it screamed as ungainly, feathered wings burst from its body, malformed and gelatinous. The horse tripped and fell, throwing him from its back as it thrashed in pain. He hit the ground hard and rolled, crying in agony as the sword blade jammed in his body twisted and cut him wider.

Sasha ripped it free and hurled it aside, falling to his knees as the pain surged around his body. Blood flooded from the wound and he knew he had only moments at best. Obscene flowers rippled from the ground where his blood fell, each one with the face of his matka, and he pushed himself upright.

He swayed and limped towards the cart bearing the coffin, dazzling lights bursting before his eyes, but he couldn't be sure if it was death reaching out to finally claim him or the power within the coffin. A blinding corona of light surrounded it and he had to shield his eyes as he climbed onto the cart and stared into its depths.

He was not surprised to see a body in the coffin, but this was one with veins that ran with fire and eyes shining with the light at the centre of creation. He felt the powerful magicks that had gone into this thing's creation: the fell, arcane science of the underfolk and the dark sorcery of Chaos.

The eyes rolled in their sockets, fixing him with a gaze that contained everything that had or might one day exist in the world. He felt himself stripped bare by its power, the flesh blackening on his bones as it consumed him. But he had one last gift for this world, one last way to achieve the atonement he craved.

His stomach heaved and he leaned forward to stare into the burning eyes of the writhing corpse of light. Its slack jaw opened and its breath was creation itself.

But if its breath was creation, his was destruction, and he spewed a froth of his deadly black vomit across its face. The light was blotted out as the viscous black liquid ate away at the corpse, burning it and melting it to stinking matter. Its malice screamed in his head, but he knew it was powerless to prevent its ending.

Sasha's world was pain as his body burned with the power of raw magics fleeing the corpse's dissolution, but he kept the black vomit coming, emptying himself before finally collapsing onto the sloshing remains.

His chest hiked and he tried to move, but there was nothing left of him.

The swordsman smiled as he saw a vision of radiant light growing from behind a slowly opening gateway. He reached out to touch the light.

And all the pain and the guilt and the terror and the anger and the trueself were swept away, leaving nothing but Sasha Kajetan, his matka's handsome prince.

There was nothing left to do.

He could die now.

III

THE DEVASTATION UNLEASHED by Anastasia Vilkova accounted for three hundred and seventy souls, most of whom were lucky to have perished in the opening moments of the swirling maelstrom. Other, less fortunate victims, were later shot down by weeping arquebusiers or otherwise put out of their misery by horrified pikemen.

Still other creatures, vile mutated abominations fled to the steppe to howl at the moon and stars in loathing for what they had become. The site of the carnage became a reviled place and within the hour that part of the camp had been forsaken, its tents left standing and every possession abandoned. No one had dared approach the wrecked cart that lay at the centre of the abandoned place, and during the night a freak ice storm of terrifying magnitude swept across the blighted ground, obliterating everything still alive, the grass, the unnatural plants and wiping away the taint of Chaos.

By morning, only a crystalline wilderness remained, and whatever had begun the terrifying events of the previous morning was now buried forever beneath an unyielding layer of imperishable ice.

It was a fitting tomb for Sasha Kajetan, thought Kaspar. A place where he would never again be tormented by the daemons of his past or those conjured within him by others.

Despite all that had happened, he could not bring himself to hate Sasha – a man who had twice saved his life. Sofia was right: Kajetan had not been born a monster, but made into one, and if his last act as a human being had been to save thousands of lives... well, that was redemption enough for Kaspar.

As to how that redemption balanced with the atrocities he had committed as the Butcherman, he didn't know, but Kaspar hoped that Sasha had at least earned a chance at absolution in the next world.

He turned away from the icy graveyard, knowing that Anastasia's body was also buried beneath the ice forever and felt the peculiar mixture of anger, sadness and guilt that came whenever he thought of her. She had been about to kill tens of thousands of people, but that didn't make the fact that he had shot a woman in the back any easier to deal with. Kaspar knew he had done the right thing, but he would never forget the look of hurt and disbelief in her eyes as she fell to the ground.

Though Kaspar had not seen the swordsman's last ride into the deadly mist of light, Bremen had told him later how there had been a final blaze of energy in the midst of the shining fog before it had quickly faded away to nothing. Whatever Kajetan had done to stop it from killing everyone was a mystery that Kaspar supposed might never be solved.

He guided his horse towards the city, riding slowly through the mass of soldiers preparing to march northwards to meet a terrible enemy. Soldiers saluted as he passed, word of his new rank having spread quickly through the regiments. Though he still wore the black and gold of Nuln, he had caparisoned Magnus in the green and yellow of Stirland to show his men that he was now one of them.

At a gathering of the senior surviving officers of the Empire forces, he had again made his offer to take command of the leaderless Stirland army. Spitzaner had made his objections plain, but with no one else capable of handling a force of such size, his words carried little weight.

It was a simple fact of war that there were those who made brilliant regimental commanders, but floundered at higher levels of command, or men who could direct the forces of an entire province, but who had no idea of how to give orders to a battalion. Within the armies of the Empire, it was common for most men who attained command to settle at their level of competency and thus far, no one but Kaspar had volunteered to take the reins of command.

The idea of leading men into battle once more sent a thrill of anticipation through him, and though he knew it was foolish and he would regret it the moment the first blood was shed, he found himself – like a new recruit – eager for battle. To reach Urszebya before the High Zar, the allied forces marched at dawn the following day; the Stirland army, which he would lead, the Talabecland army of Clemenz Spitzaner and the Kislev pulk that would fight with the Ice Queen at its head.

Twenty-five thousand fighting men, now known by the soldiers as the Urszebya pulk, to face a rumoured forty thousand. Boyarin Kurkosk was marching east with nearly twenty thousand warriors, but it was unlikely he would arrive before battle was joined, and there was no time to wait for him.

If they defeated the High Zar's army, it would be the most spectacular victory since the Great War against Chaos. But if they lost...

Kaspar still did not fully understand what power might rest within the standing stones at Urszebya, but the Kislevites obviously felt they were important enough to risk open battle with much larger force.

There was a glorious madness to all this, but Kaspar knew full well the reality of what they were marching towards. Blood and death, horror and loss. Cyenwulf had defeated every army that had stood against him and his force had grown larger with each victory.

It had never known defeat and stood poised to destroy them.

Kaspar was under no illusions concerning their chances of defeating the High Zar.

Pavel had said that people would tell tales of their bravery as far away as Magritta and Kaspar believed him.

He just hoped they were not tales of lament.

IV

THE ENTIRETY OF the embassy guards stood to attention outside the iron fence, ready to march to the city gates and join the Urszebya pulk. None of them were obliged to join the pulk, but upon returning to the embassy the previous evening, Kaspar had been met by a determined Leopold Dietz, who had spoken of his men's desire to march north with the ambassador. They had sworn an oath when they accepted the posting to Kislev to protect the ambassador's life, and they could not very well do that by remaining in the city, could they?

Kaspar had proudly accepted their offer and in turn allowed Leopold Dietz the honour of carrying the ambassador's banner. They had shaken hands, and together, his guards and Knights Panther awaited the order to march. The knights were glorious, their armour polished to a mirror sheen and their purple and gold gonfalon raised high by Valdhaas. Their mounts were fresh and clean, their caparisons bright and colourful. It was an honour to command such fine warriors.

He himself wore a practical quilted jerkin in the gold and black of Nuln with an unadorned breastplate, vambrace and cuissart. His clothes were fresh and practical, for at least a ten day march lay ahead of the Urszebya pulk before it would reach the valley of Ursun's Teeth. Wrapped in a red, gold and black pashmina of thick furs, Sofia was quiet as he tightened Magnus's saddle cinch. Her auburn hair hung loose around her shoulders and she wore an expression of barely-controlled anxiety.

'In Kislev it is customary to mourn those who ride to war as already dead,' she said as Kaspar finished preparing his horse.

'I'd heard that,' said Kaspar. 'A rather morbid practice I had always thought.'

Sofia nodded. 'Yes, so that's why I am not going to do it. I will pray for your return with each morning.'

'Thank you, that means a lot to me, Sofia,' said Kaspar, taking her hand.

She dropped her head and said, 'We never had any time, did we?'

'No, we didn't,' agreed Kaspar sadly. 'But when we defeat the High Zar's army, I will return for you.'

'You truly believe you can defeat him?' asked Sofia.

'Yes, I do,' lied Kaspar.

The lie came hard to him, but he could see the need for hope in her eyes and though it went against everything he believed in, he told it rather than spoil this last moment.

Sofia nodded and the relief in her eyes made Kaspar want to weep. She reached up and unclasped her pendant, taking Kaspar's hand and placing it in his upturned palm.

She had worn it at the Tzarina's victory dinner, a smooth blue stone wrapped in a web of silver wire, and Kaspar was touched by the simple affection of the gesture.

'Keep it next to your heart,' she said.

'I will, thank you,' he promised. He wanted to say more, but could not think of anything that would not sound trite or overly melodramatic. He could see Sofia was on the verge of tears and ached to take her in his arms and tell her that he would be fine, that he would come back and see what they might have together, but could not force the words to come.

Instead he simply embraced her and said, 'I will see you in my dreams.'

She nodded and wiped her eyes on the hem of her pashmina as Kaspar turned and climbed into the saddle.

As he lifted the reins, Sofia said, 'Promise you will come back to me.'

'I promise,' he said, though he wondered if this was a promise he could keep.

Sofia smiled sadly and stepped back as he rode through the gate to the head of the Knights Panther. He saluted in proud respect to the warriors assembled around him.

He raised his arm and signalled the advance, turning for one last look at Sofia, but she was nowhere to be seen, the door to the embassy already closed behind her.

V

THE TRIP NORTHWARD into the oblast was much easier than the last time Kaspar had made such a journey. Winter was in retreat, though snow still lay deep on the ground and the wind cut though even the thickest furs. The Urszebya pulk made good time through the wilderness, wild Ungol horsemen riding far ahead of the soldiers, scouting for any signs of the High Zar's army.

They marched through the vast expanse of the oblast, the sky a wondrous, stark blue and the hardy steppe grass providing patches of colour amid the patchy whiteness of the landscape. The sense of a land coming to life was palpable, thought Kaspar, as though it had lain dormant through the long, dark months of winter and was now waking to flaunt its savage beauty. This was wild country, saturated with a sense of ancient passions and primal emotions, and, coming from this untamed land, Kaspar found it easy to imagine how the Kislevites had become the people they were.

Over the course of their march, Kaspar had made a point of getting to know the officers who would be serving under him, needing to know their strengths, their weaknesses and their character. They were men of quality, men with the look of eagles, who he would be proud to fight alongside when the time came. They had fought two major battles recently and were hungry for more.

Some officers talked of the Ostland halberdiers and how its men were lucky to be going home, but that they would envy the honour to be won on the field of battle. Each time Kaspar heard the missing regiment mentioned, he felt a great guilt weigh heavily upon him, for that had been the regiment he had signed over to Chekatilo when he had thought Anastasia's life was in danger. He had chosen them because there was barely a hundred of them and they had been in Kislev for nearly a year, trapped in the north following the massacre at Zhedevka. Kaspar imagined that they would have been only too glad to be able to return to the Empire, but that did not assuage his guilt.

After the chaos of Anastasia's attempt to destroy the Urszebya pulk, Kaspar and Bremen had ridden to the *Chekist* and told Vladimir Pashenko every detail of the past six months. Together, they had scoured the city for Chekatilo, but to no avail. The giant Kislevite was gone. The Ostland halberdiers were gone with him and every one of his haunts the *Chekist* knew of was abandoned.

No men could be spared to hunt Chekatilo down and Kaspar was forced to accept that the bastard would probably escape the executioner's axe he so richly deserved. It irked his sense of honour that Chekatilo would not pay for what he had done, but he knew there was nothing he could do about it any more.

Every night as the pulk camped, Kaspar went round the fires of the soldiers, telling them tall tales of his previous battles and sharing food and drink with them. It was exhausting work, but his men had to know him, to get a sense for the man whose orders might well send them to their deaths.

On the morning of the twelfth day of march, as winter's last gasp of snow began to fall, the outriders brought word of Cyenwulf's army. If they were to believed, and Kaspar had no reason to doubt their word, the High Zar was less than two days from the mouth of the valley.

A nervous anticipation spread throughout the pulk as word of their foe spread, but on his nightly tour of the army, Kaspar was pleased to note the quiet courage his soldiers displayed. These men had fought and defeated the armies of the dreaded northmen before, and they would do so again. Kaspar told them he was proud of them and that the storytellers of Altdorf would tell tales of them for hundreds of years.

The snow continued to fall throughout the day and as the sun climbed to its zenith the Urszebya pulk reached the valley of its name. The land hereabouts was harsher than the steppe and in the distance through the snow, Kaspar could see twin scarps of rock rising sharply from the ground, forming a wide cut in the landscape.

A deepening valley sloped into the steppe, it sides steep and composed of a dark, striated rock. Distant cheers filtered back to him from the vanguard as they reached the valley mouth and Kaspar's gaze was drawn up to the summit of the valley sides.

Though still many miles away, Kaspar could see a jagged black spike of rock, the first of the tall menhirs that ran the length of the valley and gave it its name.

Urszebya. Ursun's Teeth.

The rugged beauty of the land was stunning and Kaspar knew he had never seen anything quite like it. But his wonder at its splendour was touched with regret for he knew that this was the last time he would look upon the valley in this way.

Today it was beautiful, but tomorrow it would be a hateful blood-soaked battlefield.

VI

THE SKY WAS turning to a bruised purple as Kaspar and Kurt Bremen made their way to the billowing, sky-blue pavilion of the Ice Queen. Despite the bitter cold and lightly falling snow, the Tzarina's guards who surrounded the giant tent were bare chested, displaying no outward signs of any discomfort. They collected weapons from every man who entered the pavilion, taking no chances with their queen's safety after the attack at the Winter Palace.

Kaspar surrendered his pistols and sword and Bremen unbuckled his sword belt. A giant warrior with long daggers sheathed through the skin of his pectoral muscles and a tall coxcomb of stiffened hair pulled back the pavilion's opening to allow them entry.

Inside, Empire officers and Kislevite boyarin were gathered around a roaring firepit where another of the Tzarina's guards turned a roasting boar on a long spit. Sweet-smelling smoke was vented through a central hole in the roof of the pavilion, and the crackling aroma of roasting meat made Kaspar's mouth water.

Tables and chairs formed of rippling waves of ice rose up from the ground and the supports for the pavilion were tall columns of fluted snow. The Tzarina sat on her golden throne, regal in a sparkling gown of icy cream. Despite the rigours of a twelve day march, the Ice Queen looked as immaculate as ever, and Kaspar wondered how much effort it took her to maintain such appearances.

But as he looked at the adoring faces of her boyarin, he knew it was not mere vanity that made her appear so ostentatious, but necessity. To her subjects, the Ice Queen was a beloved figure of aloof, regal majesty and to see her in anything less than the most delicate finery would be an anathema to them.

Clemenz Spitzaner and his coterie of staff stood as close as they were able to the Ice Queen, and Kaspar nodded in acknowledgement to his fellow general. Spitzaner bowed stiffly, still unhappy with Kaspar's presence, but having enough presence of mind not to create any kind of fuss about it.

Kaspar greeted his fellow Stirland officers and accepted a glass of Estalian brandy from a passing servant. He sipped the brandy, enjoying its fiery warmth in his belly.

'This is a civilised way to fight a war,' he said, raising his glass to Kurt Bremen.

The knight nodded and poured himself a glass of water from a jug shaped from sparkling ice. Boyarin of all description milled around the tent, helping themselves to meat cut from the boar and making loud boasts of the glory they would earn on the morrow. Kaspar saw the Tilean, Albertalli, across the fire and raised his glass in salute.

The mercenary general smiled broadly and raised his own glass, making his way around the fire to stand beside Kaspar and Bremen.

'General von Velten,' he said. 'It is good to see you again. It fill me with hope to know a man of your reputation fights alongside us.'

'My compliments to you, general,' replied Kaspar. 'I have heard good things about your soldiers while marching here. They say your men held the line at Krasicyno for five hours against the Kurgans.'

Albertalli smiled modestly. 'Actually, it more like three, but, yes, my soldiers are good boys, fight hard and well. They will do same tomorrow, count on that.'

'I will,' promised Kaspar. 'We will have need of warriors who can stand fast in the face of such brutality as the High Zar will unleash.'

'Yes,' agreed Albertalli, 'It will be grim work tomorrow.'

'Isn't it always?' said Kaspar as the Ice Queen rose from her throne and began circling the firepit. Conversations died away and all eyes turned to face her as she spoke.

'Kislev is land and land is Kislev,' she said.

'Kislev is land and land is Kislev,' repeated the assembled boyarin.

The Ice Queen smiled and said, 'Look about you, my friends. Look at the faces of the men around you and remember them. Remember them. Tomorrow these will be the men who you will be fighting alongside and upon whom all our fates depend. For we are about a great and terrible business now. I can feel the ebb and flow of the land beneath me and it cries out against the touch of Chaos. If we fail here, then the land we hold dear will pass away, never to return, and all that we once knew will be destroyed.'

Every man in the pavilion was silent as the Ice Queen passed, the crackle of sizzling fat as it dripped into the fire the only sound that disturbed the silence. The chill of the Ice Queen's passing prickled Kaspar's skin as she spoke once more.

'Tomorrow we stand before a foe many times our number. The High Zar brings warriors drunk on slaughter and victory, monsters from our worst nightmares and a creature from the dawn of the world. I have felt its every tread on the land and now it comes here to destroy us all. And make no mistake, without your courage and strength, it will succeed.

'The strength of Kislev lies in you all. The land has called you all here and it is here that you will put that strength to the test in defiance of Chaos. There is power in this land and tomorrow it will run in all of your veins. Use it well.'

'We will, my queen,' said a Kislevite boyarin solemnly.

Clemenz Spitzaner spoke next, saying, 'Tomorrow we will march out from this valley and together we will destroy this barbarian,' and raising his glass in a toast. Heavy silence greeted his words and the Ice Queen turned to face the Empire general.

'General Spitzaner,' she said. 'I think you must have misunderstood me. March from the valley? No, we will not be marching anywhere, we will make our stand right here at the end of the valley.'

'What?' spluttered Spitzaner. 'Your majesty, I would counsel against such a stratagem.'

'It is too late for any other plan, General Spitzaner. The decision has been made.'

Kaspar frowned, seeing that some of the boyarin were equally unsettled at the prospect of fighting within the rocky valley. He stepped forward and said. 'Your majesty, I think General Spitzaner's belief that we would fight the

High Zar on the steppe is shared by a great many of us. While it is true that this valley has a number of tactical advantages, it has one flaw that perhaps you have not been made aware of.'

'Not aware of, General von Velten?' said the Ice Queen. 'Then pray enlighten me.'

'There is only one way in or out of this valley,' said Kaspar. 'If we are defeated, there is nowhere to retreat to. We would be destroyed to a man.'

'Then we must endeavour not to be defeated, yes?'

'Of course, but the fact remains that we might be.'

'Do you trust me, General von Velten?'

'It is not a matter of trust, it–'

'It is *all* about trust, Kaspar von Velten. You of all people should know that.'

Kaspar felt her icy gaze upon him and realised that she was right. In battle, everything came down to moments of trust. Trust in the steel of the man next to you, trust that the officers beneath you carry out their orders, trust that the courage of the army will hold and trust that those who commanded knew what they were doing. This was such a moment, and Kaspar willingly surrendered to what the Ice Queen planned, feeling her acceptance of his trust as a cold, but not unpleasant shiver.

'Very well,' he said solemnly, 'if the Ice Queen of Kislev wishes to make her stand here, then the army of Stirland will do so as well. We will not fail you.'

The Ice Queen smiled and said, 'I have faith in you, General von Velten. Thank you.'

Kaspar bowed as General Spitzaner said, 'Your majesty, please. Regardless of what Herr von Velten says, I have grave doubts concerning this plan.'

'General Spitzaner,' said the Ice Queen. 'The decision has been made and there is no other way. We will fight together or we will be destroyed. It is that simple.'

Kaspar could see Spitzaner was angry at having been so manoeuvred, but to his credit, he knew not to cast further doubt on the Tzarina's plan in front of brother officers.

He bowed stiffly and said, 'Then the army of Talabecland will be proud to fight alongside you.'

'Thank you, General Spitzaner,' said the Ice Queen, as a servant handed her an icy glass of brandy.

'To victory!' she shouted, draining the brandy and hurling the glass into the fire.

Every man in the pavilion bellowed the same words and threw their glasses into the fire. Flames shot high into the air, mirroring the passion burning in their warrior hearts.

'Death or glory,' said Kurt Bremen offering Kaspar his hand in the warrior's grip, wrist to wrist.

'Death or glory,' agreed Kaspar, taking Bremen's hand. 'Is of no matter…'

CHAPTER ELEVEN

I

KASPAR WATCHED THE sun climb higher into the dawn sky, wondering if this was the last morning he would see. The screams of the Ungol horsemen captured by the enemy during the night had mercifully ceased, to be replaced by the braying of tribal horns.

Scraps of mist clung to the ground and Kaspar could see that the leaden sky promised more snow. His knee ached with the cold and he was glad that his rank gave him the right to go into battle on horseback. From his position at the end of the valley he could see the awe-inspiring sight of thousands of soldiers filling the valley before him: pikemen, halberdiers, archers, Kossars, swordsmen and knights in silver and bronze armour. Colourful banners flapped noisily in the cold wind blowing from the valley mouth and Kaspar felt proud to be leading these fine men into battle.

Hundreds of horses whinnied and stamped their hooves, aggravated by the presence of so many soldiers and the scent of the terrible creatures that marched with the army of the High Zar. Knights from the Empire calmed their steeds with stern words while Kislevite lancers mounted on horses painted in the colours of war secured feathered banners to their saddles. Black-robed members of the Kislevite priesthood circulated amongst the soldiers, blessing axes, lances and swords as they went, while warrior priests of Sigmar read aloud from the *Canticle of the Heldenhammer*.

He could hear a distant vibration through the cold ground, the tramp, tramp, tramp of tens of thousands of approaching warriors. The morning mist conspired to hide them from view for now, and Kaspar just hoped that it would lift soon to enable the cannons and bombards placed on the crest of the valley to fire. He yawned, amazed he could feel so tired and yet so tense, and thought back to his dream of the previous night.

He had seen a twin-tailed comet blazing across the heavens and a young man fighting a host of twisted creatures that bore the bestial features of animals yet walked upright like men. With a pair of blacksmiths' hammers, this young man had smote the beasts and Kaspar's heart had swelled with fierce joy.

But then his dreamscape had moved on, and he had seen the Empire in flames, its cities cast to ruin and its populace burned to death in the fires of Chaos.

It was an omen, of that he was sure, but for good or ill, he did not know.

Kurt Bremen and the red and blue liveried embassy guards surrounded him, his gold and black standard carried by Leopold Dietz. A dozen young men on horseback waited behind him, runners who would carry his orders to the regimental captains on the front line.

A magnificent-looking troop of Kislevite lancers, their feathered banner poles whistling in the wind, rode past and Kaspar saw Pavel at their head, his vast frame carried on an equally massive steed. Red and white pennants fluttered from their lances and each carried a quiver of iron-tipped javelins slung from their saddle horns.

He had shared a mug of tea with Pavel this morning to say their goodbyes and silently wished his former comrade luck as he passed out of sight behind a block of Kossar infantry. The tall, burly men were laughing and joking while smoking pipes and resting on their axes. Kaspar admired their calm.

Regiments of infantry covered the gently sloping plain before him, the Empire armies holding the centre of the line, thousands of men in huge blocks sixty wide and forty deep. Kaspar and Spitzaner had arranged their forces in a staggered formation, each regiment able to support another, with smaller units of arquebusiers and spearmen attached to every one. Individually, each regiment was a strong fighting unit, but working together, they were amongst the steadiest soldiers in the world.

Knights of both Kislev and the Empire sat on the flanks of the army and ahead of them, galloping groups of yelling Ungol horsemen and the light cavalry of the Empire were strung out in front of the main body of the army. When the time came to unleash them, they would harry the flanks of the enemy in an attempt to draw off warriors from the main attack.

High on the ridge behind him, braziers smoked behind gabion-edged firing pits, dug from the frozen ground by Imperial pioneers during the night. The bronze barrels of the mighty cannons and bombards of the Imperial Gunnery School protruded from the emplacements, frustrated engineers wandering along the edge of the ridge, desperate for the mist to rise.

The Ice Queen herself rode a white horse with shimmering flanks of sparkling ice and eyes like the bluest of sapphires. Her loyal guards surrounded her and she carried Fearfrost already drawn. Her cloak of swirling ice crystals hugged her tight and a ghostly mist gathered around the feet of her mount. She turned to Kaspar and raised her sword in salute to him before looking expectantly at the tall black stones atop the valley sides.

Kaspar followed her gaze, seeing the great standing stones that gave this valley its name and hoped that the Ice Queen was right to risk everything for them.

A swelling roar built from the mouth of the valley, guttural chanting from the High Zar's warriors that echoed in time with the clash of their swords and axes on iron-bossed shields.

'So it begins…' said Kaspar.

II

THE WIND PICKED up as the sun climbed higher and within minutes of the Kurgan horns being blown, the morning mist vanished and the enemy they had been preparing to fight all winter was suddenly revealed.

A line of armoured warriors stretched from one side of the valley to the other, their black furs, horned helmets and dark armour making them look more like beasts than men. They marched in a loose line, no discipline to their advance as screaming horsemen wearing nothing but furred britches and swirling tattoos streamed forwards. Packs of snapping hounds with long fangs and furry hides stiffened with matted blood ran forwards with the horsemen, their baying howls chilling the blood.

Wild horns skirled in time with their screams, but were soon drowned out as the Imperial guns opened fire. Kaspar watched as a cannonball slammed into the ground before the enemy and slashed a path through the densely packed warriors. Blood sprayed as men were smashed to a red mist by the missile, but within seconds, they had closed ranks and continued onwards. A rippling series of booms sounded and yet more bloody furrows were torn through the enemy warriors.

Kaspar felt a great pride in the men of Nuln as they loaded and fired again and again, sending iron cannonballs slashing into the enemy and huge shells that exploded in the air and sprayed them with lethally sharp fragments of red hot shrapnel. Men and horses screamed as the fearsome Imperial artillery killed them in their hundreds.

But Kaspar knew that guns alone would not win this fight as the artillery positions were once more wreathed in smoke. The wind was favouring the gunners, blowing the roiling banks of smoke behind their positions and allowing them to better target their victims.

'Those horsemen are getting too close,' he muttered to himself.

The tattooed riders galloping ahead of the enemy army stood high in the saddle, their trailing topknots streaming out behind them as they rode in close before expertly wheeling their mounts away. Each time, they would loose shafts from their powerful, recurved bows and each time a dozen men or more would fall to the ground, pierced by black fletched arrows.

They rode in again and again, tempting the warriors they fired on to charge them, but Kaspar and Spitzaner had issued clear orders that these horsemen were not to be engaged. Scattered gunfire from arquebusier regiments felled a number of the wild men, but they left behind few dead when they finally pulled away.

But as the horsemen retreated, the baying hounds hit the Imperial line. Few had fallen to the black powder weapons and they attacked in a fury of claw and fang. Those regiments attacked shuddered as men were torn from their feet, but the majority of the hounds were soon despatched by disciplined ranks of lowered halberds. Drummer boys began dragging the wounded back as the remaining soldiers closed ranks.

The black line of enemy warriors kept coming, hordes of them, and Kaspar felt a shiver of fear as he grasped the sheer scale of the High Zar's force. They came in a never ending tide of black iron and horns. Monstrous men in thick furs and brazen axes and swords. Hordes of armoured warriors on horseback rode alongside the infantry, their black steeds snorting and pawing the ground in anticipation of bloodshed. Their riders were giants of men, carrying huge-bladed war axes and pallaszes and Kaspar feared for when these awesome killers entered the fray.

A pair of massive totems on great, wheeled platforms followed them, dark idols dedicated to the terrible gods of the north. The bodies of a dozen men hung from their tops, their entrails swinging from opened bellies and feasted upon by carrion birds.

Shaggy creatures bearing enormous axes loped before these idols and hulking monsters with great clubs tramped amongst them. Three times the height of a man, these distorted creatures had oversized muscles and looked capable of tearing their victims apart with their bare hands. Something huge and dark marched before the idols, its shape indistinct and blurred, a dark umbra of lightning-pierced cloud wreathing its terrible form.

Its concealing cloud lifted and Kaspar could see the huge creature in all its terrible glory. Surely this must be the beast of ancient times the Tzarina had spoken of, a horrific monster with a dragon-like lower body of dark, leathery scales and the grotesquely muscled upper body of a man. Its torso and chest were scarred with ancient tattoos and pierced with rings and spikes of iron as thick as a man's wrist. A mane of shaggy fur ran from its crown to where its body became that of a monster. Lightning flickered around its grotesque head and huge tusks protruded from its enormous jaws.

'Sigmar preserve us,' whispered Kaspar.

'Amen to that,' added Kurt Bremen and Kaspar was surprised to hear fear in the Knight Panther's voice.

A host of armoured chariots rumbled through the army, the chanting warriors and beasts parting before their advance. Cruel, hooked blades protruded from the wheels of the chariots and Kaspar shuddered at the havoc he knew they would wreak amongst the Imperial soldiers.

He tore his gaze from the huge monster at the centre of the High Zar's army and turned to one of his runners, saying, 'Send my compliments to Captain Goscik, and order him to fire on those damned chariots as soon as he can. Tell him to aim low, I want the horses pulling them shot down.'

The runner nodded in understanding and galloped off as the distant crackle of musketry intensified. Arquebusiers fired rippling volleys of lead bullets into the advancing horde and soon the valley was filled with acrid, drifting smoke.

A huge roar went up from the High Zar's army and Kaspar watched the first wave of fur-clad warriors charge forwards. They came in ragged groups, huge swords swinging wildly above their heads and berserk screams echoing from the valley sides. With a disciplined shout, the pikes of the Imperial line lowered and the first of the enemy warriors were spitted on their lethally sharp points. Screams and shouts drifted from the fighting as men died, run through with Empire steel or hacked down with steppe-forged iron.

The Imperial line bent back under the weight of the charge, frenzied warriors hacking left and right with their massive swords and axes. But here, the very size of their weapons was their undoing. Each of the tribesmen needed a wide space around him to swing his weapon and thus avoid killing his fellow warriors, but the tightly packed ranks of the Empire allowed half a dozen men to fight a single Kurgan warrior.

The fighting was brutal and brief, and Kaspar watched the Kurgan warriors stream back from the struggle, bloodied and broken by the stout defences of his countrymen. Jeers and ululating trumpet blasts followed them as they fled, but Kaspar knew that this was but the tip of the iceberg.

The worst was yet to come.

* * *

III

GENERAL ALBERTALLI WIPED blood from his eyes and slapped the men nearest him on the back with pride as they shouted colourful insults at the retreating enemy warriors. Bodies littered the ground and he shouted at his men to close ranks. The wounded and dead were dragged to the back of the regiment and his sergeants shoved men forward with curses and the butts of their halberds.

'Are you alright, sir?' asked one of his soldiers as he wiped more blood from his eyes.

'Yes, lad, I'll be fine,' he said with a reassuring smile. 'I've had worse cuts shaving. Don't you worry about me, and anyway, I cut the bastard's head off who gave me this.'

The soldier nodded, but Albertalli could see the fear behind his eyes. He didn't blame him. For all his smiles and reassurance, that last attack had almost broken them. He and his sergeants, huge Tileans with great axes who protected the standard of Luccini, had led a brutal counterattack that had sent the Kurgans reeling back, but it had been a close run thing. Smoke drifted across the battlefield and he strained to see how the rest of the allied line was holding, but he could see nothing through the thick musket smoke and press of fighting men.

His men shouted a warning as yet more enemy warriors emerged from the smoke.

His men had courage, that was for sure, but courage could only last for so long.

IV

PAVEL OVERTOOK A fleeing Kurgan tribesman, sweeping his sword back into his face and splitting the man's skull wide open. His lancers chased down the remnants of a group of tribesmen that had broken from a clash with one of the Tilean mercenary regiments, but they were getting too close to the main body of the enemy and without support, that was not a healthy place to be.

He shouted over to his trumpeter, who blew a rising, three note blast, and hauled back on the reins. The lancers on their red-painted horses wheeled expertly and rode back to their own lines, confident that they could see off any threat that came their way.

V

THE KURGANS THREW themselves at the allied line for another hour, breaking against the disciplined lines of pikes, halberds and axes like a black tide. Each attack smashed home and killed scores of men, but was hurled back every time, leaving mounds of Kurgan dead in its wake. Dozens of heavy chariots had charged forwards, ripping into the flanks of a regiment of Kossars and scything screaming men down with their bladed wheels. Their drivers were skilled and wheeled their chariots around, driving across the front of their foes before being dragged down and hacked to pieces by the vengeful Kislevites.

Kaspar watched these men fight with pride, but knew that the battle could not continue in this way. They were killing hundreds of the Kurgans, but their own casualties were mounting rapidly, and in a battle of attrition, the High Zar had thousands more men than they did. The centre was holding, but only just. He had ordered two regiments of halberdiers forwards, men from the towns and villages around Talabheim, and they had eventually thrown the tribesmen back. Cavalry charged into the flanks of the Kurgans, cutting them down by the score, spitting them on lances or crushing their bones with heavy hammers.

So far the discipline of the Urszebya pułk was holding, but Kaspar could see that the High Zar had yet to commit his most terrifying troops to battle.

* * *

VI

ALBERTALLI SHOUTED, 'Now!' and his men lowered their halberds once again as the enemy came at them. They surged forward to meet the Kurgans, bestial men in horned helms and dark armour, and the two forces met in a brazen clash of iron and flesh. He swept his heavy sword, its edge dulled by the hours of fighting, through the neck of a tribesman and kicked another in the crotch as he clambered over bodies that lay on the ground.

An axe swept out at him and he ducked below its swing, thrusting his blade into his attacker's groin. The man screamed and collapsed, dragging the blade from Albertalli's hand. He swept up a fallen halberd and blocked a downward sweep of an axe, slamming the butt of his weapon against a tribesman's temple and reversing his grip to stab the point through his chest.

All around him, men screamed and yelled, all mores of civilization forgotten in the heat of battle. The air stank of blood and terror, ringing to the harsh clang of steel on steel and the deafening booms of cannon. He stabbed and stabbed with his halberd, sweeping it through yet another tribesman's ribs.

The standard of Luccini waved above him and he yelled encouragement to his men as the gold finial caught the sunlight

And then it was over, the Kurgans retreating into the smoke once more, driven back by the courage and discipline of his warriors. Damn, but he was proud of them. He leaned on the shaft of his halberd to regain his breath, exhausted by the fighting, when another warning shout went up. Again, so soon?

He straightened as more shapes came running at them through the smoke, and his heart skipped a beat as he saw the monstrous charging shapes. Huge, horned and shaggy beasts with slavering jaws and powerfully muscled bodies loped through the mounds of the dead with crude axes and looted swords.

'Hold fast, men. We'll see these things off!' he shouted as cries of alarm spread from somewhere close. He couldn't see from where and had no time to check as the first of the beasts thundered into their line.

Braying monsters ripped men from their feet with huge sweeps of their weapons, snapping fangs tearing mens' faces off, clawed limbs rending limbs from bodies. The beasts gorged on flesh, hacking their way through his men with ease. Albertalli chopped his halberd through the arm of a dog-headed creature, shocked when it roared and turned to face him without seeming to notice its wound.

He stabbed with the point of the weapon, the tip snapping off a handspan within its belly. The creature roared, bloody spittle frothing at its jaws, and its clawed arm swept down smashing his halberd in half.

Albertalli stumbled backwards, dragging out his pistol, but the beast was on him before he could fire, its massive jaws snapping shut on his skull and tearing his head off with one bite.

VII

THE SCREAMS OF the Tilean regiment were piteous as the monstrous beasts devoured them, but Pavel forced himself to shut them out as he spurred his horse forward. Sixty lancers followed him, leaning forward in their saddles with their lances lowered. Smoke swirled around them, obscuring all but the closest men, but he did not need to see his prey to know where to find them – they could all hear the sickening sounds of snapping bones as the creatures feasted on human flesh.

They rode from the smoke and saw the remains of the Tilean regiment, butchered almost to a man. Many of the beasts had charged wildly after the fleeing men, but many more remained, tearing great chunks of meat from the corpses of their victims.

'Charge!' shouted Pavel, lowering his lance and placing his weight into the stirrups as he leaned over his mount's neck. The ground trembled to the thunder of hooves, the shrill, shrieking whistle of the wind through their back banners driving them forward with even greater fury. The horned beasts looked up from their monstrous feast, snouts bloody and teeth bared in hunger.

The Kislevites charged into the creatures with a furious thunder of hooves and splintering lance shafts. Pavel thrust his lance into the chest of a massive, goat-headed beast, the impetus of his charge driving the tip straight through its chest. Blood jetted around the lance and the creature howled as it was punched from its feet. The lance snapped under its weight and Pavel threw aside the now useless weapon, dragging out his curved sword.

Lancers circled their horses, butchering the last of the beasts, but the damage was already done. Pavel could see that the charge of these bestial monsters had broken through the Imperial right flank. Regiments were moving to plug the gap, but a fresh tide of Kurgan warriors were already charging forwards to exploit it.

'Lancers, with me!' shouted Pavel, dragging on his reins and wheeling his horse once more.

VIII

KASPAR SENT YET more runners to order his reserve regiments forward, fearful that the attack on the right might yet overrun his forces there. But his reserves were running low and there was only so long they could continue in this way. His practiced eye swept the portions of the battlefield he could see through the smoke and the snow that had begun to fall.

The cannons were punishing the enemy and the centre was still holding. Spitzaner's army of Talabecland was fighting magnificently, and Kaspar was forced to concede that perhaps his former officer had matured into a halfway decent commander. Terrible reports of monsters attacking the mercenary regiments on the right had filtered back to Kaspar and he had been forced to reposition soldiers earmarked for the centre.

'We're too weak on the right,' he said, running a hand across his scalp.

'Shall we send Captain Proust forward?' suggested one of his staff officers.

'Aye, send his men into the gap on the right between the Ostermark pikemen and Trondheim's men,' ordered Kaspar.

The noise of the fighting was tremendous: screams, cannon fire and the discordant clash of iron weapons. He heard screaming from somewhere nearby and twisted in his saddle, trying to pinpoint its location.

'You!' he shouted to one of his few remaining runners. 'Find out where that's coming from and get back here as soon as you know something!'

He felt a strange sensation crawl up his spine and glanced round to see the Ice Queen with her hands raised, shouting into the wind in a language Kaspar did not understand. Flickering mist gathered around her, sending questing tendrils of light into the ground and he briefly wondered what sorceries she conjured.

Such thoughts were banished from his mind as the cold wind blew again and the smoke cleared long enough for him to see further along the valley.

'Oh no…' he whispered, seeing the huge, dragon creature charging towards their lines accompanied by a huge mass of gigantic horsemen. His eyes were drawn to the massive warrior who led them. Even though he was some distance away, Kaspar could see he wore shimmering armour and a helm of a snarling wolf.

There could be no doubt about it.

This was the High Zar.

IX

THE CANNON CREWS sweated despite the cold, dragging their heavy cannon back to the covered embrasure once the blackened loaders had rammed the powder charge and ball down the barrel. As the rammer cleared the barrel, the master gunner kept his leather thumb patch over the touchhole lest a stray spark or smouldering ember ignite the charge prematurely.

For the men of the Imperial Gunnery School, the battle had become little more than a series of repetitions: lload, aim, fire… load, aim, fire. They could see nothing of the battle through the stinking smoke and simply kept firing towards the enemy.

The loader hauled aside the wicker gabion in the embrasure and ducked back as the master gunner lifted the long, burning taper to fire the weapon. He pressed the flame to the touchhole and the massive gun rocked backwards, filling the emplacement with noise and smoke. The crew began hauling the gun back when the master gunner was snatched from his feet in a spray of blood.

Deafened by the sounds of battle, the gunners had not heard the howls and roars of the charging beasts that swarmed over the ridge. Dozens of monstrous, bestial creatures overran the artillery pits, tearing the gunners apart with long, bloody claws and powerful, snapping jaws.

X

KASPAR WAS SUDDENLY aware of the silence of the guns and his worst fears were confirmed when he saw his runner's horse galloping back through the smoke, its rider's headless body still clutching the reins. He saw howling beasts rampaging across the artillery ridge, smashing aside wicker gabions and hurling severed body parts before them.

The monstrous creatures were drunk on blood, frenzied to the point of intoxication by the slaughter. The beasts smashed through the gun emplacements and ran downhill towards the Ice Queen, bellowing in ferocious hunger.

Kaspar dragged on the reins of his horse and shouted, 'Kurt!'

Kurt Bremen had already wheeled his mount and yelled, 'Knights Panther, with me!'

Kaspar and the knights galloped desperately across the hard ground to intercept the charging creatures. He knew he should not be exposing himself to this kind of risk, but the old instincts of a soldier had kicked in and it was too late to stop now. The howling beasts saw them coming and altered their charge, rushing to meet them head on.

The knights smashed into the beasts, their heavy lances skewering the fierce creatures on their points. Lances broke and horses lashed out with iron-shod hooves to stave in ribcages and smash bestial skulls. Dozens of the monsters were trampled to bloody pulp beneath the heavy warhorses and as the knights wheeled their mounts, there were only four still standing.

Kaspar blew out the back of a beast's skull with a well-aimed pistol shot as the knights surrounded the remaining three creatures and hacked them down with their heavy broadswords. As the last creature fell, Kurt Bremen rode alongside Kaspar and said, 'Ambassador, that was… unwise of you.'

'I know,' said Kaspar, breathless with exertion and exhilaration. 'Don't worry, it won't happen again.'

Bremen chuckled. 'We shall see.'

Kaspar reloaded his pistol before riding back to where he had been observing the battlefield. The allied line was bending back under the force of the enemy attacks and as he watched, he saw the massive beast of ancient times finally strike his men.

XI

THE MONSTROUS DRAGON creature smashed into a regiment of Talabecland pikemen, their weapons shattering against its thick hide. Swords bounced from its ancient flesh and in reply, its huge axe swept out and a dozen men died. Another score fell with every stroke of its blade and its huge claws crushed men beneath its weight with every step. Its roar cracked the earth and lightning flared around it, incinerating friend and foe alike. There could be no standing against such a terrifying creature and the men of the Empire turned and fled, their standard falling to be trampled by the vast beast.

Nearby regiments, already hard pressed by the Kurgan tribesmen, stepped backwards despite the shouted demands of their sergeants. Seeing this horrifying god of war amongst them spurred the Kurgans to insane heights of bravery and they hurled themselves at the men of the Urszebya pulk with unremitting fury.

As the courage of the men of the Empire hung on a knife-edge, hordes of armoured horsemen, led by the High Zar himself, charged through the swirling smoke and mist and hammered into their ranks.

Against such terrifying violence, the allied soldiers broke almost instantly as the ferocious warriors killed and killed and killed. Streams of men began sprinting away from the bloody horsemen, who pounded after them and hacked them down as they ran with great sweeps of huge swords and axes.

The centre had broken.

XII

KASPAR SHOUTED AT his runners to send word to the flanks of the army. The centre had broken and enemy warriors were pouring through the gap, butchering everything in their path. Snow was falling more heavily now, deadening the sounds of battle and misting everything in flurries of white.

Kaspar felt a chill seize him worse than the falling snow, a sickening feeling that Spitzaner had been right. Fighting in this valley with no retreat had doomed them all. Even as he shouted orders to try and plug the gap in the centre, he knew it was too little too late. Hordes of heavy horsemen were charging uphill and not even the quickest regiment would be able to prevent disaster.

'General von Velten!' shouted a voice behind him. He turned his horse to see the Ice Queen beckoning him and spurred his horse towards her. He rode close to the Tzarina, feeling the skin-crawling sensation of powerful magicks surrounding her.

'Your majesty?' he said hurriedly. 'The centre has broken and I fear we are defeated.'

'You give up too soon, general. Have faith in me,' said the Ice Queen, and Kaspar could see that her eyes burned with an inner radiance, both orbs flecked with blazing winter fire. 'As we defend the land, the lands defends us.'

'I don't understand,' said Kaspar.

'You will,' promised the Ice Queen. 'Just hold the enemy back for a little longer.'

'I will do what I can,' assured Kaspar, 'but they are amongst us.'

'You must hold them, von Velten, I need only a little longer.'

Kaspar nodded as she threw her head back and white lightning split the sky above her, swirling clouds boiling and snow spinning about her in a miniature snowstorm. Kaspar and her guards backed away from the incandescent form of the Tzarina as a low moaning, sounding as though it echoed from the very centre of the earth, issued from the ground.

'Go!' shouted the Ice Queen. 'Hold them!'

XIII

STREAMS OF MEN, both Kislevite and Empire, fled before the wrath of the High Zar and his chosen warriors. Huge, armoured horsemen on giant, daemonic steeds thundered through the centre of the Urszebya pulk, killing hundreds as they rampaged across the bodies of broken men. The giant beast followed, slower as it slew and feasted on the dead it left in their wake.

Kaspar knew they could not hope to defeat the High Zar's warriors, but the Tzarina had not asked him to defeat them, merely to hold them back for a time. Storm clouds gathered above her and, though he did not know what she planned, he vowed that he and his soldiers would give her whatever time their lives could buy. Kurt Bremen and the Knights Panther stood ready to ride with him and Leopold Dietz, holding the ambassador's banner high, shouted at the embassy guards to stand to.

Kossars and scattered groups of Imperial soldiers rallied to his black and gold standard as the ground shook with the approach of the High Zar. Kaspar knew that getting men to fight was the easy part of any battle, but getting men to go back into a battle they had already run from was next to impossible, so he was filled with a humbling sense of pride as more and more warriors flocked to join them, called by some unseen signal to defend the queen of Kislev.

The dark horsemen crossed the ridge before them and Kaspar could feel the fear of these mighty warriors spread through the gathered soldiers. But not one man took a backwards step.

A swelling roar built from the throats of the men of Kislev and the Empire, and Kaspar raised his fist. His hand swept down and the Urszebya pulk swept forward to meet the High Zar, man to man, blade to blade.

The heavy cavalry smashed into the massed soldiers, their swords and axes chopping through them with terrifying ease. Screams and blood filled the air and a score of men were dead in the opening seconds of the fight. Kaspar fired both his pistols, unhorsing an enemy rider, before throwing them aside and drawing his sword.

Kurt Bremen hacked down a Kurgan rider and beheaded another, fighting with desperate skill and courage. Kaspar chopped at an enemy horseman's back, but his sword bounced clear of the warrior's thick armour.

The warrior turned and swept his sword down, the blade slashing past Kaspar's head and cutting deep into his horse's flank. Magnus reared and lashed out with his hooves, caving in the warrior's skull. Kaspar tried to rein in the pain-maddened horse, but the Kurgan's weapon had bitten deep and it was all he could do to hold on, let alone fight.

All was screaming chaos as the High Zar's armoured horsemen slaughtered them, screams, blood, noise and death. Kaspar lost all sense of direction as his horse thrashed around in agony, but it was plain to see that this battle was lost.

Another blade lashed out and he screamed a denial as a heavy axe virtually decapitated his horse. Magnus collapsed and Kaspar was hurled from the saddle, sprawling in an ungainly heap in the midst of the swirling melee.

He picked himself up as he heard a shrill whistling, but was unable to see where it came from. Bodies jostled him as he stood, stampeding horses and fighting men. He raised his sword as a huge black horse reared up before him, a length of pikeshaft buried in its chest. The beast flailed as it died and its rider was thrown to the ground.

The warrior rolled to his feet and hurled himself back into the fray. Kaspar saw from his snarling wolf helm and iridescent armour plates that this was none other than the High Zar himself. The giant tore off his dented helmet and hefted his huge pallasz, brandishing it two handed as he cut down enemies by the dozen.

Kaspar limped through the worsening snow towards the High Zar, knowing that he could not defeat such a terrifying warrior, but unwilling to lose this battle without having faced his nemesis face to face. Knights Panther and the embassy guards closed in on the High Zar, but he seemed unfazed by so many opponents.

His pallasz swept out and a knight died. A lance splintered on his breastplate and Kaspar could not believe that it had not penetrated. Another knight died as his horse was slain beneath him by the High Zar and the pallasz stabbed downwards.

Kaspar reached the Kurgan war leader at the same time as Kurt Bremen and the two men attacked the leader of the tribesmen with magnificent heroism. Bremen's broadsword clashed against Cyenwulf's pallasz in a shower of sparks and Kaspar's sabre slid from the High Zar's armour.

The giant tribesman backhanded his fist into Kaspar's chest and he collapsed, feeling ribs break beneath his armour. Hot pain stabbed into him as he fell and he saw Kurt Bremen stagger under a blow to his hip. Blood streamed down the knight's thigh where the pallasz had penetrated the mail links beneath his armour.

Kaspar tried to stand, but fierce pain flared in his chest. He pushed himself to his knees as he heard the whistling sound again and looked up in time to see a tide of red-painted horsemen thunder from the smoke, their feathered back banners and long lances glorious and heaven-sent as they charged.

Pavel rode at the head of the lancers, his sword raised high as he and his warriors charged home, lances punching the armoured Kurgans from their saddles in a crash of flesh and steel. Pavel struck left and right and Kaspar was suddenly transported back to the days when they had fought side by side as young men. His old friend was a force of nature, killing with every strike of his sword as his lancers broke through the centre of the High Zar's warriors.

Pavel's sword struck Cyenwulf's head and the mighty war leader staggered, blood streaming from his forehead. His pallasz slashed and Pavel's horse fell, its forelegs cut from beneath it. Kurt Bremen attacked as the High Zar's attention was elsewhere, but once again his armour defeated a stroke that Kaspar knew should have split him apart. As his horse screamed in its death throes, Pavel joined the Knight Panther as the battle swirled around them.

As Kurt and Pavel fought the High Zar, Kaspar picked himself up, gritting his teeth against the pain and went to the aid of his comrades. It was an unequal struggle and though they outnumbered the Kurgan chieftain, his strength and skill was vastly superior to theirs. His heart heavy, Kaspar knew they could not defeat him.

Kaspar thrust his blade towards the High Zar's groin, but his sword was easily batted aside and Cyenwulf's riposte tore into his belly. He fell, pain the likes of which he had never known before gripping his body tight, and slammed face first into the snow, rolling onto his back as blood poured from the wound.

Pavel screamed in loss and risked a high cut to Cyenwulf's head, but the High Zar was ready for him and Kaspar watched in horror as the Kurgan ducked and his mighty sword swept up and hacked into Pavel's side.

The huge pallasz shattered Pavel's breastplate and buried itself within his chest, but as he staggered under the massive impact, Pavel dropped his sword and gripped onto the High Zar's blade with both hands. Cyenwulf struggled to free his weapon from Pavel's grip, but the giant Kislevite held it firm, blood frothing from his mouth and flooding from his side. Time slowed and Kaspar saw the entirety of this battle captured in the faces of these two warriors, the brutal, unthinking hatred of the High Zar and the passionate heroism of Pavel.

As the High Zar tried to free his blade from the dying Pavel, Kurt Bremen's broadsword struck and buried itself in the centre of his face. Cyenwulf dropped without a sound, blood and brains spilling from the shattered fragments of his splintered skull.

The Knight Panther dragged his sword free of Cyenwulf's head and fell to his knees. His face was ashen and his breathing ragged as blood poured down his thigh.

Bremen smiled, content with this small victory amid such bloodshed and horror.

Then the world shook as the creature of ancient darkness stepped from the swirling snow and mist. Its massive form towered above them and lightning flared from its head as it bellowed its fury across the battlefield.

* * *

XIV

KASPAR TRIED TO push himself away from the massive creature but searing, white-hot pain seized him and he was only able to prop himself up against the flanks of a dead horse. Blood soaked his shirt and streamed from beneath his breastplate to pool in his lap. The beast towered above Bremen, easily triple his height, and as it lifted its huge axe, the knight struggled to rise, ready to fight even though there was no chance of victory.

Snow and ice lashed around the monster and Kaspar saw grooves of blood streak its massive body as the unnatural storm beat the creature back. The low moaning he had heard near the Ice Queen sounded again, much louder this time, and he looked up as the sky darkened and a rumbling tremor ran through the ground.

Whips of white lightning arced from the massive standing stones that ringed the valley, each one thrumming with barely-contained power. As he watched, each stone spewed a thick mist, venting a writhing smoke that seethed and coiled like a snake. Crackling with power, the swirling mist descended and spread across the valley floor.

His vision was blurring, but he saw shapes forming in the mist, indistinct forms fashioning themselves from the insubstantial matter into something else entirely.

All down the length of the valley the strange mist closed with the battling Kurgans and bellowed war-cries turned to shouts of panic as the tribesmen saw what approached them. Ghostly figures of mist charged them with shadow-formed axes and swords. Shaped from their most deathly fears, the mist warriors attacked the Kurgan warriors, and though their bodies and weapons were fashioned from mist and smoke, they slew whatever they struck.

Kaspar watched amazed as the shadowy warriors of the mist slaughtered the Kurgan warriors, one minute appearing as huge, bearskinned warriors of ancient Kislev, the next soldiers of the Empire and then again as primitive warriors wearing the pelts of wild animals. There was something primal and elemental about them and they drove the Kurgans back without mercy. He twisted painfully to watch the Tzarina, seeing her wreathed in a writhing snowstorm, tendrils of smoke and light stabbing through her and outwards into the land.

And Kaspar recognised who these mist warriors were in that instant, realising why the Tzarina had been so adamant that the battle be fought here.

As the Kurgan army disintegrated under the unstoppable assault of these warriors, Kaspar knew that the Tzarina had tapped into something ancient and deadly dangerous, the power of the land, the elemental energy that was the source of all her own strength. Called to defend itself, she had given the land a means to strike back at those who defiled it and sought to do it harm.

A bellowing roar of pain shook the snow from the valley sides and Kaspar watched as the misty warriors surrounded the enormous monster before him, driving it back down the valley. It may have been old when the world was young, but this land had endured throughout the ages and had a power that could not be denied.

The beast was soon lost to sight amidst the howling winds and screeching voices on the air, and Kaspar leaned back as the sounds of battle faded.

He cried out as he felt hands lift his head and groaned in pain, seeing Kurt Bremen kneeling beside him. The knight's skin was the colour of parchment and streaked with blood.

Behind the knight stood the Ice Queen, unsteady on her feet with a fading halo of winter's light surrounding her.

'Did we win?' asked Kaspar.

'I think so, Kaspar,' said the Ice Queen, her voice hollow and drained. 'The land of Kislev is unforgiving.'

'Good,' he said. 'I'd have hated to go through all this for nothing.'

'You have been a true son of Kislev, Kaspar von Velten,' said the Ice Queen, kneeling beside him and taking his hand. Kaspar expected her hand to be cold, but it was warmer than his and he smiled.

'Thank you, your majesty,' whispered Kaspar.

The Ice Queen leaned close and kissed his cheek and again Kaspar was struck by the fact that her flesh wasn't cold after all, but warm and soft. She stood and gave him a smile of thanks before turning and walking off into the gathering evening.

'Kurt,' said the ambassador, his voice little more than a whisper.

'Yes?'

'Will you do something for me?'

'Of course. You know I will.'

Kaspar reached beneath his breastplate and pulled out something from the pocket of his shirt. He held out his hand and said, 'Take this.'

'What is it?' said Bremen, opening his palm.

Kaspar placed a pendant with a thin silver chain and a smooth blue stone wrapped in a web of silver wire into Bremen's palm and closed his finger over it.

'Give this to Sofia, Kurt. And tell her...'

'Tell her what?' said the Knight Panther as the ambassador's words trailed off.

'Tell her... that I am sorry... sorry I couldn't keep my promise.'

Kurt Bremen nodded, tears coursing down his cheeks.

'I will,' he said.

XV

WITH THE DEATH of High Zar Aelfric Cyenwulf and the retreat of the Old One, the Kurgan army melted like snow before the spring thaw. As the survivors of the Kurgan horde fled the valley, the warriors of the mist faded, swirling in the spring breeze until there was nothing left of them save the distant echoes of ancient war cries.

The warriors of the Urszebya pulk watched the fleeing Kurgans, but did not give pursuit, too exhausted by the furious battle to do more than collapse and weep or give thanks for their lives.

Truly it is said that the only thing more grievous than a battle lost is a battle won. The men of the Empire and Kislev mourned together and gave thanks together as the night closed in and the pyres for the dead were built.

Too many had died and the loss was too near for there to be any thought of victory celebrations; those would come later. As night closed in, the only movement across the steppe was a lone knight riding sadly for the south.

Epilogue
Six Months Later...

I

AFTER THE GREAT victory at Urszebya, the fighting in Kislev dragged on. The days of wars being settled in one great battle were long since passed and there were many skirmishes and slaughters to take place before the final outcome of the war was decided at a place of ancient legend.

The accounts of these battles have since passed into the annals of history: the Battle of Iron Gate, the Relief of Zavstra, the Defence of Bolgasgrad, the Siege of Kislev, the Sack of Erengrad and countless others, but such are tales for a different time, and there were heroes made in these days who would live on in song for hundreds of years.

It was a time of heroes and a time of great sorrow.

Truly was it named the Year That No One Forgets.

* * *

II

VASSILY CHEKATILO HALTED his convoy of wagons at the top of a grassy rise on the slope that led down to the bustling city of Marienburg with its vast docks, sprawling mercantile houses and lively trading districts. The great forests of the Empire were behind him and he could see the glittering azure expanse of the Sea of Claws ahead of him. Tall ships with billowing sails crossed the seas here, bound for all manner of exotic ports and strange destinations. Marienburg was a wretched hive of scum and villainy, and now that he had arrived, it was time for the local criminals to watch out.

The journey across the Empire had been fraught with danger and risk, but the papers he had extorted from von Velten had seen him past the worst of it, as had the hundred soldiers he had been able to appropriate thanks to the ambassador's seal.

Most of those soldiers had since returned to the Empire, blind patriotism that Chekatilo did not understand taking them back to wars that would no doubt see most of them die in agony. It was of no matter though, he had coin enough to pay for mercenary soldiers and, since the money was good, they had protected him well enough.

The River Reik foamed downhill towards the city below, its red tiled roofs beckoning him onwards, and Chekatilo could sense nothing but possibilities opening before him. He cracked the reins of his horses and guided his wagon train downhill towards his bright new future.

But Chekatilo had not noticed the stowaway hiding in the rearmost cart of his convoy, concealed beneath an oiled canvas tarpaulin, a bloated, albino-furred rat with a strange triangular brand on its back.

Its hidden masters had marked this man-thing for death and such decrees were never disobeyed or forgotten. Fortunately the rat could sense the presence of many of its brethren below the man-city ahead.

It waited…

ABOUT THE AUTHOR

Hailing from Scotland, Graham McNeill narrowly escaped a career in surveying to join Games Workshop's Warhammer 40,000 development team, working on the Tau, Necrons, Chaos Space Marines, Daemonhunters and Witch Hunters codexes.

As well as four previous novels, he has also written a host of short stories for *Inferno!* and is planning to severely curtail his free time by writing even more. He shares a house with a life-size cardboard cut-out of Buffy who keeps watch on the place when he's away and offers advice about how best to kill daemons.

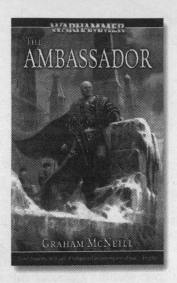

More Graham McNeill from The Black Library

THE AMBASSADOR

A Warhammer Novel

IN THE ICY Northern Wastes, a mighty army of darkness prepares to sweep southward and lay waste to the civilised lands of the Empire. In this dangerous time, retired Imperial general Kaspar von Velten is sent to Kislev as ambassador to the court of Tsarina Katarin. Unused to the power struggles and politics at court, Kaspar is forced to use all the skills and resources at his command in order to survive in this cold and hostile land. As winter draws in, can Kaspar re-forge the fragile alliance between the Empire and Kislev and prepare its troops for war before the hordes of Chaos are unleashed on the land?

More Graham McNeill from The Black Library

STORM OF IRON

A Warhammer 40,000 Novel

IN A DARK and gothic future, humanity fights a constant battle for survival in a hostile universe. Now hell has come to Hydra Cordatus, for a massive force of terrifying Iron Warriors, brutal assault troops of Chaos, have invaded the planet and lain siege to its mighty Imperial citadel. But what prize could possibly be worth so much savage bloodshed and destruction?

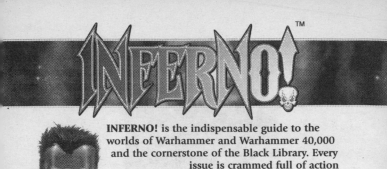

INFERNO! is the indispensable guide to the worlds of Warhammer and Warhammer 40,000 and the cornerstone of the Black Library. Every issue is crammed full of action packed stories, comic strips and artwork from a growing network of awesome writers and artists including:

- **Dan Abnett**
- **William King**
- **Graham McNeill**
- **Gordon Rennie**
- **Simon Spurrier**
- **Gav Thorpe**

and many more!

Presented every two months, Inferno! magazine brings the Warhammer worlds to life in ways you never thought possible.

For subscription details ring:

US: 1-800-394-GAME
UK: (0115) 91 40000
Canada: 1-888-GW-TROLL
Australia: [02] 9829 6111

For more information see our website:
www.blacklibrary.com/inferno